Utten
and
PLUMLEY

Utten
and
PLUMLEY

Reade Scott Whinnem

HAMPTON ROADS
PUBLISHING COMPANY, INC.

for the evolving human spirit

$2⁰⁰

Cover art: Digital Imagery © copyright 2003 PhotoDisc, Inc.
Interior art by Will Adler, Anne L. Louque, and Reade Scott Whinnem
Bucket by Maureen Kessler

Hampton Roads Publishing Company, Inc.
1125 Stoney Ridge Road
Charlottesville, VA 22902
434-296-2772
fax: 434-296-5096
e-mail: hrpc@hrpub.com
www.hrpub.com

If you are unable to order this book from your local
bookseller, you may order directly from the publisher.
Call 1-800-766-8009, toll-free.

Library of Congress Catalog Card Number: Typesetter: 2003006458

ISBN 1-57174-346-4

10 9 8 7 6 5 4 3 2 1

Printed on acid-free paper in the United States

TO WANGIE,
YOUR STRENGTH CONTINUES
TO AMAZE AND INSPIRE ME.

Acknowledgements

I would like to thank the following people:

Edelle Moss for her inspiration, imagination, and insomnia;

My fellow public school teachers, Valerie Burdette, Sarah Wheaton, Jack Harrison, and Deirdre Callanan for their reading and feedback of early versions of *Utten and Plumley*;

Scott Moore for his endless stream of great ideas;

Mary Redmond for her loving friendship and helping me find the discipline to get it all down;

My fellow writers Ingrid and Janet for their guidance;

Ryan and Sandra for their consistent support and honest feedback;

Pat Adler, my editor at Hampton Roads Publishing, who believed in *Utten and Plumley* from the very first reading;

And Carol Malaquias and her fifth grade class at the Station Avenue Elementary School in South Yarmouth, Massachusetts: Emily, Fei, Peter, Ben, Eric M., Alexander, Ryan, Steven, Chad, Kris, David, Jared, John, Mike, Kayla, Sarah, Hayley, Taisha, Eric A., Jackie, Felipe, Lauren, Seth, Corey, and Christina. They were a delightful audience and a helpful group of critics.

TABLE OF CONTENTS

EATER OF CABBAGES AND HAMMERS

1

A GENTLY ROLLING CABBAGE

A word of warning before this story begins: Plumley dies in the end. Utten himself would never tell this story without warning you of that. At the beginning of this story, Plumley is very old. In the middle, Plumley is very young. At the end, he is old again. And then, very quietly, he slips away, and he is gone. It's really nothing to be sad about, and if you read very carefully, you will see why.

Utten lives by himself in a bucket in which he travels around the world living a life of high adventure. He is magic, and when he wants to he can turn himself into a bird. He isn't very big, only an inch or two taller than a grown man's ankle. Utten's back is speckled with sooty, shiny spots, which have a strange way of rearranging themselves when you aren't looking. His belly is pale, and when something particularly exciting happens, you might see it change colors, but only slightly. Everything else about him is blue, a most unremarkable blue for a most remarkable person.

Utten isn't sure exactly where he came from or how he got his name. Someone once told him that his name came from Oton, the legendary Norwegian god of thunder and applesauce, but Utten knows that there wasn't a god named Oton in the Norse myths. Still, it is an impressive story, but one that he rarely tells people because he doesn't want them to think that he is bragging.

Interestingly enough, this story begins with bragging, or at least that's what some would have you believe. Utten claims that he was just being truthful, but Cranston, his hulky friend, claims differently.

Utten had been traveling for weeks by himself in his bucket. He had gone out on an expedition up the murky Mittauquanuck River searching for a kind of apple called a Flaming Gardner. The Flaming Gardner is so rare that some apple enthusiasts swear that it is only a myth, but those who believe claim that it tastes as sweet as roaker flowers. Because it was exotic, because it claimed to be so tasty, and most importantly because the search for it stank of adventure, Utten went off to find the Flaming Gardner apple. He didn't find it, of course, because the Flaming Gardner is only a myth.

Still, all was not lost. Utten did have quite an adventure. In fact, he was out traveling for quite some time. Being out in the bucket so long left him feeling solitary and remote, and he decided to pay his old friend Cranston a call. He sailed out down the murky Mittauquanuck, turned back up Boar's Head Creek, and then took a short path overland to find the Misery River Brook. After a few hours coasting in the stream, Utten pulled up on shore near where Cranston lived.

Utten beached the bucket right under the enormous sign that read:

CRANSTON'S TWADDLES

LOPPINGS, DEBRIS, AND FRIPPERY FOR SALE CHEAP

Utten hiked up the small hill away from the creek bed. He walked past the stacks of old dinner plates, most of which were chipped because Cranston had let him use them for sledding in the wintertime. He sidestepped the pile of plungers that Cranston claimed were "just too good to sell." He turned through bin after bin, each filled with either old rusty nails, butter hinges, damp tennis balls, odd sneakers, or rasping brackets, among other things. He tramped over rugs that had been left out to molder in the sun, and eventually found his way to Cranston's doorstep. "I hope he's home," Utten mumbled, then whistled once for luck before knocking on the door.

"Are you in there, Cranston?" Utten shouted, much louder than you'd expect from a person his size. "It's me, your pal Utten! Come on, open the door!" Utten waited for a moment outside the door, but no one came to answer him. "Come on, Cranston, open the door!" Utten waited a few more moments, and when he judged that he had waited long enough to be polite, he opened the door and went inside the little hut. It didn't take long to find Cranston. The hut only had one room, and Cranston was an enormous person. Actually, he wasn't even a person, really. He was a troll.

Cranston dressed in layers of raggedy clothes even on the hottest summer day. String after string of beads and necklaces draped his neck. Six or eight earrings hung from each ear, and a dozen bracelets wrapped each wrist. One enormous tooth grew from his lower jaw, and it was so long and so hooked that he could pick his own nose with it if he chose to. He would be quite gruesome to look at if it weren't for his one eye smack in the center of his forehead, an eye that was so simple and kind that you couldn't help but fall in love with him the instant you saw him. A monocle with glass as thick as your thumb and earhooks on either side sometimes perched on Cranston's nose. Sometimes it didn't, and when it didn't you could be sure that he couldn't see more than an inch in front of his nose. Cranston looked a lot like a pudgy, slow-witted rhinoceros, and his one dewy, happy eye was eager and attentive to anyone who offered to tell him a story.

"What are you up to, Cranston?" Utten barked. "Why didn't you open the door?"

Cranston held his finger up to his mouth, shushing him. He was sitting on a tiny rickety stool on the other side of the room, his enormous legs pulled up underneath him so that they wouldn't touch the floor. On the floor in front of him was a round green cabbage.

"What's going on?" Utten persisted.

"Please, Utten, please be quiet!" Cranston pleaded.

Rolling his eyes, Utten sat down on the floor near the door. Cranston hovered over the cabbage, and it seemed to Utten that he was waiting for the cabbage to do something. His hands were out at his sides, his fingers were twitching, and there was a little sweat on his forehead.

"It's just a cabbage," Utten suggested, not intending to be mean, but Cranston shot him a look that was so mixed with hurt and irritation that Utten decided it would be in his own best interest to remain patiently quiet. Utten intently watched the cabbage. He watched the cabbage with the same concentration that Cranston did. He watched expecting the cabbage to do something.

Which it did. Right before Utten's eyes the cabbage began to move. It shifted a little to the right, and when it did, Cranston cupped his hands to his mouth to capture an escaping squeal of delight. Then the cabbage shifted again, this time back to the left. It seemed to wobble just a little bit, and then it rose off the floor just a fraction of an inch. You could barely see it lift, but you could hear the little thud as it dropped back to the floor.

"Oh boy!" Cranston yelled, clapping his hands. He very, very cautiously stepped down off the stool, then took a few careful steps towards the cabbage. "You did it!"

Utten couldn't take it any more. "What in the name of Henry Macintosh is going on, Cranston? Have you started dabbling in magic?" He marched across the floor of the room towards Cranston and the cabbage.

"Careful, Utten," Cranston blubbered. "Watch where you step." Cranston reached down with his finger and lifted something off of the floor. He walked over to Utten and held his finger close to the floor so that Utten could see. "It's not magic, Utten. It's only my friend, Woody." On Cranston's finger sat a tiny ant. "I trained him to lift the cabbage. Can you imagine that this little ant lifted up a whole cabbage? I can't believe it myself!" Woody lifted one his front feelers to his antennae and gave Utten a silent salute.

"You trained him to lift a cabbage like that?" Utten said, trying to sound impressed.

"I did it! I did it! I can't believe it," Cranston danced in circles, blowing soft kisses at Woody. Then, realizing that he had a guest, he held his finger up to a shelf high off the ground. "You go up there and rest, Woody. You did good work!" He fished in his pocket and found a crumpled catalpa leaf and placed it next to the tiny medicine bottle that Woody called home. "Here is a catalpa leaf just for you. You rest!" Jubilantly, Cranston turned to Utten. "Why are you here, Utten?" Cranston asked. "Do you need more mushroom grease? If you do then you're in trouble, because I sold my last jar yesterday."

"I don't need mushroom grease," Utten said. "I just stopped by to say hi! And to tell you about my latest adventure."

"Just to say hi!" Cranston repeated. "Then let's have a snack and you can tell me your story!"

"Okay," Utten said. "But just a little snack. I don't want to spoil my dinner, which should be coming along sometime soon."

That's when the arguing began. Though Utten and Cranston were good friends, they often argued. Sometimes Cranston did silly things, like eating toads and salamanders and other things that he knew would make him sick. Utten would end up yelling at him, reminding him that if he didn't watch his diet, he'd get a stomachache. Likewise, sometimes Utten went off on reckless adventures, and Cranston would try to stop him before he got into danger. It didn't really matter. Cranston still went on eating things he shouldn't, and Utten still went on reckless adventures. Consequently, each had plenty to argue with the other about.

This argument was a simple one. Cranston wanted to boil up the victory cabbage and have a snack of cabbage soup. Utten complained that Cranston always had cabbage soup, even when there wasn't any victory to celebrate. Utten said that cabbage didn't taste very good in the first place, and he didn't see how anyone could eat it. He suggested that they have apple bisque instead.

Cranston was horrified at Utten's claim that cabbage didn't taste very good. He claimed that apples were really food that only worms could love. He said that cabbage was the single healthiest food in the whole wide world—

And Utten shouted that if that was true, then the single healthiest food in the whole wide world tasted like old tires—

And Cranston retorted that he'd rather eat old tires than apples—

And Utten shouted, "Fine!" and went to leave—

And Cranston said, "Fine!" and turned his back on him—

But then, quicker than you could say "snakebite roller coaster," they decided to make a cabbage and apple stew. They set the water on to boil. By the time the stew was done, dinnertime had indeed come along just as Utten had predicted, so they both indulged themselves in big bowls. Of course, Utten ate mostly apples, and Cranston ate mostly cabbage.

"The Mittauquanuck was especially murky that night," Utten began after all the stew had been eaten and the dishes piled in a frowzy heap near the sink. "I was riding along in the bucket trying to steer through the churning water. Sometimes I had to pull the wheel so hard that I thought my arms would bust!"

Cranston sat on his rickety stool across the table from Utten, listening intently to the story. He had taken Woody down from his shelf and set him in an empty half of a peanut shell so that he could hear the story, too.

"The river was pulling me in so many different directions, I didn't know which way I was going. I was just trying to keep from being dashed on the rocks!" Woody looked from Utten back to Cranston, then back to Utten again. In his tiny ant mind, he imagined that the peanut shell on which he sat was caught up in the swirling waters of the murky Mittauquanuck, and the thought terrified him.

"Just then I felt something bump hard against the bucket. At first I thought I hit a rock, but the bump wasn't jarring enough. Then I felt the bump again, and I knew that I was in trouble. I wasn't hitting against something; something was hitting against me, and it was doing it on purpose!" Utten's voice began to quiver a little as he retold his story, and without even thinking about it he began to slip into his bird form. His feet turned into bird feet, and little feathers began to pop out on his back.

Woody looked again at Cranston. He was experiencing something that many folks experience when they hear a thrilling story. He was terribly frightened, so frightened that part of him wanted Utten to stop the story altogether. The other part of him couldn't stand not to know how the story was going to end!

"Then I heard a voice calling to me from outside the bucket. '*Utten*,' it hissed, '*you're never going to make it. You'll be tossed out of that bucket into the river, and then I'll swallow you whole!*'"

Woody couldn't stand it anymore. He wished that Cranston would put him back on the shelf so that he could hide in his medicine box. He at least wanted Cranston to lift him up and place him on his shoulder, and that way he could hide behind Cranston's huge ear. Cranston, however, was too wrapped up in the story to see just how frightened Woody was.

"I knew whose voice it was," Utten continued, his arms growing long feathers as they prepared to become wings. "It was Spicklecratt, that horrible old eel who's been after me all these years that I've been sailing in the bucket. You remember Spicklecratt, don't you Cranston?"

Cranston nodded his head yes, even though he had absolutely no idea who Spicklecratt was. He was sure that Utten had told him stories about Spicklecratt before, but he couldn't remember any of them. Still, he didn't want Utten to stop the story, so he nodded his head yes and pretended he knew what Utten was talking about.

"Well, it seemed like old Spicklecratt finally had me! Every time I got control of the wheel, he'd bump his slimy body against the bucket and knock me out of control again. There was no way out! I knew the water would grab me soon, and then Spicklecratt would eat me for dinner." Just then, by coincidence, Utten burped. "Excuse me," he added, "but I'm still digesting!"

"It fit perfectly into the story line," Cranston said helpfully. "But what did you do, Utten?" He still hadn't noticed poor Woody, whose tiny body was beginning to shake with fear so badly that the peanut shell began to rock back and forth.

"I pulled hard on the wheel and knocked the bucket right into that ugly eel. I shouted out to him, 'Listen you old puddlesnake, if it's a fight you want, it's a fight you'll get!' Spicklecratt didn't like that, and with a sharp flick of his tail he toppled the bucket, sending me down into the water. But I wasn't afraid! I swam straight at him!" Utten smiled, relishing the story. By this time he was mostly bird, right down to the beak. The only part of him that was still in his normal form was his behind, which was always the last to go.

Just then, Cranston heard the light rustle of the peanut shell quivering against the table, and he glanced down to see the terror in Woody's pleading eyes. As

Utten began to speak again, Cranston leaned over and whispered something in Woody's ear.

"What did you just say, Cranston?" Utten snapped, a little perturbed at the interruption.

"I said nothing, Utten! I promise! Please finish the story!" Cranston pleaded, knowing that he was in trouble.

"I want to know what you said, Cranston!" Utten shouted, "And I'm not going to finish the story unless you tell me!"

"No, Utten! Please finish! I promise not to interrupt you anymore!" Cranston begged, but Utten sat still as stone and didn't say a word.

"I'm waiting," Utten said defiantly, but Cranston closed his mouth and refused to speak. He not only refused to speak, he refused to breathe, a trick that he always felt would help him win an argument against Utten. His face turned three different colors of red, his monocle fogged up, and it was a full minute before Cranston sucked in a huge gulp of air. Still he refused to talk. Woody looked from Utten back to Cranston, then from Cranston back to Utten. Neither of them would give in.

"Okay," Utten said. "If you won't tell me, then I'm sure Woody will!"

"He can't talk. He's mute. Once, he was sunning himself on a drive-in movie screen and fell asleep. He woke up in the middle of a Frankenstein triple feature.

He kept trying to run off the screen, but wherever he ran, there was Frankenstein's monster, or the bride of Frankenstein, or the son of Frankenstein. Poor Woody screamed himself so silly that he ruined his voice forever. He can't tell you anything!" Cranston said, and then chuckled a little at how his friend had been outsmarted. Utten hopped down from the table and over to a pile of old newspapers stacked up in the corner. He pulled the top newspaper from the stack, dragged it back to the table, and laid it out face up. The headline read,

"PRESLEY GETS DRAFTED!"

"Okay, Woody," Utten said. "This is what I want you to do. You come over here and spell out what Cranston said. You walk around this newspaper, find the letters, and tap them out, okay?"

Very hesitantly, Woody climbed down off the peanut shell and walked over to the paper. He wasn't sure what he should do, but he was very intimidated by Utten. When he was in his bird form, Utten looked just like the sparrows that used to try and gobble him up when he worked on the anthills. He didn't want to do anything to make Utten any angrier than he was already. He tapped out the first letter: **h**

"H!" shouted Utten triumphantly. "He just tapped an H!"

Woody then found an E. After that he located an **S**, an A, an *i*, and a d. Cranston leaned forward and squinted through the thick lens of his monocle.

"h - E - **S** - A - *i* - d!" yelled Utten. "Wait a second—that doesn't make any sense. What does HESAID mean?"

"He is spelling out the words 'he' and 'said,'" Cranston said, leaning back and adjusting his monocle. "He said! You are not as smart as you'd like people to think!"

"Oh," Utten said. "HE SAID! He said what, Woody?"

Woody looked up at Cranston for guidance, but Cranston just shrugged. Woody tapped out a d, then an O, an N, and a T. "That spells 'Don't'!" Utten yelled out before Cranston got the chance to make him look foolish again. Woody wandered all over the page before he found the next letter: W. Then he easily found the O again. He tapped two **r** 's, and then had considerable trouble locating the next letter: **Y**.

"Don't worry," Utten read. "Don't worry about what?"

Woody knew that the next part was the terrible part, the part that would make Utten mad. And even though Utten had by now begun to slip back into his normal form, he still looked an awful lot like a bird. Woody found the letters as quickly as he could: U . . . T . . . T . . . E . . . N . . *i* . . **s** . . . O . . . N . . . l . . . y . . . B . . . r . . . A . . g . . . g . . . i . . . N . . . g.

"'Don't worry, Utten is only bragging?' Did you really say that, Cranston?" Utten demanded.

"You were scaring Woody! I was only trying to make him feel better!" Cranston said.

Utten stomped across the newspaper, right past Woody, and shook his finger in the giant troll's face. "I'll have you know that each and every one of my stories is absolutely true! I don't lie, I don't embellish, and I don't brag!"

Cranston really didn't mean the words which next came out of his mouth. He also knew that the words weren't true, but he said them anyway. Maybe he said them because he was angry. Maybe he said them in the heat of the moment. Maybe he said them because he sometimes was jealous of Utten's exciting lifestyle. Cranston didn't get away from his hut much, only to go out into woods looking for junk that he could sell, and that wasn't very exciting. For whatever reason, he said the words, and it set in motion a terrible chain of events. He looked right down at Utten, stuck his chin out, and said, *You make things up!*

"Oh, what a terrible thing to say!" Utten gasped. Cranston had never said anything so mean to Utten before. "It's lucky for you that you're my friend or else I'd get in my bucket and leave and never come back!"

Now that Cranston's insults had started flowing, he wasn't about to stop. "You might as well leave," he said,

"If all you're going to do is tell silly stories about wrestling with eels. You never fought an eel!"

"Bring me up there so I can say this right to your face!" Utten pointed to the table in front of him, and Cranston put his hand out. Utten climbed into his palm, and Cranston brought him up close to his face. "You didn't let me finish the story! I never said that I fought with Spicklecratt!" Utten yelled, shaking his fist at Cranston's fang. "But I would have fought with him! I was going to!"

"You were not," Cranston said. "You would be too afraid!"

"I'm not afraid of anything," Utten said assuredly, not letting it show that there might be one or two things that would actually frighten him.

"That is not true!" Cranston said.

Utten turned completely back into his normal form, shaking off all resemblance to a bird. He put his hands on his hips and stood solid with his feet spread apart. His belly turned a light shade of purple. "I'll take any dare you can think up!" Utten challenged. "You name it, and I'll do it."

Cranston put Utten back on the table and leaned back on his stool. "Any dare?" he asked.

Utten hesitated, but he knew that he couldn't back down. "Yes, any dare!" he said. All of a sudden, he began to worry about what Cranston might come up with. Cranston wasn't terribly smart, but he wasn't a dummy either. He could certainly come up with something daunting.

"I need time to think," Cranston said. He took off his monocle and tried to clean it on his grimy shirt. He didn't notice little Woody, who was frantically running around the newspaper tapping out letters. But Utten saw him. Utten watched the letters he spelled out. p. . . l . . .

"Cranston?" Utten said hesitantly.

"Be quiet! I am thinking!" Cranston said.

Woody found a U . . . M . . .

"Hey Cranston!" Utten said.

"Shush up, you!" Cranston complained.

Woody found an l . . . E . . . Y . . . He stopped for a moment to catch his breath, and then he started up again. p . . . l . . . U . . .

"Cranston," Utten asked, "What's a Plumley?"

Cranston quickly put on his monocle and watched Woody do his odd dance across the newspaper. His eyes widened, and a smile swept across his face. "You got it, Woody!" he shouted. "We can make him go visit Plumley! What a smart ant you are, Woody!"

Woody stopped his dance across the newspaper and then looked up at Utten. He lifted his foreleg to his antennae in salute. Utten stepped away and sat down on the edge of the newspaper.

"Who's Plumley?" Utten asked, a shudder rippling through his body as feathers popped out of the spots on his back.

FEATHERS AND ALL

2

The House of Many Ghosts

"You tell it, Woody!" Cranston said. He knew it would take a long time for Woody to find all the letters he needed to tell the story, but he also knew that the time would only add to Utten's suspense.

"Maybe we shouldn't be so hasty," Utten suggested, smiling nervously. "That was a pretty heated argument, Cranston."

"You said any dare! You said any dare!" Cranston yelled, almost singing the words as he savored Utten's discomfort. Meanwhile, Woody began to dance out the story of Plumley:

O...l...d...M...A...N...p...l...U...M...l...e...y

..i...s...T...h...E...M...e...A...N...e...s...T...

M . . . A . . . N . . .W . . . h . . . O . . .

E . . . V . . . E . . . r . . . l . . . *i* . . . V . . . E . . . d . . .

Utten walked up right to the edge of the newspaper. "If he's so mean, how come I've never heard of him?"

"Because you are not as smart as you think you are," Cranston offered.

h . . . E . . . *i* . . . s . . .

W . . . *i* . . . C . . K . . . E . . . d . . .

T . . h . . E . . r . . E . . . *i* . . s . . .

A . . . h . . . U . . . g . . . E . . f . . . E . . . N . . . C . . . E . . .

A . . . r . . . O . . . U . . . N . . . d . . .

h . . . *i* . . . s . . . h . . . O . . . U . . . s . . . E

h . . . *i* . . . s . . . y . . . A . . . r . . . d . . . *i* . . . s

C . . . O . . . v . . . E . . . r . . . E . . . d . . .W . . . *i* . . . T . . . h

p . . . r . . . *i* . . . C . . . K . . . E . . . r . . . s . . . A . . . N . . . d . . .

W . . . E . . . E . . . d . . . s . . . T . . . h . . . A . . . T . . .

s...M...E..l..l..l..*i*..K...E...

g...A...r..l...*i*...C...

"Hey Woody, you're a pretty good speller," Utten piped, hoping that it might win him some clemency with either Cranston or Woody. Woody didn't even pause to acknowledge the compliment.

T...h...E..h...O...U...s...E...*i*...s.

A...l...w...A...y...s..d...A...r...K

...*i*...N...s...*i*...d...E...

Utten gulped. "Even during the day?" Utten asked.

E...V...E...N...d...U...r..*i*..N...g...

T...h...E..d...A...y...s...O...

T...h...E...y...s...A...y...

"So who says?" Utten asked.

T...h...O...s...E..W..h...O...

h...A...v...E..g...O...T...T..E..N...

21

O . . . **U** . . . T . . . A . . . l . . *i* . . . **v** . . . E . . .

Woody paused for minute, looking the paper over for a very specific punctuation mark. He finally spotted it in an advertisement for a brand new kitchen tile cleaner. He ran over and tapped it. . . . ! . . .

"This is silly," Utten said. "There's no such guy as Plumley!"

i . . . N . . . **s** . . . *i* . . . d . . . E . . . T . . . h . . . E . . .

h . . . O . . . **U** . . . **s** . . . E . . .

p . . . l . . . **U** . . . M . . . l . . . E . . . y . . .

s . . . T . . . O . . . r . . . E . . . **s** . . .

h . . . *i* . . . **s** . . . T . . . h . . . *i* . . . N . . . g . . . **s** . . .

Woody emphasized the word "things" by slowing his pace and tapping harder with his foreleg on the letters. The effect was quite dramatic. Utten asked the obvious question, "What kinds of things?"

O . . . h . . . y . . . O . . . **U** . . . K . . . N . . . O . . . W . . .

Woody tapped, and then slowed down his pace to add even more drama. As he hit each letter, he looked up at

Utten and opened his eyes wide. T . . . h . . . *i* . . . N . .
g . . . S . . . Each time Woody made eye contact with
Utten, a feather popped out of the skin on the top of
Utten's head.

Woody tapped faster as he detailed the *things* that
Old Man Plumley kept in his house. He knew where
most of the letters were now, and could find them with
ease. He also started pausing at times so that they could
better see where one word ended and another began.

SKULLS . . . SNAKE SKINS . . . TORTURE RACKS

"Do not forget the dead birds on sticks!" Cranston
offered.

**DEAD BIRDS ON STICKS . . . BIG BLOODY JARS
FULL OF BUGS . . .**

"There are also shovels that he likes to steal from
graveyards!" Cranston said.

BUT THAT'S NOT THE WORST OF IT . . .

"What's the worst of it?" Utten asked. He really
didn't want to know. He had learned enough about
Plumley to realize that he didn't want to go anywhere
near the old man's house.

**HE HAS A PET WOLF NAMED CORCORAN . . .
CORCORAN CATCHES KITTIES FROM THE
NEIGHBORHOOD . . . HE BRINGS THEM HOME . . .
THEN THE OLD MAN GETS OUT SOME OF HIS
MOLDY STINKY CHEESE AND MAKES A BIG CAT
CASSEROLE!**

en realizing it, Utten squawked. He imag-
with an eye patch, a peg leg, and an old
d around his waist. At his feet sat a crazy
...g wolf, and next to the wolf lay a big sack full of
squirming kitties. Plumley fumbled through a giant
recipe book, flipping with grimy fingers through page
after page as he searched for the right casserole recipe.

Just to taunt Utten, Woody added one extra fact. He
wasn't sure that the fact was true, but it fit the story very
well. **WHENEVER HE CAN CATCH ONE HE ALSO
EATS BIRDS . . . HE EATS THEM RAW . . . FEATHERS
AND ALL . . .**

"No way!" shouted Utten. "There's no way I'm going
over that guy's house!"

"You said any dare, Utten," Cranston reminded. "You
said you were fearless. You said you would do anything."
As Utten listened to his friend, he wished that he hadn't
gotten so hotheaded during their argument. Cranston continued, "This is the dare. You fly up the brook to where it
bends. You go to Old Man Plumley's house. You sneak
inside. You find him, and you pluck a single gray hair off
his scaly head and bring it back here to me and Woody. If
you don't then you are just a little blue chicken."

"Fine," Utten said. "I'll go in the morning. It's too
late tonight—"

Cranston leaned forward, and the lens of his monocle made his eye look like it was bulging out of his head.

"No way! You go tonight. You go in the dark! You be back by dawn! That is the dare!" Cranston said.

Utten thought for a minute. If only he hadn't gotten so riled up before. If only he had thought before opening up his big blue mouth. Then he wouldn't be in this situation. "Okay," he finally said. "A dare is a dare. You watch my bucket until I get back." Utten turned into his bird form and flew out the window of the little hut, away up Misery Brook to where it bent.

Cranston and Woody smiled as Utten left. "This will teach him a lesson!" Cranston said. They settled back to wait for Utten's return. But Utten wouldn't be coming back that night, and he wouldn't be back at dawn either.

The moon was just beginning to rise on Misery Brook. "A dare is a dare, a dare is a dare," Utten kept saying to himself as he flew over the brook. "A dare is a dare." He could not admit to Cranston and Woody that the story of Old Man Plumley had spooked him, but he had to admit it to himself. His body felt electric, as if his nerves had all started prickling at the exact same time. "My," he said out loud to himself. "This certainly is exciting!" Utten flapped his wings bravely. Surely Woody had exaggerated his tale of Plumley a little. The old man couldn't be all that bad.

But Woody hadn't exaggerated, at least not about the house that Plumley lived in. Utten found the house with ease. The enormous mansion stood by itself in the middle of the woods far away from any main road. An old driveway overgrown with withered grass wound away towards the road. A high fence surrounded the yard, and the lawn was covered with weeds. Utten could smell the weeds' garlic stench as he circled over the top of the house.

Utten had rarely seen a house so big. In fact, the only houses that Utten had ever seen that were bigger than Plumley's were the houses of sultans and kings and presidents that Utten had met in his travels around the world. The rooms of the house seemed to be pushing on the outside walls, pressing through with odd angles and creating twisted corners. Likewise, the roof was covered with gables, dormers, and mazes of drainpipes. Boards hung from the siding. Shingles dripped from the roof. The gutters were rusted through or stuffed up with leaves. The house seemed to breathe, and it decayed a little more with every stale breath it expelled.

Last but not least, it was incredibly dark, though it looked like there were very dim, flickering lights in some of the windows. Utten had never seen a house that looked more haunted. It was the kind of place where, if you woke up in the middle of the night at just the right hour, you might hear the laughing of tiny, eternal ghosts as they flitted from room to room playing hide and seek with each other. You might lie awake on such a night and hope that none of them had decided to hide under your bed while you had been sleeping . . .

Utten landed on the roof, and though he tried to slip back into his normal form, his excitement wouldn't allow him to lose all the feathers on his back. He dropped down to a windowsill and tried to look inside, but he couldn't see a thing. He pulled upon the window, and it opened with ease. He sneaked inside.

Utten found himself in a long hallway. Many doors led off of it, some of them open and others not. Then the hallway turned, and Utten couldn't see where it ended up. The hall resembled the entrance to an enormous maze, and Utten wondered how he was ever going to find Old Man Plumley with so many rooms to check. More important than that, he wondered how he would avoid Corcoran, who at that very instant might have caught a whiff of him and started down one of the many passageways to find him.

Utten held his breath and tiptoed down the hallway. He was very careful not to make any sound at all as he peeked into the many rooms he passed. Some of the rooms had nothing at all, while others were filled up with old furniture. One room was stacked floor to ceiling with musty mattresses; another was full of desks with all their drawers pulled out. A thick carpet of dust on the floor had only been disturbed by the cautious footsteps of tiny frightened mice.

The first place that Utten found that looked even slightly lived in was an enormous library. Filled with stacks and stacks of books, the library took up four huge rooms in the house. Utten couldn't understand how one man could read so many books. Someone had even arranged the books by alphabetical order and placed letters on all the stacks so that they could find the books more easily. Looking at the arranged volumes, Utten realized that one person couldn't possibly read all the books that Plumley had at his disposal. Even if a hundred people spent their entire lives reading Plumley's collection, they still couldn't get through all the books that sat on those shelves.

In the last room of the library, Utten found a remarkably cozy den. A thick rug lay comfortably under his toes, and a sloppy, well used chair stood ready next to a large fireplace. The fireplace had been used recently; a bed of black coals still radiated a little heat. In front of the chair was a small table, and Utten climbed up onto the seat of the chair to examine it.

A thin folding wooden chessboard sat on top of the table. It looked like someone was in the middle of a game. Utten looked around the room, but there were no other chairs to be found. If Plumley was playing chess, then who was he playing with? Upon closer inspection, Utten saw that a lot of the pieces were mismatched. The black pieces were mostly made of marble, but a number of them were missing. In their place were odd objects. A peppershaker was the king, and one of his bishops was a spool of thread. On the white side, the queen was an aspirin bottle, and three of her pawns were only acorns. A small piece of worn wood off to the side of the board had the words **White's Turn** scratched on its surface. Utten flipped the piece over, and on the other side it said, **Black's Turn**.

"This is very strange," Utten whispered out loud. Since he had turned the wooden piece over, he thought it would be only polite to make the move for white, so he studied the board intently for a few minutes. When he was sure he had chosen the best move, he shifted one of the rooks forward five paces. Satisfied that he had done right, he dropped off the chair and made his way further down the hallway.

Utten reached the stairwell. The stairwell went down to a lower floor, and then further down beyond that. Utten couldn't see exactly how far the stairs went down, because just a few steps below the next landing the stairs disappeared into blackness. The lower floors were so dark that it looked as if that portion of the house were filled with black, sooty water. Then Utten heard a sound that made his feet turn to talons and caused his mouth to stretch into a beak. Somewhere down those steps on one of the lower floors, somewhere deep down in all that liquid darkness, something was crying. At least, it sounded to Utten like something was crying or wailing.

No, it wasn't a cry. Nor was it a wail. It was a mew. Something was mewing down there. And that could only mean one thing. Plumley and Corcoran had captured a bunch of cats. They were downstairs somewhere, probably in an old burlap sack trying desperately to get out before Plumley woke up and chose a recipe from his casserole book. They mewed and mewed, and Utten knew that he had to go down there and let them free.

Utten dropped down the stairs one at a time until he hit the second landing. Still the mewing came from below. If Utten were going to save the cats, he would have to go into that inky blackness. Just as he began to step down, he noticed a dim light coming from one of the doorways. He hung close to the wall, made his way down to the door, and peeked inside.

The room was lit by a tiny nightlight, and Utten could barely see by its dimness. The furniture was sparse. A dresser leaned against the far wall on the left, its top decorated by nothing more than a comb, a pair of nail clippers, and a single gray sock. Warped hardwood floors had not even a rug to warm them. A bed stood near the door, a dingy bathrobe hanging off one its four wooden posts. There were no pictures on the walls, and no family photos stood in frames on top of the dresser. It was almost as if the occupant had no personal treasures at all. As Utten glanced around the room, he sensed a life so narrow and so bare that it wasn't worthy of a single personal treasure.

A loud thump jolted Utten, causing him to jump against the wall just inside the door of the room. A book had fallen from the edge of the bed onto the hardwood floor below. Utten pressed himself against the wall and held his breath. Atop the bed, the large lump that was Old Man Plumley shifted under the covers. A withered hand reached down from the bed and grabbed the edge of the book. Utten could just barely make out the title of the book: *The Wizard of Oz* by Frank L. Baum. The hand snapped the book closed. The lump under the blankets settled again, and its breathing became slow and even.

Plumley fell back to sleep, and Utten sighed with relief as he stepped away from the wall and back out into the hallway. If Utten could just free the cats quietly, then he could sneak back upstairs and pluck a hair off Plumley's sleeping head. He could do it so fast that he could fly up and out the window before Plumley even opened his eyes.

Of course, this plan would only work if the great wolf, Corcoran, didn't find him first. Utten had found Plumley, but Corcoran could be anywhere, and he might not be asleep.

Utten made his way down three of the steps that led to the ground floor. The next step down would take him into the shadows. Even close up, it looked to Utten like he was standing on the edge of a lake of blackness, so much so that he held his nose as he dropped over the edge. The room was pitch black. There wasn't even moonlight coming in from the windows. If Utten were going to find and free those cats, he was going to have to do it blind.

From the darkness the mewing continued. But now there was another sound with it. Along with the mewing of the cats, Utten could hear the breathing of a larger animal, a dog—

No, not a dog. A wolf.

Utten thought that maybe it was time to forget the whole thing and go back to Cranston's hut, but he dismissed the idea. He couldn't leave those poor cats out there trapped in that sack. He stepped away from the stairwell into the dark room.

His arms out in front of him, he felt his way along. He took each step carefully, hoping that he wouldn't bump into something big and hairy. Each step forward could mean certain death, but Utten refused to stop. He kept going forward, trying to locate the source of the mewing, but the source kept moving. When he stepped closer to the sound in front of him, another would pop up behind him. Try as he might, he couldn't figure out where the sack of cats might be. By the time he got out into the center of the room, the mewing seemed to come from all around him.

Suddenly, something brushed up against Utten. Whatever it was, it was large and it was furry. Utten panicked. Without even thinking, he slipped into his bird form and let out a loud squawk. He flapped his wings and lifted up off the floor, immediately colliding with a lamp. It tipped over, pulling him with it as it smashed onto the floor of the room. Stunned, Utten lay on the floor of the old mansion and tried to regain his bearings. He couldn't tell which way was up or down, but he could hear three new sounds floating to him through the blackness of the room.

First was a large animal growling right next to him.

Second was a click as the upstairs hall light was turned on.

Third were the footsteps coming down the stairs.

"I LIVE IN A BUCKET."

3

THE CAT WRANGLER

A figure of a man paused when it reached the bottom of the stairs, and Utten could discern only his outline in the dim light cast by the upstairs hall light. He had wrapped himself in a bathrobe, and the few hairs he had on his head were scraggly and frazzled. He placed his hand on the banister to steady himself.

"Who's there?" he asked the darkness angrily.

Utten lay perfectly still, not knowing what to say.

"Who's there?" Plumley called again, stepping out into the dark. If Utten didn't know the story of how terrible and mean Plumley was, he might have thought that Plumley sounded a little afraid. "I am just an old man, and I have nothing for you to steal."

"I'm no thief!" Utten shouted, expecting Corcoran to gobble him up the instant he opened his mouth.

"Then why have you come to my house in the middle of the night? Why do you hide in the dark? Do you mean me harm?" Plumley asked.

Utten began to feel a little bad. He had sneaked into Plumley's house in the middle of the night. He had made a ruckus and woken Plumley up. Utten's sympathy for Plumley lasted only for an instant, and then he remembered that Plumley ate cats.

"I've come for the cats!" Utten shouted from the dark. "I've come to free them!"

"Oh have you?" Plumley asked, his voice rising. He stepped forward and clicked on the light switch. Utten quickly hid inside an old slipper next to the couch. "I can't see you," Plumley said. "Where are you hiding? Come out; I'm just an old man, and I can't hurt anyone."

Utten wasn't about to be fooled by Plumley's "I'm just and old man" trick. This man was vicious and cruel, and he could not be trusted. Utten peeked out at him from inside the slipper. To his surprise, he saw that Plumley didn't have a peg leg. He didn't even have an eye patch. In fact, he didn't even look all that mean.

"Please come out," Plumley said. "You've startled me, and I'm a little frightened." Plumley hesitantly pulled back one of the curtain windows, checking behind for the intruder.

"Just let the cats go and I'll be on my way," Utten demanded, trying to make his voice sound deep and intimidating.

"I'd be happy to let the cats go, but they won't leave," Plumley explained, checking behind an old arm chair. "I never wanted them here in the first place, but they seem to love my dog Corker for some reason. They follow her home all the time, and they won't leave. I keep expecting that someone will come to claim at least one of them, but no one seems to want to come by my house."

Safely hidden inside the old slipper, Utten pondered whether or not this could be true. "It looks like a haunted house," Utten pointed out.

"It used to be nice, but I let it go a little. Then I began to get old, and I couldn't fix it up anymore. Then the cats came, and now I spend all my time refilling saucers of milk and cleaning kitty litter. It's terrible! If you want the cats, you can take them!"

Utten peeked out of the slipper a little more. Plumley was right close by peering over the back of his sofa. Next to him stood Corcoran. Actually, according to Plumley, the animal wasn't even called Corcoran; he was called Corker. Also, he wasn't a *he*—he was a *she*.

Corcoran wasn't a wolf at all. She was just a dog named Corker. She stood a little taller than Plumley's knee, and she was sleek like a hound. Her fur was a mixture of deep browns and tans which blended together in a brindle which looked like carefully polished wood. She stood at Plumley's side sniffing the air to try and locate the stranger who had invaded their house. Around her circled five cats, all rubbing up against her and purring.

Corker came from a long line of hounds that were expert hunters. Her sense of sight and smell excelled even by dog standards. Utten's head wasn't out of the slipper for a second before she spotted him. She immediately ran over and sniffed the slipper, then looked up at Plumley.

Very cautiously, Plumley walked over and lifted the slipper from the ground. "I'm sorry, old girl, but I don't think anyone could possibly fit in there." He turned the shoe and peered inside.

Feeling the slipper in Plumley's grasp, Utten knew there was no escape from him. If what Woody had told him was true, Utten would surely be eaten alive, but Utten was beginning to doubt everything about Woody's story. He shyly poked his head up from inside the slipper. "Hello," he piped, trying to sound as cheerful as possible.

"Oh my," Plumley said quietly. "Oh my, oh my." He sat down on the edge of the sofa and stared at Utten. "What are you?"

"I'm Utten," Utten explained. "I live in a bucket. I'm magic, and when I want to I can turn myself into a bird."

Corker stepped over and sniffed at Utten in the slipper. The scent of him confirmed her suspicion that Utten was no real danger. Satisfied, she lay down at Plumley's feet.

Seeing her up close, Utten sensed how lucky he was that Corker didn't see him as a threat. Though not a wolf, underneath her beautiful coat moved a powerful, muscular frame. She was more than capable of defending her master if the situation called for it.

"Live in a bucket, eh? Is that so?" Plumley said absently. "Then I must be dreaming."

"Nope! Sorry!" Utten said. He climbed out of the slipper and looked around the room. There were cats everywhere. Utten's first thought was to try to count them, but they were moving around so much that he couldn't tell one from the other. Many of them were milling around Corker. Plumley must have had every cat in town living on the first floor of his house.

"If I'm not dreaming, and you really are an Utten, then you're a very rude little Utten!" Plumley snapped. He was recovering from the alarm of having an intruder in his house, and irritation began to grow in the place his diminishing fear left behind.

"I'm not rude!" Utten protested, but he knew that he had been a little rude.

"What right do you have to be squawking around people's houses in the middle of the night? I'm a respectable citizen! I pay my taxes! I should just call up the local police and have them come out here and arrest you," Plumley said, his voice growing more irritated.

"Wait, let me tell you exactly what happened," Utten

said. He proceeded to tell Plumley the whole story. He began with his expedition up the murky Mittauquanuck, and about how he wanted to go visit his friend, Cranston. He told him about Woody and the cabbage. He told him how he tried to tell Cranston and Woody about Spicklecratt, but that Cranston called him a liar. He told him about the dare. He told how he only wanted to sneak into the house and steal a hair off Plumley's sleeping head. "But then I heard the cats mewing," Utten explained, "And I had to free them before you ate them."

"Pollywog snot!" Plumley shouted, so loud that it startled Corker. "I don't eat cats! I don't keep bloody jars of bugs in the corner, I don't have any torture racks, I don't play with dead birds on sticks, and I certainly don't steal shovels from graveyards! I'm just an old man who wants to be left alone!"

Utten felt terrible. "I'm sorry," he said, and he meant it.

"I don't have time to be up in the middle of the night with such silliness!" Plumley scowled as only old men know how to and pointed to the front door. "Now go!"

Utten very slowly climbed down off the couch and headed for the door. He turned back to Plumley and asked, "Can I just have one hair—"

"No!" Plumley shouted. "If you haven't come for the cats then get out and leave me alone, you little blue what-ever-you-are!"

Utten had almost reached the door when his guilt

handed him an idea. "Hey Plumley," he said joyfully, "I think I know how to take care of your cat problem!" He walked back to the couch, climbed up onto the cushions, and sat down next to Plumley again.

Plumley ran his fingers through his frazzled hair and snorted. "You're sure you're not a nightmare, a hallucination of some kind?"

"I don't think so," Utten replied, slightly confused.

"I might have had too much mustard on my sausages at dinner, and it's bubbling down there in my belly and giving me bad dreams," Plumley suggested.

"I'm pure, unfiltered reality!" Utten beamed. "Poke me if you're not sure!"

"That won't be necessary," Plumley replied. He reached out to pet one of the many cats that lay on the couch. "I might as well stay up and listen to you," he sighed. "I'd probably never get back to sleep anyway. But this better be good! What's your plan?"

Utten told Plumley the plan, and Plumley agreed that it was a pretty good plan. Utten said he was full of good plans, and told him the story of when he helped the Sultan of Polania, who was strapped for cash, build a combination observatory and cafeteria for the same price as it would have cost him to build an outhouse. That story led to the story of how Utten was once trapped in an outhouse way out on the tundra when the outhouse door froze shut and locked him inside. That story led to another, and that one to another, and before either of them knew it the sun was rising.

"I think we're ready," Utten said. He climbed up on Corker's back and straddled her neck. "Head 'em up!" he said. As the rising sun tried to filter through the closed shutters of the mansion's windows, Utten and Corker climbed the main stairwell all the way up to the top floor. They went from room to room waking up all the cats and shooing them downstairs.

"Heeyah!" shouted Utten. He had a long twig that he had taken from a weeping willow he had found in the yard, and every time he shouted "Heeyah," he snapped it in the air, creating a crack like a tiny whip. "Move it on, kitties!"

The cats didn't think much of Utten's cowboy routine. In fact, they ignored him. However, they were fascinated to know what Corker was up to, so they followed along dutifully. As they cleared out every room upstairs, Plumley closed the doors to the rooms so that the cats couldn't go back in. After the third floor was cleared, they went to the second. Nearly thirty cats had joined the group by the time they came downstairs.

The majority of the cats were already on the main

floor. When Corker led the procession downstairs and all the cats were in the main room, their ranks swelled to an army. They circled around, purred at, and rubbed up against Corker. She really didn't like all the attention, but she was a very polite dog, and she didn't want to do anything that might hurt their feelings. Still, she quietly hoped that Utten's plan would work.

"Okay, Plumley, now we're ready to head them all back to town!" Utten declared.

"Oh no," Plumley said. "I won't be going to town. You don't need me for this plan."

"What?" Utten blurted. "But this is your chance to prove to the whole town that you're not a nasty old cat-eater!"

Plumley's lips soured into a frown. "Let them think I eat worms for all I care! Who needs 'em!"

"Please, Plumley, it's going to be fun!" Utten prodded.

"Pollywog snot! It's a long walk to town, and I'm a very old man. I'd tire out and slow you down, Utten. You go have fun." Plumley picked up a small chair and carried it towards the door.

"How old are you?" Utten asked.

"Oh, I don't know. Old enough to be a father for sure, if I had a son. Old enough to be a grandfather I guess, but I have no grandkids. Even old enough to be a great-grandfather, I would venture to bet, but I have no great-grandkids." Plumley opened the front door and set his chair outside in the sun. "You go on your own, Utten. You don't need an old man to slow you down." He brushed off the chair, sat down, and rubbed his hands together. "Now, let's get this show on the road!"

Corker agreed by whining quietly. The cats had decided to give her a cat bath, and about a dozen of them were licking her head and back. She was ready for peace and quiet.

Utten climbed up on the mantel over the fireplace and surveyed the scene. The entire room was a mass of happy cats climbing over each other to get at Corker. In the middle of it all Corker sat patiently. To Utten, she looked like a rock star who had been dropped into a pit full of adoring groupies.

"Ready, Corker?" Utten asked. Corker barked once and cocked her head. Utten threw his arms out to his sides. His left hand began to quiver, and tiny feathers popped out along his arm. Feathers appeared on his right, too. His mouth pointed into a beak, and his feet thinned into talons. Feathers rolled down his belly. Utten flapped his wings and flew out into the room over the throng of cats. "Come and get me!" he shouted.

The cats ignored him. They couldn't have cared less about a bird so long as Corker was in the room. "It's not working!" Utten said.

"What's the hold up?" Plumley called from the doorway.

"They're not taking the bait," Utten called back. "It doesn't make any sense! Cats love to catch birds!"

"Try swooping at them," Plumley suggested. Utten swooped down at the cats, but they refused to notice him. He spun in the air, flipped, and flew figure eights. He even pecked one of the cats on the head, but they were simply not interested.

"They only care about Corker!" Utten said. "This will never work!"

"Wait!" said Plumley from the doorway. "I have another suggestion. Corker, bark at Utten. Pretend he's bothering you!"

Utten flew over Corker's head, and she rallied a storm of barks from her lungs. She barked as angrily as she could and snapped at Utten with her jaws. Her bark was so fierce that even Utten was surprised, and judging only by the force of her snapping jaws, he thought that she might as well *be* a wolf like Woody's rumors had suggested.

Corker's show was enough to convince the cats. Believing that she was truly annoyed, one of the cats swiped at Utten with his claws. Utten flapped out of its way, but soon other cats joined in. Each one of them wanted to knock the blue bird out of the air to please Corker.

"It's working!" Utten shouted. He flew circles just out of reach of the crowd of cats, barely avoiding the paws that tried to tag him.

"You've got 'em, Utten! Head for the door!" Plumley shouted.

Utten flapped his way to the door, and the entire mass of cats followed after him, desperate to capture him and appease Corker. "They sure do like you, Corker!" Utten said. He flapped straight out the door, and the mob of cats followed after him.

It had been a long time since Plumley had ever seen a show like this. Majestic in his bird form, Utten sure knew how to fly. He got just close enough to the cats to keep them interested in the chase, but not close enough to get nabbed by their claws.

Away down the driveway they went. The tiny blue bird flapped like an aerial daredevil followed by hundreds of desperately jabbing paws. In their wake they left nothing but a cloud of dust . . . and, of course, peace and quiet.

Plumley and Corker hadn't known peace and quiet in a long time. Corker came out and sat at Plumley's feet. He scratched her head, and she looked up at him. For a moment, Corker thought she saw the old man smiling, but he dropped his chin into a frown as soon as he saw her looking at him. "That Utten sure is something, isn't he?" Plumley asked his dog.

They waited there in the sun for a half an hour. When Utten returned, out of breath but extremely excited, Plumley held out a finger for Utten to land on. "You should have seen it, Plumley! We got to the center of town, and one by one everybody came out of their houses to see what all the commotion was about. There I was in the center of the street with all those cats leaping up at me! The people were so happy to see their cats that they ran out and started scooping them all up. I shouted at the top of my lungs, 'Plumley doesn't eat cats! Plumley doesn't eat cats!' They were so excited to see their pets back that they didn't even realize that it was a bird talking. They just started telling each other, 'Hey, did you hear that Plumley doesn't eat cats?' Then someone else would say, 'No, I didn't know that but it must be true.' What an adventure! Amazing!" Utten flew off of Plumley's finger and landed on Corker's head. He slipped back into his normal Utten form and slid down her back to the ground. "That was great fun!" he shouted, still a little out of breath. Corker leaned over and gave Utten a big thank you lick, and Utten's belly turned pink in embarrassment.

"It is nice that they all got their cats back," Plumley said. He stood, walked to the door, and looked inside his mansion. "It's nice and quiet in there, don't you think? The house seems empty with all our kitty friends gone, doesn't it, Corker? How's an old man going to breathe life into this broken down house?"

"With my help!" Utten said. He slipped back into his bird form and flew up to land on Plumley's shoulder. He then slipped back to his normal form and sat down next to Plumley's collar. "We can have all kinds of adventures in here!"

The trio spent the afternoon clearing bushes away from the largest of the windows downstairs. Plumley found an old pair of loppers in the shed, and he let Utten borrow a pair of fingernail clippers so that he could help out. As they pulled away the branches, Corker picked them up in her jaws and placed them in a pile by the fence.

"You'd better let me get into the bush first," Utten warned. "There may be a sylberpodder nest in there."

"Sylberpodder? I've never heard of such a thing!" Plumley growled as he snipped at the enormous bush.

"A sylberpodder is a terrible, terrible creature. It has a body like a spider, but it has wings like a fly. It has claws like a lobster, and it has pinchers like an ant. And it's got an ugly little face that's not like anything you've ever seen before."

"Really," Plumley said, genuinely interested. "And you've seen such things?"

"They're very rare," Utten said, trimming at the smaller twigs with the fingernail clippers. "But you never know. It's best to be careful. A sylberpodder can be a nasty beast if it gets at you."

Plumley snipped a large branch, and when it fell a great portion of the window became exposed. "What will a sylberpodder do if it gets at you?" Plumley asked.

"They wait until you go to sleep, and then they fly up inside your nose and build a nest. You won't even know they're there because the nest is so light and fluffy. You'll just think your nose is stuffed up. Then at night when you sleep, the sylberpodder will go out and fly around and find food that she'll take back up your nose and eat."

"I did feel a little sneezy this morning," Plumley confessed. "I might have a sylberpodder up there right now and not even know it!"

"There's only way to find out for sure," Utten said. "Lower your head down here." Plumley brought his face right up close to Utten. With his left hand Utten grabbed Plumley's nostril, and with his right he reached up inside Plumley's nose and felt around. Then he did the same with the other nostril. "Nope, you're all clear!" Utten said when he had finished.

"Thank you, thank you very much," Plumley said, wiping his nose with his finger.

"No problem! You also have to worry about choates, which are almost as bad as sylberpodders, but not quite. And don't forget flobbleworms!" Utten said with a shudder.

"Tell me about them," Plumley said.

They passed most of the afternoon away like this, and

Utten listed all of the creatures of the world that he felt Plumley should watch out for. By the time he was finished, the window was clear, and Utten, Plumley, and Corker went inside to see their handiwork.

The room looked completely different. A huge shaft of sunlight fell into the room, creating a lagoon of light around a dusty armchair. Tired, Plumley sat down in it, and Corker lay down with her head resting on his feet.

"Let's go out and cut down some more!" Utten suggested.

Plumley shook his head. "You have so much energy," he sighed.

"Yeah, I'm a pretty lively guy!" Utten said.

Utten looked around the room. Now that the cats were gone and there was some light to see by, the room looked quite nice. The curtains were old but beautiful, and the windows were very tall. The furnishings were comfortable. It looked more like a pleasant lobby to welcome people into the mansion than a living room.

"This is a pretty nice place once you let some light in," Utten said, but Plumley had fallen asleep in the warm sun. Utten climbed up the side of the chair and stood on Plumley's shoulder. He waved the fingernail clippers in the air. "Don't worry Plumley," he whispered, "If there are any sylberpodders about, I'll get them!" He pretended that a sylberpodder was trying to fly up Plumley's nose and stabbed at the imaginary bug with his clippers. "And I'll get the choates and yinkers, too!" Waving the clippers like a madman, Utten listed off the creatures he was capable of defending the old man from. Meanwhile, Plumley sank into a deep, restful sleep.

ALL MAGIC HAS A BALANCE

4

MAGIC IN THE BIRCH

Early the next morning, Utten and Corker cleared away a small area of the weeds in the backyard. Utten then went upstairs to the library and took all the chess pieces off the chess table. Together he and Corker managed to carry the small table down to the clearing in the backyard.

Plumley claimed that he wasn't interested in playing chess. While Corker carried down the chessboard in her mouth and placed it on the table, Plumley grabbed a chair from inside the house, set it up in the newly made clearing, and brought out a newspaper to read. With the exception of the year, the newspaper had the right date. Its headline read,

DEWEY DEFEATS TRUMAN!

Meanwhile, Utten opened up one of the windows in the library and began flying the pieces down one at a time. He placed them in the exact locations they had been in on the board when they were up in the library. Finally, Utten brought down the wood piece that said, "Black's Turn" and placed it next to Plumley.

"It's not black's turn, it's white's turn. You've got it all wrong," Plumley said, barely looking up from his newspaper.

"Nope, I made a move for white the night I first came here," Utten explained. "So now it's black's turn."

"You what?!" Plumley shouted, his frown growing deeper. "You can't move for white! I'm playing the white pieces!"

"Fine," Utten said agreeably. "Then I'll play for black."

"Pollywog snot!" Plumley shouted, equally enraged. "You can't move for black. I move for black!"

Puzzled, Utten stared at the board. "How can you move for black and for white? That doesn't make any sense!"

"That's why I have that little piece of wood. It helps me keep track of whose move it is. Besides, when I play against myself, I always win!" Plumley explained.

"But you also always lose!" Utten pointed out.

"Who am I supposed to play with, the dog?" Plumley said. He rattled his newspaper. "Darn bugs! Get off my paper! I should have stayed inside!"

"I'll bet that Corker is a fine player," Utten said, sitting down on the edge of the board.

"She's a dog! Dogs don't play chess!" Plumley said, and he whacked the newspaper with the back of his hand. "I hate ants!"

Utten looked down at Corker. She cocked her head and lifted her ears, interested in what Utten had to say. "It's your move, Corker." Corker barked twice, and Utten moved one of the black pieces. "She says she'll play for black. It's your turn!"

"Darn ant!" Plumley barked. He stood up, threw the newspaper to the ground, and raised his foot to stomp on it.

"Wait!!!" Utten shouted, but Plumley's foot fell on the paper. He twisted his foot from side to side to mash the little bug into the ground. He sat back down again, leaving the paper on the ground.

"Oh well, I've read that one about fifty times before," he said. He folded his arms and looked down at the chessboard. He surveyed the pieces, and then he moved his aspirin queen. "Take that, dog!" he shouted at Corker.

Utten leaped from the table down to the squashed newspaper, but he found no evidence of an ant anywhere. He read the headline on the paper. "Hey Plumley, why do you read a paper that's so many years old?"

"The news is the same, more or less, whether you buy a new paper or read an old one. There's always a politician in trouble for something, there's a war about to break out somewhere, or there's an earthquake down in South

America. What difference does it make to me if the news is old or the news is new? It's not going to change my life either way," Plumley explained.

Utten looked the paper over completely, looking for a trace of the ant that Plumley had tried to crush. Finally, he found him cowering behind a blade of grass.

Woody shook terribly. He walked over to the paper. Being careful to stay on the crumpled underside out of Plumley's sight, he spelled out the following:

WE WERE WORRIED ABOUT YOU. I CAME TO FIND YOU. DO NOT LET HIM GET ME!

"Don't worry," Utten whispered. "He won't get you. He's not so bad a guy, once you get used to him."

Plumley growled at Utten from his chair. "Hey, you little blue goober! It's the dog's move! Get up here!"

"Hold on a minute," Utten whispered to Woody. He walked back to the game, climbed up on Plumley's shoulder, and listened to Corker bark her move out. Then he walked down Plumley's arm to the chessboard. He grabbed Corker's rook and moved him forward. "Make way, make way!" Utten shouted at the other chess pieces as he carried the rook across the board. "Coming through here! Make way!" He captured Plumley's aspirin queen and carried her off the board. "Nothing to see here," he shouted as he carried her off to Corker's side of the board. He paused to address one of the knights on horseback. "Mind your business!" he shouted up at him, then placed the aspirin queen on Corker's side of the board.

"You captured my queen!" Plumley howled.

"Nope," Utten corrected. "Corker captured your queen!"

Plumley rubbed his chin with his hand. "Dogs can't play chess! They're not smart enough!"

"Then why are you losing?" Utten asked. At this, Corker barked once in agreement.

Plumley snarled. "How do I know you're not moving the pieces for her?"

Utten placed his hands on his hips, and his belly turned slightly purple. "In case you haven't noticed, I'm not even paying attention to the game," he said indignantly, then shouted, "Your move!" as he jumped down from the table and walked over to the newspaper.

Plumley carefully stared at the board. "It's been a long time since I've played anyone," he said. "This is tough!"

Utten whispered to Woody, "Why don't you let me introduce you to him?"

Woody ran very quickly back and forth between two letters: **NONONONONO**.

"Okay!" Utten reassured him. "Go back and tell Cranston not to worry. I'll come back to see him soon. You won't believe the story I've got to tell!"

Woody tapped out **OKAY** on the newspaper and then ran away as fast as he possibly could. Utten climbed back up onto Plumley's shoulder just as Plumley made his next move.

"Hah!" snapped Plumley. "I've got you now!"

Corker immediately barked to Utten, who climbed down and moved her queen across the board. When he had completed the move, Corker barked again, and Utten translated. "She says, 'checkmate!'"

Plumley stared at the board in disbelief. "I've been beaten by my dog!" he bellowed. "I must be getting senile! Play me again!"

They played a second game. Plumley led early with his aspirin queen and tried to pin back both of Corker's rooks, but she sneaked in from the side with her knight and broke through the lines. Then Plumley captured both her bishops, one right after the other. Corker countered by knocking out the aspirin queen and all three acorn pawns. Plumley came back and made a run straight for her black pepper king, but Corker captured Plumley's king before he could execute all his moves, beating him for a second time.

Plumley ordered a third game, and this time the match stayed pretty even all the way through. Both sides lost their queens early on, and both players kept things lively by hopping their knights all around the board. Finally, after taking a long time to make her decision, Corker made a bold move with her spool bishop and placed Plumley's king in danger.

Plumley stared at the board . . . and stared . . . and stared. He tried to concentrate, but his eyes grew tired. Before he could make his next move, he fell fast asleep in the chair. Utten stood up on Plumley's shoulder, and using his keen eyes kept a sharp lookout for errant sylberpodders who might try to take advantage of the situation and fly up Plumley's nostrils, which flared in and out as he piped out regular, raspy snores.

When Plumley awoke an hour or so later, Corker was lying in the sun in the tall weeds nearby. Utten sat on Plumley's shoulder staring down at the board. Through bleary eyes, Plumley examined the chessboard. He could see that the game had been finished. "What happened?" he asked.

"I finished playing for you, Plumley. Guess what? You won! Congratulations!" Utten said.

"I did?" Plumley mumbled, still a little cloudy from sleep. He looked the board over carefully. "So I did!" he exclaimed. "Utten, that was so much fun! I wish I hadn't fallen asleep. I'm sorry. But I get so tired sometimes."

"That's okay," Utten said. "Want to play again? I'll play you this time."

"No, thank you, Utten. I'm still very tired. I think I'll just sit here for a while." The two of them sat in silence for a time, and then Plumley said, "I never wanted to grow old, Utten. I remember when I first learned that I had grown old. I went into town to buy some aspirin, that bottle right there, as a matter of fact," he said, pointing at the aspirin queen. "When I went up to pay for it, the lady at the counter asked me if I wanted a senior citizen's discount. I was insulted! Then I went home and I looked in the mirror and realized that I really had grown old. But it seemed that it happened all at once! I thought that maybe I just needed to comb my hair and shave and put on nicer clothes, but when I did all these things it was still an old man looking back at me in the mirror.

"It seemed that every time I went into town, people's patience got shorter and shorter. It got harder and harder for me to hear young people because they spoke so quickly and my ears were getting older. One day I tried to buy some groceries, and the cashier asked me a question. I couldn't hear her, so I asked her to repeat it. She gave me such a look! Then I noticed the long line of people standing behind me—each of them was glaring at me, tapping their feet, and waiting for me to hurry up. I reached for my money, and the change spilled out all over the floor. I may be a grizzled old man, but I tell you I was embarrassed, and I just wanted the floor to open up and swallow me whole so that I wouldn't have to see the looks on their faces anymore! I never went into town again!

"Here I am in this old house all by myself, and my life has gone by without my even noticing. All I've done is read books and play chess by myself. I didn't think I needed anybody! Now suddenly I'm an old man and I have no friends! It's my own fault—nobody wants to hang around with a grump," Plumley confessed. "So I went to the local pound and got Corker to keep me company. She's a good dog, but I was still lonely."

Plumley held his finger up to his shoulder, and Utten

crawled up onto it. Plumley pulled Utten closer to him so that his old eyes could see Utten more clearly. "Now you come along. You have so much energy, and I just can't keep up with you." Plumley placed Utten on the chessboard. He rose from his chair. "I wish I'd met you ten years ago, or seventy years ago, for that matter. But I was cranky then, too," Plumley said. He held out his old arms. "Look at me," he said. "I wish I'd met you when I was twelve, Utten. We could have had some wild adventures when I was young. I was an angry boy, Utten, and I could have used a friend like you."

"What were you so angry about?" Utten asked.

Plumley looked up at the house. "This. This whole place. I was angry about my whole life, but most of all, this *house*. Then I got older and I made a lot of wrong decisions, Utten, and I would love to be able to go back and change things. But what's done is done. I've wasted my whole life being a cranky old fool, and now I'm just a sick old man with no time left."

Plumley sat down next to Utten again. "Time . . ." he said, then repeated himself. "Time . . ." He stared off into the distance.

"Time! That's it, Utten!" Plumley jumped up. There was so much excitement in his voice that he almost sounded like a twelve year old. "You're magic, right Utten?"

"Of course!" Utten replied.

"Can you travel through time?" Plumley said expectantly, and he held his breath waiting for the answer.

"Well, yes, sort of . . . but it's not very comfortable," Utten said hesitantly.

Plumley's eyes lit up. "If you went back through time, then you could have an adventure with me when I was a boy, and then maybe things would have turned out, or will turn out, differently—"

"Whoa! Hold on there Plumley! It's not that easy! I can't just run around through time as I please. Nobody can do that!"

Plumley began to frown again. "Then how do you go through time?"

"By accident, of course!" Utten exclaimed. Discouraged, Plumley plopped back down next to him. "In order for me to travel through time, certain things have to happen. First, I have to find an object. The object only needs to have two things true about it. First, it has to be an object that somebody has lost. And second, it must be an object that the owner treasured very, very deeply." As Utten explained the circumstances under which Utten could travel through time, Plumley's face grew longer and longer.

"If I touch the object, then amazing things start to happen, and before I know what's going on I get sucked back through time to when the person lost the object. Usually I just show the person where the object is, and it makes them very happy. I've had some amazing adventures that way!"

Plumley's face had dropped so low, his cheeks looked

as if they'd melted. "So how do you get back?" he asked.

"Oh, that's easy. When I go back through time, there's got to be another Utten back there somewhere floating around in a bucket having some kind of adventure, right?"

Plumley nodded. "Unless you go back before you were alive."

Utten looked puzzled. "I don't think that's ever happened. Anyway, to get back I just find the other Utten and shake his hand. Together, our magic can do wonders. I get to go back to wherever I want!"

Plumley furrowed his brow. "So the only way to send you back through time to when I was twelve is to find something that I loved when I was a boy but then lost?"

"Yeah!" Utten exclaimed. "That's not impossible!"

"If I knew where something was that I lost over seventy years ago, I'd just go and find it! Then it wouldn't be lost! This is silly." Plumley angrily swiped the chess pieces off the board into the grass. "Blast it! I thought I had something there."

"Come on, Plumley," Utten said. He turned into his bird form and flew up to perch on Plumley's head. "My bird eyes are pretty good, so maybe I can spot something that you lost better than you can. What did you love when you were twelve? Did you have a baseball glove?"

"Nope," Plumley said. "I never much liked sports. Sports were too . . . too *social*." Plumley dropped the word *social* off his tongue as if it were a bug that had gotten caught in his mouth.

"What about a fishing pole?"

"I fished a little, but I never caught anything. Nope, I can't say that I ever loved a fishing pole," Plumley reasoned.

"What about a doll?" Utten suggested.

"Certainly not!" boomed Plumley. "Boys don't play with dollies!"

"Some do," insisted Utten.

"Well, not me!"

Corker barked twice to Utten, and Utten snickered. "What? What did she say?" Plumley demanded.

"She said that it's too bad we couldn't find your sense of humor," said Utten defiantly. Plumley seemed honestly hurt by what Corker had said. She felt so bad that she went over and lay down by Plumley's feet. "You know, Plumley, you're not being very helpful!" Utten said.

"I'm sorry Utten," Plumley said, stroking Corker's fur. "I have lived here most all my life. Anything I've ever lost must be around here somewhere. Let's take a look around and see what we can find."

It took most of the day to search the entire grounds. First they searched the woods near the house. Plumley and Corker fished around in the bushes while Utten surveyed the scene from the air. The only thing they found was an old moldy football which Plumley frowned at and threw farther back into the thorn bushes. They then moved inside the house, and they searched every single room on all three floors. Utten climbed underneath every sofa, chair, and bed, but all he found was some dust. Once, he found some old marbles, but they didn't do anything. In another room he found an old leather satchel full of books.

In an old, unused room on the third floor, Corker found the most promising objects so far. Using her very keen sense of smell, she detected some paper under the floorboards in the corner. Utten found that the boards were loose, and when he pulled them up they found a secret cubby underneath. "I think this is it, Plumley!" Plumley got down on his knees and pulled out a bunch of old comic books, an old yoyo, and a stack of baseball cards wrapped up with a rubber band.

"Wow!" Utten shouted. "This has got to be it!" He was about to slap his hand on the yoyo, but Plumley pulled it away.

"Nope," Plumley said. "None of that stuff is mine. This house is full of other people's junk." He placed the board back and stood up to leave. "It's hopeless, Utten. Thanks for trying."

Utten wasn't sure what to say. "Do you want to play chess again?" he suggested.

"No, thank you. I'm tired now, and I think I'll go have a nap," Plumley left the room, and Corker followed after him so that whatever chair he decided to sit in, she could lie down at his feet.

Utten didn't like to see Plumley so sad, and he knew that there must be something he could do to cheer him up. Finally, he made his mind up. He climbed up onto the windowsill and opened the window. He turned into his bird form and took off into the sky.

After a short visit during which Utten told Cranston and Woody the story of Plumley and the cats, Utten went down to the brook to retrieve the bucket. As he pushed the bucket off the side of the bank, he shouted out to Cranston and Woody, "See you later, guys! Remember, Plumley doesn't eat cats!" He didn't want to spend too much time sailing, so he fired up the bucket's water engines and cruised upstream to the bend in the creek where Plumley lived. When he reached Plumley's house, he engaged the land wheels and chugged the bucket up the creek bank, through a break in Plumley's fence, and into the little clearing where the chessboard, tables, and chairs still sat. The bucket coughed to a sputtering stop. Utten withdrew the land wheels and set the brakes. There was a sound from inside the bucket like someone stepping on a rubber clarinet, and then Utten climbed out. "Hello, it's Utten! Anybody here?" Seeing that neither Plumley nor Corker were around, he went to work by himself.

Utten removed a tiny anvil from inside the bucket, then grabbed his hammer and laid it on top of the anvil.

He disappeared back inside the bucket, and reappeared a few minutes later carrying what looked like a tiny coin.

As Utten climbed out of the bucket, the engine coughed as if it were about to start up on its own. Utten picked up his hammer, whacked the bucket on its side, and the engine grew quiet again.

Utten laid the coin on the anvil. He banged at it a couple of times with his hammer, and each time he did, a different colored spark arose from the anvil and flew away across the yard to the white birch tree. Utten held the coin up to the light and let the sun hit it. He watched very carefully to see how the light's rays reflected off the surface of the coin, then placed it back on the anvil and whacked it again. Again the sparks danced away, one for each swing of the hammer. Around the old birch the sparks began to chase each other. It looked almost as if they were playing tag.

Utten checked the coin again, then molded it more with the hammer, then checked again by the light's rays. Again and again he checked and molded, and each time he hit the hammer a tiny spark flew away and joined the others in the tree. He had been working for almost an hour when Plumley and Corker came out of the house to see what Utten was up to.

"What are you doing, Utten?" Plumley asked curiously. Plumley sat down in his chair next to the chessboard and leaned over Utten to watch him work.

"See this?" Utten said, holding up the coin. "This is a Farnswoggle's Coin. It's called that because it was invented by Alexander Graham Farnswoggle."

"That's very interesting," Plumley said as Utten began thwopping the coin with the hammer again. As the tiny sparks flew away, Corker chased them all the way back to the birch tree, then barked at them as they flew around its pale branches. "But what is it for?" Plumley asked.

"Remember how I said that I lived in a bucket?" Utten said.

"Yes," Plumley answered.

"Well, that's the bucket right there," Utten said.

"I gathered as much," Plumley admitted. "But what's with the coin?"

Utten checked the coin against the light, and the effect amazed Plumley. The coin almost seemed to gather the sun like a light magnet, then cast it back down on Utten in deep, rich red rays. Utten was getting closer to the desired shape, but he still had plenty of work to do.

"Remember how I said I was magic?" Utten continued as he laid the coin on the anvil again.

"Yes," Plumley said, his curiosity growing. He watched the tiny sparks fly away to the birch. Under the tree Corker barked and wagged her tail as the lights swooped through the branches.

"Well, different beings do magic in different ways. Some people do it with odd chemicals and herbs. Others do it with food. Others do it by carving shapes in wood or wax or stone."

"Continue," Plumley said eagerly. "Please continue."

"I do it with my hammer and anvil. Some magic I can do with just my hammer and anvil, but for others I need coins. At times I can even use shattering crystals such as ice or diamonds. But usually I use coins. It's safer with coins anyway. There are different kinds of coins, and they were all made many, many years ago by secret blacksmiths who imbued them with magic powers. All I need to do is find the right coin and shape it just the right way and I'll have a magic spell."

Away under the white birch, a group of daring sparks flitted down and hovered over Corker's tail. Corker turned around and around trying to catch them, but she ended up only chasing her tail. The sparks circled with Corker until she got dizzy and fell down, and then they flew around her muzzle just to tease her. They disappeared back up into the tree.

"So what kind of spell are you cooking up, Utten?" Plumley asked.

"I have to be very careful," Utten said seriously. "If I get the spell wrong then awful things can happen. The harder the spell, the worse the disaster if something goes wrong. You need to know that before you agree to anything."

"Okay," Plumley said. He was completely fascinated by Utten's work. "What kind of disasters?"

"Most are silly disasters. One time, I met this little girl who wanted to be able to turn into a bird like me. I made the spell, but there was a dent in the coin that I didn't see, and instead of becoming a bird like me, she became a big green turkey!"

Plumley laughed as he pictured the little girl turned into a turkey. "You turned her back, right?"

"Oh, of course. The spell will begin to wear off just as soon as I take the coin away from you. But she was a green turkey for a full day. She could fly, but she wasn't very graceful," Utten said. "You see, with any kind of magic, there's some give and take. I have to mold it so that I get the right balance, or the spell could be disastrous. One stray dent can throw everything out of whack!"

Plumley couldn't stand it any longer. "What kind of spell are you making for me, Utten?" Plumley demanded. He tried not to sound too grouchy about it. Utten was the first person he had met in a long time that he really liked, so he was trying very hard to be nice. It was difficult for him, though, because he was so practiced at being cranky.

"How would you like to be young again?" Utten asked.

Plumley sat back slowly in his chair and stared at Corker as she leapt at the sparks. "Oh my," Plumley said quietly. "Oh my, oh my."

"You wait until this is done," Utten said. "I'll do my best to get it right!"

Plumley sat back and considered what Utten was proposing. If he could be young again, he could make so many changes in his life. If he could be young again . . .

Utten kept hammering away at the coin until the sun touched the horizon, at which point he felt that the coin was done. By the final rays of sunset, Utten checked the shape of the coin. The light gathered in the curves of the coin and spilled down Utten's arm. Without a word, he handed it over to Plumley. Silently, Plumley accepted the solemn gift and placed it in his pocket. The two of them watched the sunset. Down at the birch tree, Corker continued to play with the sparks, which glowed brighter as the sun's light faded. Dusk rolled in, and the pale old birch came alive with hundreds of tiny swirling lights.

"Do you think it will work, Utten?" Plumley asked hopefully.

"It's working already," Utten said. "You just can't see it yet."

One by one the sparks in the birch flew off down the brook. When the last of them had left, Corker returned to the house, and the three of them went inside for the night.

Utten had crafted an exceptional coin for Plumley. In fact, he only missed one tiny dent.

THE DANGER OF LOST THINGS

5

Sizzling Salamander Spit

The next morning a wide pool of gentle sunlight filled Plumley's living room. Curled under a cloth napkin, Utten slept peacefully on the seat of the stuffed armchair. As the morning sun hit him, he tossed off his napkin and turned on his back, allowing the sun to warm his belly. The warmth from the sunlight sent him off into a deeper sleep, and he dreamt of climbing mountains made of crusty, warm apple pie. He slept peacefully until the screaming started.

The first wail jolted Utten from sleep, and he sat bolt upright on the chair. He had never heard anything quite like it before. At first he thought that maybe one of the cats had come back and was wailing to get back into the house, but no cat could ever scream that loud.

The screaming was not only loud, it was constant. In fact, it was more like a cry mixed with a scream. It was the sound that could only be created by a baby!

Utten ran upstairs to Plumley's room. There on the bed, wrapped up in Plumley's pajamas, was a screaming infant. Corker, though noble and strong, cowered under the bed, her paws covering her ears and her face buried in one of Plumley's bedroom slippers. Utten climbed up on the bed and dragged a pillow over next to the baby. He climbed up onto the pillow and looked down into the baby's eyes. When it saw him, the baby grew quiet, and a distinct look of hope came over its face.

"Is that you, Plumley?" Utten asked. "Boy, I never expected this to happen!" Plumley started to wail again, and Utten dropped off the pillow and started pulling on Plumley's pajamas. "The coin's got to be here somewhere!" he said. "I'll take back the coin, and then you should start turning back to your old self." Hearing that, the baby quieted down. Utten continued to rifle through the pajamas looking for pockets. Suddenly Utten stopped, climbed back onto the pillow, and gazed wide eyed at the little baby Plumley. "Wow!" he said, "This certainly is exciting!" Plumley answered him with another mighty wail, and Utten hurried back to his work.

"Hold your horses!" Utten said. Finally, Utten located the breast pocket of Plumley's pajamas. In it was the Farnswoggle's Coin. Utten took it from Plumley's pocket and climbed down off the bed. "You should be better in no time!" he said, climbing up to the windowsill. He held the coin up to the light and turned it into the sun. He looked it over for a full two minutes before spotting the tiny dent. "Here's the problem! Why, if I weren't looking for it, I never would have spotted it in a million years!" He climbed down from the windowsill and back up onto the bed. Corker came out from under and jumped up on the bed next to them.

Utten hiked back up the bed sheets and onto Plumley's pillow. He held up the Farnswoggle's Coin. "Now look, Plumley. Here's the coin. I've got it now, so you can just relax and wait until you return to your old self."

Utten expected Plumley to calm down, but instead Plumley gritted his teeth and wrinkled his brow. "What's the problem?" Utten asked, but of course Plumley couldn't answer. Then Utten realized.

"Now listen, Plumley, you'd better not! You'd better not. I know you're mad at me right now but for the love of pennies you'd better not do what I think you have to do! I do not have any diapers, and I wouldn't change one even if I had one to change you with!"

Corker jumped down and hid back under the bed.

"I'm warning you, Plumley! I'm just a little Utten. I can do a lot of things, but I have my limitations!"

Plumley gritted his teeth harder, his brow wrinkled even more.

Utten did some quick mental calculations. "Look, Plumley, if you can just hold out for an hour or so, then you'll be about seven years old—at least I think so—and you'll be able to handle things the way normal people do."

Plumley's face twisted, he kicked his legs.

"Don't do it, Plumley!" Utten shouted.

But Plumley was, after all, only a baby, and Utten was forced to make do. He folded a makeshift diaper out of a clean bed sheet he found in the hall closet. He grumbled the whole time he changed Plumley, but he did a pretty good job.

Within twenty minutes after this "incident," Plumley was able to talk again. He looked to be about three years old, but he still spoke with Plumley's old man voice. Utten found this quite amusing.

Plumley didn't find it amusing at all. He tried to get up and walk around, but after toppling over a number of times he decided to crawl. "I don't care how funny you think this is! Look at me! I thought you'd make me about twenty or so. Maybe ten! I never dreamed that you'd—"

"Look Plumley," Utten interrupted. "I didn't plan for this to happen. I told you, magic is a very tricky thing. Sometimes, I get it right. Sometimes, I get it wrong. This time, I got it a little wrong—"

"A *little* wrong? A *little* wrong? Look at me! I'm an infant!" Plumley blurted in his gravelly old man's voice as he crawled in circles all around the bed. He was aging by the minute. Utten felt that if he looked at Plumley carefully enough, he could see him changing.

"I'm sorry, Plumley. I gave it my best shot. I can try to reshape the Farnswoggle's Coin—"

"No!" Plumley yelped. "I'll be perfectly happy to be my old self again." Plumley stopped crawling for a moment, and his face turned greenish. "Oh my," he said. "I think I'm going to throw up. I used to throw up all the time when I was a toddler."

"I'll get a trashcan, old pal!" Utten said cheerfully. He climbed down off the bed and looked around for a trashcan.

"I'd rather use that bucket of yours," Plumley grumbled. "Just leave me alone, Utten. I'll be fine. I'll come downstairs when I'm a little more presentable."

"Whatever you say, Plumley," Utten said. He and Corker left the room and headed downstairs.

When Plumley came downstairs an hour or so later, he looked to be about twelve years old. He was able to walk without stumbling, and he seemed to be in better spirits. "I'm sorry I got mad at you, my friend," he said. "I know you did your best."

"You're sure you don't want to try the Farnswoggle's Coin again?" Utten suggested. Corker cocked her head, afraid to hear the answer.

"No, I think that I'll be happier when I'm my own age." Plumley looked himself over. "To be twelve again. It's a wonderful age, twelve. Just beginning the walk into manhood, but still enough of a boy to enjoy the simple pleasures, like running. This is an old man's dream, but I'm growing so fast it'll be over before I know it. I don't even have time to find other kids to play with. I'm going to go outside, Utten. I'm going to go outside and run. I'm going to run around in circles. I'm going to climb trees. I haven't done those things in so many years. Let's make the most of it while we have it."

"Sure!" Utten said. He slipped into his bird form and flapped behind Plumley and Corker as they darted out the door into the back yard.

Within two hours, Plumley was in his twenties, and he didn't feel like running anymore. Instead he felt like working on the mansion, and he and Utten cleared away most of the bushes around the foundation, mowed the lawn, and pulled the weeds in the driveway. The yard looked pretty good by the time they were done, but Plumley was not a young man anymore. It was late afternoon, and he was beginning to tire. Utten thought he looked about fifty. They went inside to sit for a while and talk. Utten told one of his favorite stories, which detailed the time he got lost in the Goorusoonami Desert for three days with no water or apples and was then taken prisoner by a band of desert outlaws. It was a long story, and by the time he finished, the sun was dipping below the horizon. Plumley was an old man again. The final light of the fading sun cast an orange glow on Plumley's wrinkled, weary face as he sat in his chair and examined his arms once more. "So, Utten, we can't send you through time, and you can't make me forever young. That's okay. This is the way I was meant to be, I guess. But I want to thank you, my friend. Thank you so much for trying."

"No problem!" Utten replied. "Don't worry, Plumley. You may not be twelve years old, but we can still have lots of adventures!"

"I don't know," Plumley said. He rose and headed for the stairs. "I'm very old, and I don't think I have very many days left here on earth." Plumley turned back to Utten. "I've never known anyone quite like you, Utten. As late as it is in my life, I'm thankful you came along to be my friend." Plumley turned his back and headed up the stairs to bed.

Utten couldn't turn back the clock for Plumley, but that didn't mean he didn't have another idea for cheering the old man up. In the morning, he woke Corker up early. "Corker, can you come with me? I want to do something for Plumley, but I'll need your help." Corker agreed, and the two of them walked downstairs and out into the back yard where the bucket was waiting.

"Give me just a minute," Utten asked Corker. He climbed inside the bucket and pulled a series of levers to activate the bucket's engines, but nothing happened. Utten reset his controls, then activated them again. Far away, down in the gears of the main drive section, he heard a very low whizzing noise which slowly trailed off to silence.

"Waddling marshmallows!" Utten yelled, then added apologetically, "Sorry, Corker, I know I shouldn't curse like that, but this bucket sure knows how to get my feathers ruffled." He grabbed his hammer and climbed out of the bucket. He placed his ear up against its curved metal exterior. "It's a very finicky machine," Utten explained to Corker. He felt all around the outside of the bucket with his hands, listening carefully. Finally, he found the spot he was looking for, and he whacked at it as hard as he could with his hammer. The engines roared to life, but as Utten attempted to climb into the bucket, they died again. Thick orange smoke issued from the tailpipe, and Utten knew that the bucket simply did not want to start.

"You'd better start!" Utten shouted. "I need you to work today!" He prepared to swing the hammer again, but Corker interrupted him with a bark.

"Yes, we absolutely need the bucket. I want to get some presents for Plumley, and we'll need the bucket to carry them back," Utten answered her. Corker barked at Utten again, and Utten pointed off into the woods. "We're going that way," he answered her.

Corker picked up the bucket's handle in her jaws and

set off in the direction that Utten had pointed. "Great idea!" Utten beamed. He slipped into his bird form and flew after her. He landed on her back, looking forward to the ride.

Corker and Utten didn't have too far to go, just down the brook to Cranston's twaddleyard, but in parts the brush was thick and it made for difficult travel. Still, it took them less than an hour, and soon they were knocking on Cranston's door.

Corker had never seen a troll before, but she kept herself very composed and did not look at all surprised when Cranston opened the door.

"Cranston, this is the vicious, horrible, cat-abducting wolf named Corcoran," Utten said.

Corker looked up at Cranston, cocked her head, and folded her ears back. "But she is no wolf! This is not Corcoran! I have seen the wolf myself, running through the woods. He chased me all the way home one day when I was out in the woods looking for junk! I saw it!"

"You saw nothing!" Utten yelled. "You probably had just forgotten to wear your monocle again."

"But I—"

"This is Old Man Plumley's dog, Corker, and as you can see she's not a vicious wolf!" Utten insisted.

"Maybe you are right, Utten. Sometimes I get chased by things, and then they catch me and it turns out it was only a rabbit or a squirrel," Cranston confessed. He leaned his great body over and patted Corker on the head. "Hello, wolf!" he smiled.

Woody looked over the edge of his shelf down at Utten. Utten turned into his bird form and flew up to say "hi," but Woody got scared and hid in his medicine tin. "Hey, Cranston," Utten said, returning to his normal form and sitting down on the edge of the shelf, "we need your help. I want to get a couple presents for Plumley, and I figure you've probably got what I'm looking for."

"I do not give credit," Cranston said. Cranston leaned over and spoke directly to Corker. "He always wants to buy things on credit."

Utten turned into his bird form, flew across the room, and landed on Corker's head. "I never said anything about credit! I just want to know if you have what it is that I'm looking for!"

Cranston shook his finger at the little blue bird. "You always want credit. You want things but you say, 'Cranston, I'll pay you later,' or 'I'm sorry, Cranston, but I can't pay you until next week,' or 'what if I just borrow this for a while?' That is not fair. Do you have money today?"

"Well," Utten hesitated, "no, but . . ."

"I knew it! I knew it!" Cranston hollered. "So how are you going to pay?"

Utten turned back into his normal form and sat down on the top of Corker's head. He rubbed his chin with his palm and tried to think of a way to pay Cranston. "What if tomorrow I—"

"No! No! No!" Cranston yelled.

Utten thought some more, and then Corker came up with an answer. She barked it to the two of them without even dropping the bucket.

"Hey, that's a good idea!" Utten said.

"I do not know, Utten," Cranston said. "I do not think I would want that."

"Maybe you wouldn't," Utten said, and he scratched Corker affectionately behind the ear. "But maybe I could do it for Woody!"

Hearing his name, Woody came out from his medicine can. Cranston lifted him off the shelf and placed him on the table, which was already covered with newspaper. "What do you think, Woody? Do you want Utten to make a spell for you?"

Woody cocked his head and rubbed his left feeler with his foreleg. He crossed the paper and tapped out his response. SURE . . .

"The question is, what kind of spell do I make?" Utten hopped down into the bucket, and Corker placed the bucket on the floor. Utten lifted his anvil and the hammer up to Cranston, who placed them on the table near Woody. Utten turned into his bird form momentarily and flew up to the table, startling Woody.

"Woody, you don't have to worry," Utten said, seeing

Woody's nervousness. "I'm not going to eat you even if I am in my bird form." Woody relaxed, and he tapped out **WONDERFUL** . . .

"So what do you want, Woody?" Utten said, lifting his hammer. He pounded once on the anvil, and a tiny spark flew away, circled the table, and went right up Cranston's nose. Cranston coughed, then giggled as the spark tickled him from the inside. "How about I try and give you your voice back?"

NO THANKS . . . Woody responded. While he enjoyed Cranston's company, he didn't relish the idea of having extended conversations with him. Many times during their friendship, he had come to see his muteness as a blessing in disguise.

Corker barked a suggestion. "Yeah, Woody, how about a pair of wings? Then you could fly like me."

Woody shook his head and spelled out **NO** . . .

Utten scratched his head. "How would you like to be invisible?"

NO . . . Woody answered.

"Would you like to be able to grow a perfect cabbage all year round?" Cranston suggested.

NO . . . Woody answered, quite quickly.

They all sat in silence for a moment, and then Woody began to spell. **I WOULD LIKE TO BE ABLE TO BREATHE FIRE!**

"Wow!" Utten shouted, and his excitement ran a ripple

of feathers down his back. "What a great choice! I don't even need a coin for that one, just some salamander spit!"

Cranston jumped up and ran over to his spice shelf. "I have some! I have some!" He squinted through his monocle at all of his bottles and eventually found the salamander spit.

"Cranston, what are you doing with salamander spit?" Utten said indignantly. "You know your stomach can't handle something as spicy as that!"

"I only use it every once in a while," Cranston said sheepishly. He uncorked the bottle of salamander spit and a whiff of steam poured out. Cranston dropped a single drop onto Utten's anvil. It popped and fizzled when it landed on the metal.

"Come here, Woody, and stand right in front of the anvil," Utten said. "Now open your mouth." Woody lifted up his head and opened his mouth.

Utten raised his hammer and brought it down onto the anvil with all his might. It slapped into the sala-mander spit, and a tiny red spark rose dizzily from the anvil. It spun around twice in the air, then went straight down Woody's throat. "Great!" said Utten. "It's work-ing!" He swung the hammer twice more, and twice more dizzy sparks rose from the sizzling salamander spit and found their way down Woody's gullet. After ten swings, the salamander spit had evaporated, and Utten stopped swinging.

"Now you go sit someplace quiet for about an hour, Woody. You'll be roaring flames in no time!" Woody spelled out **THANKS**, and Cranston placed him back up on his shelf where Woody could wait for the magic to take effect. Cranston then placed Utten, the hammer, and the anvil back into the bucket.

"That was really nice of you, Utten," Cranston said. "Now what can I get for you?"

"I need some chess pieces!" Utten declared.

"Is that all?" Cranston said, honestly surprised. "I would have given you those for free!" Cranston steered his great body out through the doorway and into the twaddleyard. He paused for a moment, trying to remember where the chess pieces were. "I know!" he shouted, and walked off down one of the many paths that led through the expansive piles of junk.

"Don't forget the bucket," Utten yelled to Corker, who quickly grabbed the bucket by its handle and followed Utten and Cranston down the path.

"I think it is down this way," Cranston said, as Utten circled around his head. He stumbled through the maze of pathways. At times, he seemed to know exactly where he was going. Other times, he looked completely lost and had to turn back and take another path. Finally he got to his destination.

The path led to a small open square. Chessboards of different shapes and sizes laid out edge to edge covered every inch of the square. Across the chessboards stood hundreds of chess pieces.

"This is exactly what we're looking for," Utten said. He swooped down low over the pieces. "So many different kinds to choose from!"

Corker barked three times at Cranston, who answered, "I got them all by looking. I look through the humans' garbage cans. I go through their dump at night. I find things they lose in the woods. I have been doing it for many years, so I have a pretty large collection."

Utten flew by the bucket and dropped in two pawns. "These are almost like the ones that Plumley has in his set already!" he shouted.

Corker held the bucket in her mouth and began to carefully step through the clearing. She tried not to knock over any of the pieces, not because she didn't want to make a mess of things, but rather because there was something about the chess pieces that was making her nervous. Whatever it was that was bothering her, Utten didn't seem to notice at all. He just continued flying gleefully from piece to piece, checking to see if it would be right for Plumley's chess set. He found a good black bishop and dropped it in the bucket. "So much for the spool!" he shouted as he flew away. Still, Corker remained nervous, and the hair on her back began to prickle.

Utten found a black king to take the place of the pepper shaker. "Now all we need is something to take the place of the aspirin queen!" He landed among the pieces and reverted to his normal form so that he could get a better look around.

"Please be careful!" Cranston shouted. "I spent a long time setting them up!"

"Stop worrying!" Utten shouted. He found a number of queens, but either they were too small, too cheap, or too fancy. Many of the pieces towered over Utten, peering down on him with hollow, lifeless eyes as he weaved his way through them.

Suddenly, Corker got a very strange feeling in her belly. She heard Utten cry out, "Here she is!" Corker whirled around, knocking over a few pieces with her tail.

"She's beautiful!" Utten sang. "The set's complete. Boy, won't Plumley be surprised when he sees this!" He placed his hand upon a beautiful white marble queen. The hair on Corker's back raised up in a sharp ridge.

A tiny spark flew out from Utten's hand when he touched the marble, and he jerked his hand away. "Oh no," he whispered, backing away from the queen. The spark flew around Utten in circles, and Utten tried to shoo it away. "No, no, not now!" he shouted at it. Corker barked, and the bucket swung back and forth in her jaw.

The spark split into two, then four, then eight. Like tiny bees they buzzed around Utten. "Help, Corker!" Utten yelled. "Give me your tail!"

Corker held out her tail for Utten to hold on to. The

sparks kept multiplying, and soon there were thousands. Cranston could barely spot Utten underneath the buzzing sparks.

"Do not go!" Cranston yelled.

"I'm trying not to," Utten yelled. "Pull, Corker!" Corker pulled with her tail, but it felt as if Utten were being sucked into a hole. She couldn't pull him out.

"Oh no!" Utten shouted. A number of the sparks had started to climb up Corker's tail. She spun around and snapped at them, but it felt as if her tail had gotten caught in a powerful vacuum cleaner. Where Utten had been, she saw only a mass of swirling sparks. She tried to pull away, but the sparks held her. Soon she felt herself going through the hole as well, and there was nothing she could do to stop it.

His one eye bulging with horror, Cranston watched this whole situation from the edge of the chessboards. He knew that there was nothing he could do. He watched as the tiny sparks covered Corker and the bucket. Soon there was no more Corker, just millions of little lights in the shape of a dog and a bucket. Then, all at once, the sparks disappeared, and everything was quiet.

"That's not fair!" Cranston shouted, sitting down in the dirt path and frowning. "Utten never takes *me* with him when he travels through time!"

One tiny spark remained behind where Utten and Corker used to be. It spun around twice, then lazily flew off into the woods.

FLIPPIN' WHISKERS

6

THE MAN WITH SPIDER FINGERS

As far as Corker was concerned, the journey that the sparks sent her on was one of the least pleasant things ever to happen to her. She had absolutely no idea what was happening, and this frightened her. She also felt a little sick. Later she would describe it to Utten as follows: "It's very hard to put into words. It was almost as if the part of my stomach which is normally on the inside was suddenly on the outside, and the outside on the inside. Also, my front legs felt like my hind legs, and my hind legs felt like my ears, except that they were moist like my nose. My tail felt like my tongue. Also, I had absolutely no hair, and that was the least comfortable of all, because I am a dog and I like my fur."

When she woke up, she thought that the experience had made her blind. She opened her eyes and saw absolutely nothing. It took her a few moments to realize that she couldn't see because her head was stuck inside the bucket. She still felt sick all over, though all of her body parts seemed to be in the right place. She pulled her head from the bucket and tried to sit up, but she fell over sideways in a dizzy heap. She decided to simply lie on the ground and wait for the feeling to go away. There was one thing Corker knew for sure when the experience finally passed—she never, ever wanted to go through it again.

She lay on the ground in some bushes. She saw Utten nearby, and it was clear that the experience had not been pleasant for him either. While her body had only *felt* like it was turned inside out, Utten's had actually morphed into something ghastly. Though half Utten and half bird, his bird parts were mismatched. His beak was where his belly-button was supposed to be, and one of his bird talons was sticking out of his forehead. Both his wings were where his ears normally were, and he only had one eye. He sat in the dust and flapped his silly ear wings, trying to get himself back into a more presentable form, but he couldn't seem to get a correct bearing on what he was supposed to be.

"Flippin' whiskers!" he shouted. "I hate to curse like that, but this certainly is uncomfortable! Are you okay?"

Corker half barked, half whined back at him to let him know that she felt terrible and that she desperately wanted to know what was going on.

"Remember how Plumley wanted to send me through

time?" Utten asked. "Well, he got his wish! Here we are! The only question is where and why, but that will make itself clear in just a moment." Utten tried again to right himself, but he only fell over backwards. He would have landed smack on his bottom if his bottom had been where his bottom was supposed to be. "I give up!" he finally shouted, and turned himself into a small ball of jelly. From this shape, which was basically nothing at all, he slowly reformed into his normal self one limb at a time. Finally, after a few minutes of great effort, he got himself back into his normal form. He breathed an exhausted sigh of relief and fell backwards into the dirt and dust. This time, he landed on his bottom, which was back where bottoms should be.

Corker too had begun to regain her bearings. She sat up and shook her head, trying to drive out the last of the time travel brain bugs. "It was the queen," Utten explained. "It makes perfect sense! I don't know why I didn't think of it earlier! Plumley was missing pieces from his chessboard, right?"

Corker yapped her agreement with Utten's theory.

"He must have lost them in the woods near the house, and then Cranston found them one day and put them in his collection . . ." Utten's voice trailed off. Something nearby had caught his attention. "Give me a boost?" he asked Corker, then climbed up her back and stood on the top of her head. Corker lifted her head and looked over the bushes.

They recognized their surroundings immediately, but that didn't stop them from being shocked by what they saw. There in front of them stood Plumley's mansion, only it wasn't the least bit run down. In fact, it looked marvelous. All of the shingles lined up neatly, and fresh paint coated the mansion walls. The gutters were clear, and the brush around the windows had been neatly trimmed to let the light in. The recently mowed lawn showed no signs of weeds. Whoever was in charge of the grounds attended very carefully to the details.

As much as the mansion and the yards surprised them, they weren't nearly as surprising as the people who were in the yard. Near the back of the house, the yard had been cleared away to make a large playing field. About twenty boys had gathered to enjoy a game of football. The most shocking thing of all was the sign which hung over Plumley's front porch. It read:

THE LIVERSTANES

BOARDING SCHOOL
FOR BOYS

BALSEM T. LIGGIT, HEADMASTER

"Liverstanes Boarding School?" Utten said. "What's going on here?"

Fairly close to the bushes that Corker and Utten were hiding in, a young boy, perhaps twelve years old, sat on a wooden chair in the sun. He leaned forward, his arched back curling up to his bowed head. Below his furrowed, frustrated brow sat two eyes carefully examining a frail table set before him. On the table, a chess game was in progress.

Chess is a game for two players. However, the boy sat alone.

"Plumley!" Utten whispered to Corker. "You watch. Something is about to happen, and it will explain how we got here." Within seconds, something did happen. The boys playing the football game began to get rowdy, and their playing got rougher. Their passes got longer and longer and longer, and it wasn't long before a pass arced out of the field, over the heads of the players, and began to drop towards Plumley. Corker yelped a quick warning to the boy, but it was too late. The football struck the small table, and chess pieces flew in every direction.

The white queen sailed into the bushes and struck Corker on the bridge of her nose.

"That's it!" Utten yelled. "That's how we got here! Now all we have to do is . . ." Utten's voice trailed off. Something else was happening, something he didn't expect.

Instead of helping Plumley pick up the pieces of his chessboard, the boys that were playing the football game began to laugh at him. "You think this is funny?" Plumley shouted. He picked up their football and held it up for them to see. "You ruined my game!"

As the boys laughed louder, Plumley shouted, "You shouldn't do that! You shouldn't do that!" But the fact that he repeated himself only made their laughter louder.

The largest of the boys stepped forward. "Listen, Dumbley Plumley, nobody cares about your little chess game."

"You ruined my game!" Plumley said again. He couldn't think of anything else to say.

"Can you even hear right? I said, 'Nobody cares about your little chess game.'"

Plumley looked down at the ball in his hand. "You shouldn't have done that. I wasn't bothering you," Plumley whined.

The tall boy smirked. "Why don't you just give us the ball back, Dumbley?"

Plumley hesitated for a moment, then gripped the ball tighter. "Give us back the ball!" the tall boy ordered.

From the bushes, Utten and Corker watched as Plumley reached back and hurled the ball into the air. Having never thrown a football before, he was unable to send it spinning through the air like a football should. Instead, it tumbled end over end through the air, and a few boys stepped back to grab it as it came down. They stopped just short of the edge of the field, and watched the ball land far back into a thick patch of thorn bushes. One of the boys caught a slight smirk crossing Plumley's lips and shouted, "He did that on purpose!"

The tall boy lurched forward from the group of football players and stood about a yard away from Plumley. He spoke quietly, but underneath his soft words violence threatened. "Dumbley, you're going to go into those thorns and get our ball back . . . or else."

Plumley didn't budge from his spot. "You make me," he ordered defiantly.

The tall boy's eyes seemed to light with fire, and he stepped closer to Plumley. He reached up with his fist, then suddenly seemed to grow calm again. He glanced cautiously up at the mansion and stepped back away from the smaller boy.

"You'll get yours, Dumbley," he warned. He looked back up at the mansion, searching the windows to see who might be watching. Finally he turned and the group of boys walked away.

Plumley righted the table and picked up the chess pieces. He placed them all very carefully in their start positions on the board. One by one the pieces were retrieved, and Plumley's little black and white armies reformed their ranks. Those that had gotten dirty in the fall he wiped clean on the tail of his shirt.

Plumley found all the pieces except his white queen. He ventured into the bushes to find her, but she was not there. He looked in the exact spot where he thought he saw her land, but she simply was nowhere to be found. Nor, for that matter, was there a bucket, a dog, or a tiny blue man, but of course Plumley didn't notice *their* absence. He wasn't looking for them.

As Plumley stepped from the bushes, he noticed something strange on the board. A new piece stood in the queen's place. Plumley approached cautiously. The piece was blue instead of white, and dark spots covered its back. Its belly was paler than the rest of it. It stood as still as if it had been carved of marble. Plumley picked up the piece and examined it more closely. "What's this all about?" he asked out loud to no one.

Entranced by the new blue chess piece, Plumley didn't notice the thin figure approaching him from across the lawn. A voice as harsh as the sound of two bricks being ground together called at him. "Mr. Plumley!" it grated, causing Plumley to jump.

"Yes, Headmaster Liggit?" Plumley's voice shivered. He stuffed the blue figure into his pocket.

Dressed in a dull black suit which his thin body could not quite fill, Headmaster Liggit towered over the boy. He purposely raised his pointed chin to make his face appear more angular and aloof. At his sides, his long-nailed fingers twitched, making his bony hands look like pale quivering spiders. "Follow me, Mr. Plumley," he said, his voice chilled. "I would like to see you in my office immediately." Liggit turned his thin chin back towards the house, and the rest of his body followed obediently. Plumley followed the long sweeping legs of the dark crane of doom back towards the house.

The inside of Liggit's office was sparsely decorated. Because Liggit preferred bare wood, no rug covered the floor. Because Liggit preferred to leave his charges standing, there were no chairs apart from the old wooden kitchen chair in which Liggit himself sat. And because Liggit valued order above all else, his desk rarely held more than one stack of three or four papers. Two windows graced adjoining walls. One looked out over the playing fields, from which the headmaster could keep a wary eye out for the misdeeds of those in his charge. The other looked towards the front walk that led to the entrance of the school. From that one Liggit could watch new pupils as they arrived at the school for the first time. In the short time it took for a nervous arrival to get from the front gate to the front door of the house, Liggit could read that boy's fears. By the time the boy had been led into his office, Liggit would have devised a way to manipulate that weakness.

Only one piece of artwork hung in the office, a large charcoal drawing of Liggit himself, dressed in his black suit with his chin held high. Below it on a label of steel was written a single word: "LIGGIT."

Liggit seated himself behind his desk and clacked his fingernails on its hard wood top. "Mr. Plumley, do you have the right to disrupt the entertainment of others?"

"But, Headmaster Liggit, they—" Plumley began, but Liggit lunged forward in his chair.

"You know my expectations, Mr. Plumley!" Liggit screeched. "I ask only very simple questions of my pupils! You will reply with courteous answers in either the affirmative or the negative! Do you understand?"

Plumley locked his teeth together and swallowed all his explanations. "Yes, Headmaster," he said.

Liggit settled back in his chair. "Mr. Plumley, do you have the right to disrupt the entertainment of others?" he repeated.

"No, Headmaster," Plumley murmured.

"And yet I saw you toss a perfectly good football into the thorn bushes. Bushes from which one could not possibly hope to retrieve it with any measure of success. Did I not see this just now?" Liggit said.

"Yes, Headmaster," Plumley replied again.

Liggit paused before speaking again, allowing ample time for Plumley to grow more uncomfortable. "Do you have any idea what the cost of a football is in this day and age, Mr. Plumley?" Liggit mused.

"No, Headmaster," Plumley said, shifting his feet.

"So, you shamefully stole a football from the other pupils. With no regard for its cost, you callously threw the football into the least hospitable place you could find. You ruined the other pupils' good time, and you recklessly destroyed perfectly useful school property. Is this true?"

Now it was Plumley's turn to pause. This was not his first time in Liggit's office. He did not want to say, "Yes, Headmaster," but he knew what would happen if he made any effort to explain himself. He used this pause to shout inside his head, "They ruined my game! I got mad, and they laughed at me! They were mean to me! They're always mean to me!" Inside his head, Plumley said all the things he longed to say to Liggit, things which if said out loud would only make his punishment more severe. As he shouted, he grabbed at the mysterious marble chess piece in his pocket.

"Yes, Headmaster," he finally said out loud.

"Do you know what your problem is, Mr. Plumley?" Liggit asked. Plumley wasn't quite sure how to answer Liggit's question, and he was thankful when Liggit didn't give him the chance to reply. "What plagues you, Mr. Plumley, is that you are antisocial. You don't seem to appreciate other folks!" Liggit leaned forward and pointed his long, buck-knuckled finger at Plumley. "You have been a student at the Liverstanes Boarding School for Boys for four months now, and you have not made a single friend here.

"Now, you may, in your own ridiculous and silly way,

believe that the other boys deserved to have their precious football thrown away. You may feel those boys are cruel, possibly even mean. But if you made the extra effort to be more pleasant, then you might find that they would be less nasty to you!"

Liggit sat back, very pleased with himself. "Am I making myself clear?" he asked.

"Yes, Headmaster," Plumley said, though he didn't believe a word that Liggit had said.

Liggit stared at Plumley for a long time. When he was satisfied that he had said all that he could, he stood and opened the door to the office. "One week of yard duty, Mr. Plumley," he sentenced as Plumley exited. "And let this be the final time I see you in this office!" He slammed the door shut behind Plumley.

Plumley entered the main floor common room, the room that would one day be his living room, and slumped into a chair. Trophies won by other boys cluttered the obnoxious walls around him. "First Place in the County Canoe Building Contest: Liverstanes Boarding School." "Honorable Mention in the National Tulip Growing Competition: Liverstanes Boarding School." "Silver Medal in the Statewide Origami Fold-Off: Liverstanes Boarding School." Plumley hated all the trophies. He hated all symbols of school pride. The worst was the school motto, however. Carved in a long piece of solid, polished oak, it hung over the mantel of the large fireplace:

LIVERSTANES,

A PLACE WHERE BOYS WILL BE BOYS . . . BUT ONLY FOR SO LONG.

Plumley pulled his fingers in to form tight fists. He placed his elbows on his knees and leaned forward, using his fists to shield his eyes from all that was Liverstanes. "I hate this place so much," he said. "I wish I'd never been brought here." He sat that way for a long time. After a while he remembered the curious object in his pocket and brought it out.

The strange little statue resembled his other chess pieces in size and shape, but its markings were very different. First of all, it was blue. Plumley had never even seen a blue chess piece before. The ones he saw were always black and white. Also, it had strange spots on its back. It didn't seem to be made of marble or plastic or wood, and yet it was rigid. Plumley supposed that if he never found his white queen, he might be able to use the little blue figure as a substitute.

But still he wondered where it came from . . .

In an attempt to discover the nature of the object, Plumley held it by its base, leaned over, and rapped its head on the coffee table in front of him.

"Ouch!" the figure bleated. Plumley wasn't sure which alarmed him more, the fact that the figure suddenly changed texture, turning into what felt like a squirming frog in his palm, or the fact that it spoke.

"Augh!" Plumley screamed, dropping the blue figure.

"Ouch!" barked the blue figure again when it hit the hard wood floor.

Immediately Liggit's office door opened, and the headmaster stepped out into the common room. "Is something awry, Mr. Plumley?" Liggit asked, a light squeal piping in his voice. His piercing eyes scrutinized the boy.

"No sir," Plumley said, kicking the blue thing underneath his chair with the heel of his foot. The blue thing let out another tiny exclamation of pain.

Liggit leaned forward and looked at the floor in front of Plumley. "I thought I heard an hysterical outburst," Liggit questioned further.

Plumley's mind scrambled, grabbing the first explanation to materialize in his head. "Merely a belch, sir," Plumley explained.

"A belch?" Liggit said disapprovingly. "Belching is one of the many diseases of immaturity, Mr. Plumley, and it will not be tolerated." Liggit pointed a bony finger at the school motto: *Liverstanes, a place where boys will be boys . . . but only for so long.*

"Learn to control the contractions of your digestive bunker unless you plan to grow up to be a bungler, a drunkard, or a fool." Like a sand crab, Liggit retreated to his office, closing the door behind him.

Relieved, Plumley leaned over and looked under the chair. "Are you under there?" he asked.

"Yes," a voice replied. "But I'd rather not be knocked into anything anymore, thank you."

"I am sorry about that," Plumley said. "But you shouldn't go around startling people!"

Having turned back to his normal form, Utten marched out from underneath the chair. "I wouldn't have startled you if you hadn't knocked my head on the coffee table!" he said, shaking his finger up at Plumley.

Though shocked to see a tiny talking blue man, Plumley didn't let it show. "I didn't know you were alive! I thought you were a statue!" he growled, shaking his finger back at Utten. "I don't know who you are or what you're doing here, but if you came to be nasty with me, then I'll just kick you right back under this chair because I've had just about all I can stand today!"

"Well," Utten said, his voice suddenly growing calm, "it seems that we haven't gotten off to a very good start." Though he didn't say it out loud, he realized that this wasn't the first time that he and Plumley had gotten off on the wrong foot.

"Let's try this again," he said calmly. "My name is Utten. I live in a bucket. I travel the world. I'm magic, and when I want to I can turn myself into a bird."

"Or a little statue?" Plumley asked, his voice still a little angry.

"Or a little statue, or a blob, and a couple other things. But mostly just the bird."

Plumley's brow furrowed. With his face all wrinkled with disapproval, the boy looked remarkably similar to Old Man Plumley. "What do you want? Why did you hide on my chessboard?"

Utten wasn't quite sure how to answer that question. He certainly couldn't tell Plumley the truth—that he had stumbled through time to meet him because he'd grow up to be an unhappy old man. Besides, Plumley had never explained exactly what he had wanted Utten to change about his life. Truthfully, Utten wasn't exactly sure why he had come back through time. All that Old Man Plumley had said was that he wished he had an adventure with Utten when he was a boy.

Utten couldn't tell the truth, but he also couldn't make something up. It wasn't in Utten's nature to tell an outright lie.

"I guess I'm not really sure," he said. "I was in the bushes when those boys spoiled your game, and maybe I felt a little bad for you. I wanted to meet you, and this seemed like such a creative way to go about doing it!"

Plumley seemed somewhat pleased by Utten's answer. It soothed him a little to have someone acknowledge what the boys had done. He was about to respond when Liggit's office door opened again.

"Mr. Plumley, are you still here? Get outside in the open air! Boys mope, men recover!" Liggit shouted, then backed into his office and slammed the door.

"We should go," Plumley said.

"I know a spot," Utten said. "Take me back out into the woods to where you lost your chess pieces." Though squeamish at how frog-like Utten felt, Plumley picked him up and placed him back inside his pocket.

Content that no one saw him enter the bushes, Plumley sat on the ground and took Utten out of his pocket. "There's somebody I want you to meet," Utten said. "You'll like her!"

There was some movement from the bushes, and Corker emerged carrying the bucket in her teeth. "This is Corker," Utten said. "She hangs out with me sometimes. Corker, this is Plumley."

Corker put the bucket down, and walked cautiously up to Plumley. For obvious reasons, meeting the boy struck her as very strange. Apart from the brief morning when Old Man Plumley had been turned into a boy, Corker had only known the old man. Now she was meeting the young boy, and she worried if he would be the same.

She decided the best way to find out was to sniff him.

She sniffed his hands and then his feet. She sniffed his belly. Then she tried to sniff his face.

"Stinky dog! Quit sniffing me!" Plumley barked, pushing her away.

Corker barked back at him once, then retreated. She placed her head inside the bucket and pulled out the white queen. She dropped it in Plumley's lap, barked once again, then went to lie down on the other side of the bucket facing away from Plumley.

Utten's mouth curled into a tight, toothy frown. "I wish that had gone better," he said. He decided the best thing to do would be to change the subject. "Listen Plumley, I was thinking . . . Would you like to have an adventure with us?"

"What do you mean an adventure?" Plumley asked.

"You know! An adventure! Fun! Running around in the woods! Climbing mountains! Setting sail on the high seas! Exploring haunted castles! An adventure!" Utten suggested.

Plumley sat and thought for a moment. Slowly, his brow began to wrinkle again. The more Plumley's brow wrinkled, the more Utten's frown twisted downwards. "When?" Plumley asked.

"Well," Utten said, trying to think of the best way to word his offer. "How about right now? We could head off down the brook out to the river to where it meets the sea! There's bound to be boats shipping out to far off places!"

"Pollywog snot!" Plumley snarled. "You're a cornball! Run off to the sea? Explore a haunted house? That's the most cornball thing I've ever heard! I can't just run away like some juvenile delinquent!"

"But you hate it here! I heard you say so! You can't stand this place! We could have a great time!"

A cold, familiar voice interrupted from outside the bushes. "Mr. Plumley, what are you up to in those bushes?" Liggit called.

Plumley glared at Utten. "You're just here to get me into more trouble, aren't you?" he whispered angrily.

"I'm coming, Headmaster Liggit!" Plumley called, then turned back to Utten. "I don't even know who you are! I'm not going anywhere with you! Be on your way, and don't bother me anymore, you and your wet-nosed, sniffling dog!"

Plumley stood up and marched away. When he was gone, Corker got up and sat next to Utten, who was so perplexed by the situation that he didn't even realize that his back had gone feathery. "Well, Corker," he sighed, "this isn't going to be as easy as I thought."

WHERE BOYS WILL BE BOYS...

7

FLYING PEAS AND DRIED MUD

Corker advised Utten to keep an eye on Plumley. When Utten started to walk out into the open beyond the bush, she suggested that maybe he should be a little more discreet. Utten agreed, slipped into his bird form, and flew from tree to tree listening in on the conversation between Plumley and Liggit as they marched back to Liverstanes Mansion.

"We do not creep around in the bushes here at Liverstanes, young Mr. Plumley," Liggit reprimanded. "We are not squirrels, and we do not grovel for nuts and berries. Do you have anything to say for yourself?"

Plumley had stopped to gather his chessboard together, and so had to run to catch back up with Liggit. "I was looking for a lost chess piece, Headmaster," Plumley explained, a little out of breath. Even after he caught up with him, Plumley had to maintain a swift gait to keep pace with the headmaster.

"Is that so?" Liggit asked.

"Yes sir," Plumley breathed.

Liggit fell silent for a moment. "Still, I will extend your yard duty by one week. If you want to go poking around in bushes, you might as well make yourself useful while doing it." Liggit reached the door to the house. He stood aside so that Plumley could open it for him. "You seem a little out of breath, Mr. Plumley. Might I suggest that you spend less time fiddling with your chess pieces and more time running and jumping about—"

Liggit's scolding of Plumley continued, but they had passed inside the house and Utten could hear them no more. Utten flew to the window that looked in on the main room and watched while Liggit shook his finger a number of times at Plumley. Plumley nodded and said little, and soon was dismissed.

Plumley went up the main stairwell, and Utten flew all over the house looking into various windows as he tried to keep track of the boy. Rooms that had been shut up and dusty when Utten first saw them were now classrooms filled with desks. Other rooms were dorm rooms, lined up with beds and reading desks. These rooms were all full of boys, some of them doing some last minute studying, others simply talking with friends. Many of the boys seemed to be combing their hair and straightening their shirts, and Utten realized that dinner time must be approaching.

Plumley passed many boys in the hallways, but spoke to none of them. Very few even acknowledged that he was there. The few that did acknowledge him did so with a look of contempt, and Utten recognized most of those boys as the afternoon football players. Plumley finally ended up in a large room on the third floor all the way at the end of the house. The room housed five bunk beds, and Plumley sat down on the lower bunk of one of those beds. He pulled out a small trunk from under his bed, opened the lock, and placed the chessboard carefully inside. He closed the trunk, returned it to its spot, and then took a comb from his nightstand and combed his hair. He removed from his shirt some briars that he had picked up in the bushes with Utten. When he was confident that he had done all he could to make himself presentable, he began the long trek back down the stairs to the main dining room.

Utten circled around the house and landed on a windowsill that looked in on the main dining room. A long line of boys stretched out the door, snaking all the way back to the main stairwell. At the front of the line stood Headmaster Liggit, who carefully examined each boy for proper hygiene before he allowed them into the dining room. He made sure that their hair lay flat. He made sure that their faces were free of smudge or dirt. He made sure that shirts were clean and neatly tucked in. For every ten or twelve pupils that passed him by, Liggit was sure to send at least one back to his room for further cleaning just to set an example for the others. Occasionally, Liggit would pull a white glove out from his pocket, place it on his hand, and run his finger harshly behind a boy's ear. Liggit would examine the gloved finger, and if it showed any grime Liggit would hold it up for the rest of the boys to see before sending the shamed, dirty-eared boy back to his room.

Plumley got the white glove treatment, but luckily he passed and was admitted to the dining hall. He got his tray and sat alone at a far table near the wall. Utten landed on the sill of an open window near Plumley.

What Utten heard amazed him. Never before had he heard a room full of boys be so quiet. There was very little conversation, and what conversation there was was kept to a low murmur. The only real sounds to be heard were the light tappings of the forks, knives, and spoons as they struck the plates. Those taps were overpowered by the crisp clicking of Liggit's heels as he paced the room overseeing the operation.

Plumley did nothing except eat. He spoke with no one, and no one spoke with him. No one even sat with him. He had been sitting quietly eating for about five minutes when the first pea struck him on the head and dropped onto his plate.

Plumley looked around to see if he could spot who

had shot the pea at him, but all the other boys appeared to be minding their own business. Liggit was at the other end of the dining hall, carefully scanning the room for any sign of trouble. Whoever shot it was careful enough not to get caught by the headmaster.

A second pea landed inside Plumley's ear and lodged there. Plumley scooped it out with his finger and continued to try to locate the aggressor. No one even glanced in his direction or let out a giggle.

Utten spotted the boy with the third shot, a pea which sailed over Plumley's head and out the window that Utten was resting on. It was the tall boy from the football game who had referred to Plumley as "Dumbley." This time when Plumley looked around the room the tall boy met his glance and snickered at him. Plumley's mouth fell open, and the large boy shot a fourth pea which went straight down Plumley's throat, causing him to gag. When he had finished coughing, Plumley stood up and shouted, "Just what do you think you're doing?"

Because Plumley's shout had been so loud, Utten expected all the boys in the dining room to take notice. No one did. A few glanced up, but then went back to their business as usual. Even the boy who had shot the peas pretended that Plumley had said nothing at all.

"I said, 'Just what do you think you're doing?'" Plumley repeated, pointing at the large boy. By this time, Liggit was standing in front of him.

"Calm yourself, Mr. Plumley," Liggit warned. "You

have had quite a day already. I would hate to see you face further punishment by disrupting the dining hall."

"Headmaster Liggit, that boy threw peas at me!" Plumley demanded.

"Which boy? Where?" Liggit asked, and followed the direction of Plumley's finger. "Stand up there, lad, and face your accuser!"

Mock innocence struck the boy's face as he stood. "Me, sir?" the older boy said. "I don't think so. I am merely talking here with my *friends*." His emphasis on the word friends was purposeful, reminding Plumley that he had no friends. "Why would I disrupt my dinner and the dinner of my fine *friends* just to bother that person sitting way over there by himself? It doesn't make sense, sir."

Liggit turned his pointed chin back at Plumley. "He makes a good point, Mr. Plumley. It would be silly of him to ruin his own nice meal just to bother you."

"But he did, Headmaster," Plumley persisted. "He hit me with three peas."

"Then where are these peas, Mr. Plumley? If the boy hit you with peas, then surely there would be evidence! I see no peas on the floor, and no peas on the table near you. Did he shoot invisible peas at you?" Liggit mused.

"One landed on my plate. One landed in my ear, and I smushed it with my finger. One went in my mouth. That's the truth!" Plumley explained.

Liggit looked at Plumley, then back at the large boy,

pondering what to do next. The older boy interrupted his pondering. "If it please you, sir, may I continue with my meal? Du—, I mean Plumley's silliness shouldn't keep us from enjoying our dinner."

"Certainly, young man," Liggit said, granting his request. "Mr. Plumley, you will come with me. I will not have you disrupting the dining hall."

Plumley abandoned his tray and followed Liggit out of the dining hall. As he passed the other boy's table, a fifth pea was lobbed, striking Plumley in the back of the head. Plumley did not even turn around.

Plumley was banished to the library for the remainder of the evening. While it might not have seemed like too harsh a punishment at first, it prevented Plumley from joining in on the night's activities. It was movie night at Liverstanes, the pupils' favorite night of the entire week. That evening all the boys would be in the common room on the main floor watching Ronald Reagan in *Bonzo Goes to College*, a movie about a man who adopts a monkey and teaches him not to be a thief. Liggit had chosen it because it conveyed a strong moral message.

The outcast Plumley would be left alone with only books to entertain him for the rest of the night. Utten stayed with him the entire time, though Plumley didn't know it. Utten perched on the sill of one of the windows of the library and watched Plumley as he read by himself. Utten was beginning to feel really bad for Plumley. Sure, he was a grumpy young boy, possibly even grumpier than he was as an old man. But Utten didn't think that anyone deserved to be as alone as Plumley was, and he watched him through the window for hours.

Utten finally returned to the woods when Plumley put on his pajamas and began to brush his teeth.

"I don't know, Corker," Utten said when he had landed at their hiding place. "I can't figure young Plumley out! The Old Man said that he wished he had had an adventure when he was a boy, but the boy doesn't seem to like the idea at all."

Utten was so confused by the situation that he forgot to change back into his normal form and simply paced around the dirt in his bird form. "He didn't even give it a chance! He just said that I was a 'cornball.' I don't even know what a cornball is! Do you?"

Corker let out a confused whine, telling Utten that she did not. In truth, she did know what a cornball was, but she figured it would be better to tell Utten later. There was no sense in hurting his feelings while he was already so upset.

"The funny thing is, Plumley hates it here! I heard him say so. I saw some of the other guys pick on him. He has absolutely no friends! No one at all! It doesn't make any sense!"

Corker howled lightly, and her answer made a lot of sense to Utten. "You might be right," he agreed. "The Old Man purposely avoided people too. Maybe young Plumley doesn't have any friends because he doesn't want any friends. But why would a boy not want any friends?"

With three barks Corker brought up the larger mystery. The Plumley she knew had never had any friends, and she was used to that idea. Only Utten, who loved to meet people and learn their stories, would find such an idea strange. Corker wanted to know why the mansion was a boarding school. How could it end up being Plumley's home later on if he was just a student there now?

"I don't know," Utten replied. "The house is definitely a school, though. There's classrooms and dorm rooms all over the place. All those rooms that used to be closed up in Plumley's house . . . wait, I mean, all those rooms that Plumley will one day close up . . . . Oh, tadpole rodeos! I'm getting all confused!"

Utten flopped down onto the ground and flapped his feathers in the dust. "I'm sorry, Corker, I know I shouldn't curse like that, but time travel always does this to me. I can't tell what happened before and what's going to happen next." This whole business was too disturbing for him. He had thought for sure that Plumley would have wanted to run away and that by now they'd be knee-deep in danger. Instead, nothing was going right. He and Corker were stuck out in the woods in the middle of the night, and their real home wouldn't even exist for another fifty years.

In an effort to clear his cluttered little mind, Utten flapped his wings. At least they worked right, and he took comfort in that.

Back at the house, young Plumley brushed his teeth. He usually spent a lot of time at night brushing his teeth. He found it was a good time for thinking. There was something about the regular vibrations of the brush over his teeth that soothed his brain. Plumley had been thinking all day, mostly about the little blue frog-creature and its dog friend, whose names he couldn't quite remember. He thought about them when the first pea had struck him on the head and distracted him. He thought about them all through the hours he sat in the library. And now, he thought about them as he brushed his teeth. It was during this time, this teeth brushing time, that he finally put his day into perspective.

He wasn't the least bit upset about his confrontations with Liggit. He had known for months that Liggit didn't like him and that Liggit would go out of his way to find reasons to punish him. Despite his best efforts to keep to himself and not disturb others, at least once a week something would happen that would upset the headmaster, and that always meant trouble for Plumley. But Plumley didn't care. He could do yard work for hours and hours so long as everybody simply left him alone.

The punishment was nothing new to Plumley. But finding a little statue that turned into a tiny, blue frog-like creature that talked—that was not something that happened every day.

"Perhaps," thought Plumley as the brush massaged his gums, "I have lost my mind. Perhaps this terrible place has finally gotten to me and I have lost my mind. That is why I saw the little blue frogman and his stinky dog."

But what if they were real? And more importantly, what if they were sincere? It seemed clear to Plumley that the blue man had wanted to be his friend, and no one had wanted to be his friend for a good long time. Plumley had gone out his way to make sure that no one would want to be his friend, and it had worked. It had taken a lot of effort to muster up such grumpiness. Of course, Plumley had assumed that once others discovered that he didn't want any friends, they would leave him alone. He never expected them to treat him the way that they did.

It had started simply enough. First came the nickname, "Dumbley." That didn't bother Plumley because he was in fact rather smart. Then the others started making quiet jokes about him when he walked into the room. They hid his books on him so that he couldn't do his homework. They tied his clothes together so that untangling and ironing would make him late for breakfast in the morning. One time, they even filled his shampoo bottle with mayonnaise. Plumley had marched down to the Headmaster's office in his towel and presented the shampoo bottle to him, but instead of finding the boys who had done it Liggit had given Plumley two weeks laundry duty as punishment for stealing mayonnaise from the dining hall.

Lately, the other boys' jokes had grown in severity. Plumley honestly believed that they had purposely destroyed his chess game that morning, and that was more than he could bear. Chess was the one thing that soothed him. It forced him to focus his mind completely, and all the problems of his life disappeared as he tried to defeat the worthiest of adversaries—himself.

What if the little blue man had wanted to be his friend? Why would he want to?

The rhythm of the brushing calmed Plumley's mind, and the resolution came to him. It didn't matter what the blue man wanted, or his sniffling dog for that matter. Plumley didn't need any friends. Let them go on their cornball adventure without him. All he needed was to be left alone by everyone and everything.

Plumley spat out the toothpaste foam and wiped his

mouth. He left the washroom and walked down the hall to his dorm room. Most of the other boys were already asleep in their beds.

Plumley could tell that something was wrong long before he got to his bed. First of all, the sheets were slightly rumpled, as if someone had tampered with his careful bedmaking. Second, there was dirt all over the floor. Plumley looked around the room. All the other boys appeared to be asleep. But Plumley knew they were only pretending. Whatever had happened, his dorm mates surely knew about it, and they were staying awake to see Plumley's reaction.

Plumley pulled back the sheets on his bed. One boy let out a little chortle, which infected other boys. The dorm room filled with snickering.

Written on the bottom sheet in thick mud from the football field was a single word: DUMBLEY.

Plumley considered pretending that nothing was there and crawling into bed anyway. Then he considered calling the headmaster, but he knew that he'd be blamed for the mess. He considered shouting at all the boys in the room, but he knew the commotion would bring the wrath of Liggit down upon him once again.

He couldn't just get into the bed, nor could he do anything to the boys who had done this to him. He had absolutely no idea what to do next.

Plumley left the room.

Plumley found his way down the stairs without alerting any of the hall monitors, but he had to find a way out to the back yard without alerting Liggit. He couldn't just walk by Liggit's office; the headmaster possessed supernatural senses and would surely detect him. Deciding that the best way to escape was to try to sneak through the kitchen, Plumley went down through the back stairway, in through the back kitchen door, and out into the dining hall. Luckily, the window in the back of the hall was still open. He slipped out and stood free in the night air. Plumley easily found his way in the dark back to the bushes near the football field.

"Are you out here?" he called quietly, looking into the bushes. He could see nothing in there, but still he kept looking. "It's me, Plumley! Are you out here?"

Plumley shrieked as a bat flew by his ear. He instinctively swatted at it, knocking it to the ground.

"Ouch!" said the bat. It wasn't a bat at all. It was a blue bird.

"Is that you?" Plumley asked. "What are you doing flapping around at night? I thought you were a bat!"

"I told you I could turn into a bird!" Utten shouted. He was tired of being smacked around by Plumley. He turned into his normal form and led Plumley back into the bushes to the hiding place.

"Plumley's back!" Utten exclaimed to Corker, rubbing his head. Corker barked once, and Utten said, "Hey, that's a good question! Why are you back? Have you decided to come on the adventure with us?"

"Certainly not!" Plumley snapped. "I just . . . I just . . . wanted to know for sure if you were real or not. You are, aren't you?"

"I'm pure, unfiltered reality!" Utten said. "Poke me if you're not sure!"

"That won't be necessary. I want to know something, and I want to know the truth. Why do you want me to go with you on this adventure? You don't even know me," Plumley said.

Utten paused and looked at Corker, not sure what to say next. Luckily, he never got a chance to answer. The voice of Liggit called out into the darkness. "I know you're out there!" the headmaster screeched from the back door of the mansion. "You may think that you got out of here undetected, but I heard you leaving! Come out now, or the consequences will be dire!"

Plumley couldn't breathe. In the past, every time he had been in trouble with Liggit, someone else had done something that he had gotten blamed for. This was the first time he had actually broken a school rule and gotten caught.

"You are in violation of curfew, whoever you are, and that is a serious offense here at Liverstanes! You will come back inside this minute!" Plumley and Utten peered out through the bushes together. They saw the thin silhouette of Liggit in the doorway across the field. In the rooms above him, lights were coming on one by one. Windows were pulled up, and boys on all floors looked out to see what all the commotion was about.

"I will find out who you are! You're only making it worse by hiding!" Liggit cried.

"What do I do?" Plumley asked Utten. Every dorm window on the back side of the mansion was open, and boys from the other side had crossed the hall to get a better look at what was going on.

"You will never see the end of your punishment if you do not return right this moment!" Liggit shouted.

"He can't stand there all night," Utten explained. "When he goes back inside, maybe you could sneak back up to your room. All we have to do is wait." Plumley knew that Utten's plan would be difficult to pull off, but he couldn't think of anything else to do. He had to just wait it out.

"I have a good idea who you are, and I'll know for sure soon enough," Liggit cried. His anger began to cause his voice to crack. He turned to all the boys in the windows. "Everyone back in their rooms! We're going to do a bed check!"

The boys saved him the trouble. "It's Plumley, Headmaster," a number of them called down together.

"I knew it!" Liggit howled. "I knew it! Mr. Plumley, you had better come out now! I plan to give you every duty under the sun! Nobody at Liverstanes breaks curfew! Nobody!" Liggit began listing off the weeks of duties that Plumley would have to perform. He began with floor polishing, listed all the indecencies of bathroom scrubbing, and went on to coal shoveling. But Plumley wasn't listening.

"What's your name again?" he asked the little blue frogman.

"Utten!" Utten shouted.

"And her?" Plumley asked.

Corker barked, though Plumley couldn't understand her.

"I hope this adventure of yours is no fake, because I can't go back to the house now. I have no choice," Plumley explained reluctantly. "I'll come with you."

Very carefully, they crept deep into the woods away from the mansion. When they had gotten a safe distance away (not too far, coincidentally, from the spot where Cranston would one day build his twaddleyard), they settled down to rest for the evening.

AUNTIE COLLIDA,
CHASER OF WICKETS AND RUDELIES

8

Captain Hobart's Traveling Ocean Circus

They began walking early the next day. Utten flew ahead trying to spot the easiest path through the woods. Corker followed after him, carrying the bucket. Plumley walked a safe distance behind and talked very little to either of them. Occasionally he called out to the two of them, saying things like "Slow down up there!" or "Wait for me!" But for the most part he walked alone and scowled.

By noon they reached the main river, and they stopped to rest. Utten found an apple tree nearby which provided lunch. Plumley ate quietly, sitting away from Corker and Utten. When he had finished his apples, he stood up and brushed himself off. "This is some adventure so far. Briars and thorns all morning long, and nothing but apples for lunch. This is not what I had in mind."

"Don't worry, it's sure to get better!" Utten exclaimed,

trying to be as positive as possible. "Adventures sometimes start slow, but once they gain momentum you'll
find yourself longing for these simpler, more relaxing
times!"

"Pollywog snot," Plumley said glumly, and began to
walk off down the river. As he walked away, Corker confessed to Utten that she liked Plumley much better when
he was old and grumpy rather than young and grumpy.
Then she picked up the bucket and walked after Plumley.

Utten let her go on ahead and allowed himself a few
minutes of guilt. Plumley was not having a good time,
and if Utten didn't find a way to connect with the boy
then he surely couldn't help his friend the Old Man. Not
only that, but poor Corker wasn't supposed to be along
with them in the first place. If he hadn't grabbed her tail
when he started to drift through time, she wouldn't be
trudging through the woods carrying a broken down
bucket with her teeth.

"Something had better happen soon," he thought.

Something did happen soon. By mid-afternoon, they
had reached the city of Port Oscar. Within fifteen minutes they had met Captain Hobart and had signed on as
shipmates on his travelling ocean circus.

An impressive port, Port Oscar boasted twelve full
docks, each capable of holding a full size tanker. On the
afternoon that Corker, Utten, and Plumley walked out of
the woods, there was only one boat docked at the pier,
but it was an enormous boat. She had no name. At one

time she did, and if you looked carefully at her side, you could just make out the letters of the name that she used when she served in the cruise line fleet before Captain Hobart bought her. Those letters had been whitewashed over, and in their place were written the words, "Captain Hobart's Traveling Ocean Circus."

Captain Hobart sat on a rough plank bench on the dock in front of his pride and joy. In his hand he held a tiny piece of wood and pocketknife, and at his feet had gathered a pile of loose wood shavings. He glanced up as Utten, Corker, and Plumley walked by, then went back to whittling. One might think that the captain would be surprised to see a little boy in ragged, dirty pajamas, a tiny blue man that looked a lot like a very ugly frog, and a dog with fur colored like the mixed layers of polished wood, but he wasn't. Captain Hobart was a circus man, and in his day he had seen so many strange sights that nothing shocked him much anymore.

"Are you the Jumping Orlando Brothers?" he asked.

Plumley, who was very tired from all the walking, very bored from the lack of adventure, and very grumpy just by his nature, replied rather coolly, "Do we look like the Jumping Orlando Brothers?"

"No," answered Captain Hobart, not seeming to mind the nastiness of tone which Plumley used. "But one can hope, can't one?" Utten stepped closer to Captain Hobart to try to figure out what exactly he was whittling. "The reason I ask is because we were supposed to set sail two hours ago, but the Jumping Orlando Brothers, whom I just recently signed on as a new act, have not shown up yet. If they don't show up soon, I'll have to set sail without them."

To Utten, the whittling looked like nothing much at all. "What are you whittling there?" he asked, quite interested.

"It will be what it will be," Captain Hobart said wisely, and Plumley humphed. "Where are you folks headed?"

"It seems that we're headed right here," Plumley said. "Our little adventure has not been well planned out from the start. So far it has turned out to be nothing but stomping about in creeks and bushes. I for one am just about ready to turn around and go back to where I started."

Captain Hobart still did not look up from his whittling. "A little adventure?" he asked.

"Yes," said Plumley. "A poorly planned adventure."

Still whittling, Captain Hobart replied, "It will be what it will be."

Plumley humphed again.

"I have been on many adventures," Captain Hobart said. "Why, when I was just a little older than you I went on my first adventure. My father, who was not a very nice man, sold me to the captain of a merchant ship for ten dollars. Only it turned out that it wasn't a merchant ship at all, it was a pirate ship."

Utten, sensing that a story was coming, shifted into his bird form and flew up to perch on Captain Hobart's knee. "Come on up, little blue man," Captain Hobart said. "There's plenty of room." Corker, too, was ready for both a story and a rest, so she placed the bucket on the dock and lay down at the captain's feet to listen.

Plumley's mouth turned into his sour frown again. "Pirate ship? Pollywog snot! There's no such thing as a pirate ship, not in this day and age."

"Well, yes and no," Captain Hobart replied. "There are pirates. Not the peg-legged kind who wear eye patches and search for doubloons, but there are pirates. They look just like any other ship, but really they're marauders. They'll stop any ship on the high seas and try to steal her cargo. It doesn't matter if the other ship is carrying bananas or wheelbarrows. If the pirates can steal it and sell it on the black market, they'll steal it."

Captain Hobart paused in his whittling and his story just long enough to check the shape of his object, then continued. "I wasn't given any special job on the boat. I did all the jobs that no one else wanted. If something got spilled in the galley, the pirate captain would yell, "Hobart, go get a mop and clean that up!" If there was a rat loose in the hold, the pirate would yell, "Hobart, take a stick and chase him out of there!" And if one of the other pirates got seasick, the pirate captain would yell, "Hobart, go get a bucket for that man!"

"Sounds horrible!" Utten exclaimed.

"Sounds silly to me," Plumley said, digging his foot into the dirt. "Who ever heard of a pirate getting seasick?"

"One day, the pirate captain boarded a freighter bound for San Diego, California, and took every single box in her hold. At first I didn't know what the other ship was carrying, but the next day the pirate captain sent me down into the hold to fetch some Epsom salts from the storage locker. The captain had terrible, terrible calluses on his feet, you see, and he often had to soak them for hours at a time."

Plumley didn't even bother to scoff at the idea of a pirate with calluses. He was tired of scoffing, and just wanted the story to end.

"Every single box was full of yo-yos! Every single one. There must have been thousands of yo-yos down there in those boxes! I asked the Captain what he planned to do with the yo-yos, and he told me that he was going to take them to Minsk where they'd be melted down and turned into plungers."

"Imagine!" Utten said. Even Corker lifted her head up and cocked it to one side.

"I couldn't let that happen!" Captain Hobart said. "All I could think about was all those thousands of kids in San Diego, California who wouldn't be getting their yo-yos, and it made me want to cry. I was still a young man then, and I knew the joy a good yo-yo could bring."

"What did you do?" Utten asked, his feathers beginning to ruffle as the excitement of the story grew.

"Well," said Captain Hobart, checking his whittling once again, "first I went into the kitchen and got myself a long hose. I attached the hose to the sink, and pushed the other end up into the ventilation shaft. Then I found a sledgehammer in the engine room—"

"A hammer?" Utten blurted. "*I* use a hammer!"

"I went back up to the kitchen, and I swung the hammer as hard as I could into the wall of the ship. It let out a boom that you wouldn't believe. Then I turned on the hose full blast. I ran through the ship yelling, 'We're hit! We're sinking!' At first, the pirates didn't believe me, but then they saw the water come spurting up through the vent shafts and they panicked. 'Abandon ship!' I shouted. 'Abandon ship!'

"The pirate captain, who was a coward at heart, ran for the nearest life raft. 'Hobart,' he shouted at me, 'you try and keep her afloat!' All the pirates clambered into the lifeboats, and I set them all adrift. Once they were all gone, I went down to the kitchen, turned off the hose, and set sail full steam for San Diego."

"Pollywog snot!" Plumley shouted, unable to contain himself.

"The mayor of San Diego was so pleased he gave me a reward for saving the yo-yo shipment. I used that reward money to buy my own boat and get my circus started, and I've been sailing the high seas bringing my circus from port to port ever since."

"Wow!" Utten said. "What a story!"

Politely shooing Utten from his knee, Captain Hobart stood up and brushed off the last of the wood shavings from his trousers. "Now if you folks will excuse me, I have to get my circus floating. We're due in Schnaibleville the day after tomorrow." He lifted his piece of whittled wood to his lips and blew with all his might. A shrill blast came from the tiny wooden whistle he had created, and four heads looked down at him from the deck of the ship. "Let's set sail, boys!" the captain yelled.

"Aye, Captain!" the sailors shouted, and within a minute the great engines of the cruise ship roared to life. Captain Hobart walked up the gangplank towards the main deck.

"Wait!" Utten called out. "Is there room?"

Captain Hobart turned around and asked very seriously, "Are you afraid of a little work?"

Before Plumley could answer, Utten shouted, "No sir!" and flew all the way up to the deck railing. Corker didn't wait for Plumley's protest either. She grabbed the bucket and darted up the gangplank to join Utten.

Plumley didn't move. He didn't even look up at the ship. He just continued to dig in the dirt with his foot. He looked back at the woods they had just walked through and weighed his choices.

Plumley didn't even flinch when the Jumping Orlando Brothers ran gleefully past him up the gangplank onto the ship. It was only when two sailors appeared on deck to pull up the gangplank that he finally stepped off the dock and walked up to the deck of the ship.

Utten hoped that he and Plumley and Corker would be given jobs as actual circus performers. He thought that possibly they could accompany the Jumping Orlando Brothers, or maybe perform a solo act in which Utten demonstrated his dancing prowess. Instead, the three of them were given crew jobs. As a matter of fact, they were given the most menial jobs on the ship. Utten didn't mind that so much. He had served on a number of ships himself, and he knew that it was important for new crew hands to prove themselves at some of the more boring jobs before they got moved up to something really exciting.

Plumley, on the other hand, was not pleased with the occupation he was given. He couldn't complain that much, however, because one of the first things Captain Hobart did was to feed them all a good hot meal and find some clean clothes for Plumley to wear. He also assigned the three of them a pile of hay where they could sleep at night.

Captain Hobart gave Corker a fairly important job for a first-time crew hand, but it was a job that she was very well suited for. Because of his history with pirates, Captain Hobart kept a wary eye on not only the ocean's horizon but also on the very decks of the ship. Pirates can be very tricky people, and a captain never knew if there might be a stowaway on board waiting to cause trouble.

A good captain remains ever vigilant. Captain Hobart took Corker aside and told her to roam the decks and keep an eye out for intruders. Along the way she could visit whomever she wanted, get her ears scratched, engage in conversation, and accept treats. As the job promised a lot of social interaction, Corker was thrilled to have it.

Utten and Plumley became flappers. Flappers hung around in the hold with all the elephants, giraffes, and mules. They were given large flyswatters, and if any bugs tried to molest the large animals, it was their job to swat at them. They were put to work that evening before they even had a chance to see much of the ship.

Utten really looked forward to the job. He stood next to their hay pile just before he and Plumley went on their first rounds and practiced swatting with the flyswatter. Though it was a bit too big for him, he soon learned to manage it well, and boastfully listed off all the dangerous bugs he could think of swatting. While Plumley made up his mind that he would only swat at flies, gnats, and mosquitoes, Utten dedicated himself to eradicating sylberpodders, choates, and yinkers as well.

"There's no such thing as choates, yinkers, or sylberpodders!" Plumley shouted at him when Utten explained his plans. "I'm sticking with bugs that I know!"

"I already told you about sylberpodders!" Utten shouted, but then realized his error. Sure, he had told

Plumley about them, but he had only told the Old Man. Young Plumley knew nothing about them.

"Listen, Plumley," Utten began again. "This ship is set to sail all over the wide ocean. We're bound to encounter all kinds of things you've never heard of before, so it's important that you know all about them." Utten explained the physical characteristics and mode of attack for choates, yinkers, and sylberpodders. He even touched on gungyfish, though they lived mainly in stagnant freshwater ponds. Young Plumley's reaction remarkably resembled that of the Old Man's.

"You mean these things fly right up inside your nose and live there and you don't even know it?" Plumley asked.

"Of course!" Utten said.

Plumley immediately thrust a finger deep into his left nostril and felt around for a sylberpodder web. He repeated the same on the right side as well. "I think I'm clear," he said. "But how can I protect myself when I'm sleeping? That is when they attack, isn't it?"

"I'll keep a look out for you," Utten said.

Plumley almost said thank you, but stopped himself before he let his appreciation show. "That certainly would be nice," was all he said. He turned around to begin his rounds and shrieked.

Plumley believed for a moment that he was staring straight into the face of giant yinker, because this creature, though a hundred times larger, was just as creepy as the yinkers Utten had described. Dressed in a long black and orange shirt and skirt, it stood barely five feet tall. Its feet were bare, and its pink painted toenails were long like talons. Its hair was knotted and gray. One of its eyes, glazed and chalky, stared off lazily in an odd direction. But the other eye was vibrant and lovely, and it shined with youthful energy.

The creature smiled. It had very few teeth. Plumley screamed again. The creature laughed. Sure that he was about to die, he yelled, "Please don't kill me!"

The creature reached out with its hand and affectionately touched Plumley's chin. He whimpered. "I always get that reaction," it said. Its voice, though as old and parched as its skin, was very pleasant. It laughed again. "My name is Collida, but you boys can call me Auntie Collida. Everybody else does!"

"Hello, Auntie Collida!" Utten said happily. "I'm Utten, and this is Plumley. We've run away from an awful boarding school. Pleased to meet you!"

Still frightened, Plumley backed away from her. "Oh, you'll get over my appearance soon enough, boy," she reassured him. "Corker already told me all about what happened at the school. What a pleasant dog she is! And quite witty!"

Suddenly Plumley became less afraid. If this woman was capable of having a conversation with a dog, then clearly she must be just as nuts as she was ugly. She wasn't a giant yinker after all. She was just a crazy old lady.

"I'm the witch of the circus, and I have an act that I

think you'll both enjoy. It's one of the most popular attractions that we have! Did you know that I'm the oldest living person alive on earth?"

"Wow!" Utten squawked, turning immediately into his bird form and perching on Auntie Collida's head. "How old are you?"

"Oh, Utten," she replied, not seeming to mind that he had landed in her hair. "It isn't polite to ask a lady her age! Come on, let me introduce you to the circus!"

With Utten perched on her head, Auntie Collida walked down a long hall, through the main ballroom, and up the stairs that led onto the main deck of the ship. Plumley followed her cautiously, but he couldn't hide his amazement at what he saw on the deck of the ship. Both Utten and Plumley were astounded. Activity kicked and wailed from every corner of the deck. Almost a hundred people and animals ran around on the deck. Most practiced their acts. Some just socialized. Others simply horsed around.

Just as the three of them stepped out onto the deck, a motorcycle raced by. The occupant wore a long yellow cape and a helmet that said "Rolo." Auntie Collida explained. "That's Rolo, one of our trick cycle riders." Rolo ran the bike up a long ramp and jumped over the pool, landing safely on the other side and stopping just before he drove into the rear deck railing. Auntie Collida pointed down at the pool. "Those are the elephants, Phillip, Bryant, and Arabica. You'll be working closely with them, as they tend to attract quite a few bugs. Hello, folks!" The elephants stopped their splashing and raised their trunks to her and her companions.

A one-armed man walked past, and Auntie Collida introduced him. "This is Maxwell, our lion tamer,"

Maxwell extended his one arm. "Actually, I prefer the term Feline Choral Director, but you can call me a lion tamer if you wish," he said, then shook both their hands and continued on his way.

"Over there are the Jumping Orlando Brothers. I believe you met them earlier," Auntie Collida observed. Over on the port side, identical triplets stood on the deck railing. One after another, they leapt into the air, flipped once, and landed back squarely where they had begun. The third in line faltered slightly, almost falling over into the ocean, but his brother caught him by the shirt and righted him. "Oh my, I hope they're as good as we've been told," Auntie Collida added with concern.

A shrieking chimpanzee darted up to Auntie Collida and ran circles around her. He held out his hand and dropped a pair of silver earrings into her palm. "Oh, Gipper, aren't these lovely. But they're not mine. They belong to someone else. I think you should return them." She handed the earrings back, and Gipper shrieked off as quickly as he came.

"Over there are the clowns." Plumley and Utten looked over to see a group of men, their faces only half painted, rehearsing a clown funeral.

"That doesn't seem very funny to me," Plumley complained.

"Oh, they make it funny and sad at the same time. Only the best clowns can do that," Auntie Collida suggested.

Captain Hobart himself walked past and gave a wave. "How are we doing, boys? Like the place so far?"

Plumley humphed. Utten waved back with one of his wings. "Great so far, Captain!"

Auntie Collida walked over to one of the hatches, then proceeded down a stairwell to the lower decks. For her age, she quite nimbly traversed the narrow stairs. She led them down another hall, then through the nightclub and into the old casino.

The old casino wasn't a casino anymore. All of the gaming tables had been removed, and now it was simply a large open area where all of the animals could hang around, munch on hay, and socialize. Auntie Collida led them past several gorillas and a half-dozen zebras before finally stopping at an enormous elephant. Next to the elephant sat a rather beautiful, rather fat, young woman. "Hello, grandmother," the young woman said.

"This is my granddaughter, Frehley," Auntie Collida said, then she placed a hand on the elephant. "And this big girl next to her is my friend, Kashmir." The elephant reached around with her trunk, clasped Auntie Collida's hand, and moaned. "Oh, I know!" Auntie Collida responded, stroking the big elephant's side. "How can you possibly be comfortable in your condition? I know from experience!"

Auntie Collida pulled up a chair for Plumley and set some water on a small stove. When the water was hot, she poured it into cups for tea. She sat down next to Frehley, and Utten flew from her head down to her knee. "So tell me, boys. Tell me all about this adventure you're on."

Auntie Collida failed to impress Plumley. He refused to join in the conversation. He only drank half his tea, then rudely rose and walked off, absently whacking at gnats with his swatter. He spoke to no one, though he did enjoy looking at the animals and the various people practicing their acts. He saw a lot of things that he had never seen before in his life, and for that reason he felt that the evening was not a complete waste. Still, when he settled onto the hay pile to sleep that night, he told himself that his life certainly would have continued along just fine if he'd never seen those things at all. So what was the use?

Utten was so enamored with Auntie Collida that he forgot all about swatting bugs that evening. He sat on her lap and talked with her for hours. Eventually she became tired and had to go to bed, and Utten returned to the pile of hay that he and Corker and Plumley would call home.

"Wow! Wasn't she amazing?" Utten said after he woke Plumley up.

"Amazing? I thought she was creepy!" Plumley said tersely, turning away from him. "I don't know how you could ride around in her hair like that. She was gross!"

"She's lived a lot longer than you have, Plumley," Utten suggested, switching back into his normal form.

"So?" Plumley barked.

"So? So she has a lot more stories to tell! You can't imagine all the things that she's done!"

"I don't care what kind of stories she's got. She's still old and creepy, and she gives me goose bumps."

Utten hesitated. Under the circumstances, he wasn't sure that what he was about to say was wise. Then again, he knew it was the truth. "You might be old one day, too, Plumley."

"Maybe," Plumley replied. "But I won't be old and creepy like her. Now can I get some sleep?"

There wasn't much more that Utten could say. He knew that Plumley would not only be old, but that by reputation alone he'd be the creepiest guy in his neighborhood. But he certainly couldn't tell the young Plumley that. "Good night, Plumley," was all Utten said.

Plumley didn't answer.

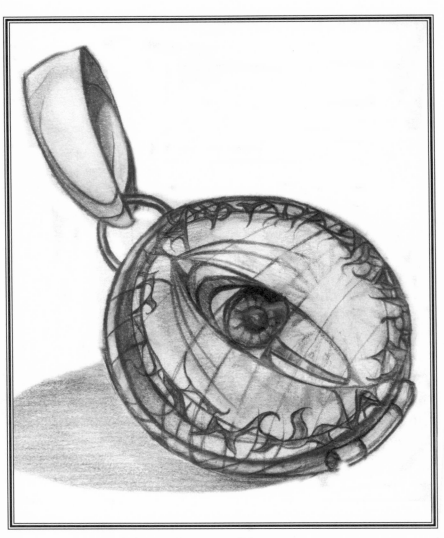

THE EYE OF KARLOFF

9

The Voodoo Priestess of Magnimarf

Late the following evening they arrived in Schnaibleville. Utten performed his flapping duties well that day, so well as a matter of fact, that one of the elephants complained that he was a little too overzealous. When his work was completed, he went to visit Auntie Collida and Frehley, and spent the whole afternoon sharing stories with both of them.

Plumley, on the other hand, put in extra hours at his flapping. It wasn't because he loved the job, nor because he was any good at it. He simply lost track of time. Even with his sour attitude, he couldn't help but get caught up in all the action that went on around the ship. By the time they reached Schnaibleville, he had seen many remarkable things that he had never seen before. He watched clowns putting on their makeup. He saw monkeys playing a game much like volleyball in the indoor pool. He saw a woman hang spinning from a rope by her teeth while Rolo rode around her in circles on his motorcycle shooting flaming ping-pong balls into the air. He saw the Jumping Orlando Brothers bounce on trampolines and throw daggers at each other. These things made him almost . . . almost pleased that he had come along.

All these things were also mere practice for the following day when the performers put on the real show for the people of Schnaibleville. And if the performers themselves were to speak truthfully, they would admit that their own acts were nothing compared to the show that Auntie Collida put on. Auntie Collida never practiced her show. Her very special ability could only work if she had a live subject to work on, and it was far too serious a matter to ever practice.

In the morning, Corker's duties increased as crowds of circus goers began to stream onto the ship from the city of Schaibleville, and Captain Hobart kept her close by his side as he made his rounds. Utten and Plumley, however, were released from their flapping duties early on, and the captain suggested that they take in some of the shows. There was no doubt where Utten wanted to go first. Auntie Collida's act had been shrouded in mystery since they had gotten on board. She refused to reveal what it was about, and the other performers only said, "She's our most popular show! Especially among folks who have kids."

"Well, there certainly isn't anything better to do," Plumley sighed to Utten. "I guess I'll come along with you." In fact, there were plenty of things to help Plumley pass the time, but he was as curious about Auntie Collida's act as Utten was.

Auntie Collida's act took place in an old room down deep under the waterline near the bow of the ship. Utten and Plumley went through the crew's quarters so that they could avoid the crowds on the upper decks. They arrived just in time; Auntie Collida's show was about to start and space remained for only two folks to stand in the back.

The room didn't hold that many people, maybe just fifty at a time. Auntie Collida said that a crowd any bigger would be too big for her show. A small stage had been set up at the front of the room, and a giant maroon curtain spotted with quarter moons and stars hung in the back. Across the top of the curtain were written the words, "*So much for the wickets and the rudelies.*" From his spot on the floor, Utten couldn't see the action at all, so he turned into his bird form and perched on Plumley's shoulder.

Plumley's first instinct was to brush Utten away, but he didn't. Utten was beginning to become familiar to him—not likeable, and certainly not friendly, but familiar. He decided to let Utten remain there.

Suddenly a large belly appeared through a break in the

curtain with Frehley following close behind it. She placed her hands on either side of her stomach and called out to the audience. "Ladies and gentleman! I am pleased to welcome you to this afternoon's show. I ask you to keep in mind that during this show you may see some very strange and awesome sights. All of us together in this room will pass from the world that we know into the world of the strange and mysterious. If you, by chance, feel the hairs on the back of your neck begin to prickle, do not be alarmed! If you, by chance, see a misty shape flit by, do not be alarmed! If you, by chance, hear a strange voice from beyond that seems to call out to only you, do not answer! Do nothing that would disturb the spirits!"

Frehley looked around the room. "I see we have many children here with us today! I see many unhappy parents! That is good. That is when Auntie Collida does her best work! Ladies and gentlemen, children of all ages, the hottest show on Captain Hobart's Traveling Ocean Circus:

AUNTIE COLLIDA!"

The room went pitch black and stayed that way for a full thirty seconds. One of the audience members became afraid and let out a little whimper. Then, from the darkness, they heard someone chanting. The lights came up slowly, so slowly that for a long time Plumley could only make out the dim outline of a person on the stage.

When the lights finally became bright enough, Plumley could see Auntie Collida sitting cross-legged and swaying back and forth as she chanted from center stage. Her eyes were closed, and she held a tiny metal bowl in each hand. In each bowl sat a small smoking, smouldering coal. She wore an eyepatch over her bad eye, and around her neck swung a large silver locket.

Suddenly, Auntie Collida began to speak out loud, though she spoke as if she were held in some kind of trance. "Oh, by the power of autumn and her promise of winter, I calls out to you! Oh, with the yellowed leaf that marks the arrival of the sage, I welcomes you! Oh, like the crow's feet planted on the husks of a ripe melon, I anticipates you! Ohhhhhhhhh . . . ." Auntie Collida swayed so far to the side that Utten feared she might fall over. "In this time of glorious senility, I hails you with both hands, and kisses you with salutations!"

"Why is she talking like that?" Plumley whispered to Utten.

"For the effect!" Utten whispered back. "Isn't it chilling?"

"Pollywog snot!" Plumley replied.

Auntie Collida opened her eyes, stood up, and faced the crowd.

"Ladies and gentlemens, please do not be afraid! It is I, Auntie Collida, mistress of the ages, the oldest woman alive, the high voodoo priestess of Magnimarf, the buddha of Alaska, the channeler of ancient potency, and the exorcisor of all the wickets and the rudelies!"

The audience began to clap, but Auntie Collida hushed them. "I appreciates your courtesies, but we musts remain hushed, lest we accidentally scares away the little invisible peoples which guides me in my works!"

"What is this hogwash?" Plumley asked, but Utten ignored him.

"I can sees many folks in my audience today. Many folks has come here with their little childrens! They come with looks all so hopeful on their faces! Well don't you worry, because I am here to help you all!" Auntie Collida waved one of her arms out towards the crowd, and a wisp of smoke floated out over them. For a second, Plumley thought he saw a face appear in the smoke, but it drifted away into nothingness as quickly as it had come. Whatever it was, the rest of the audience must have seen it as well, because a low murmur ran through the crowd.

"Many folks out there are thinking right now, 'Auntie Collida, my little boy, he don't do his homework no matter how many times I asks him!' 'Auntie Collida, my little girl, she spills the milks all over the table and won't gets a rag to wipe it up!' 'Auntie Collida, my little boy he just watches that doggy-goned TV all the whole day!' 'Auntie Collida, my little girl she chases the kitty around all day with a tennis racket!'" Each time Auntie Collida recited a parent's woe, a different family in the audience became restless. It was almost as if Auntie Collida had read their minds.

"Some of you just have childrens with you that's simply mean and nasty and grumpy and sour. That is why I am here! I can drives the wickets and the rudelies out from any child! Is there anyone out there who is with such a child?"

Hands shot into the air all around the room. Utten's wing shot into the air as well. "Hey," Plumley said, his voice sounding honestly hurt. "Put that down!"

Auntie Collida picked a family from the front row. She took a ten-year-old boy by the hand and led him up onto the stage. "What is your name?" Auntie Collida asked.

"Theodore, but don't call me Theodore. Everyone calls me Riggles. And your silly magic won't work on me!" Riggles replied, stamping a foot.

"A perfect case to starts with!" Auntie Collida sang. Frehley emerged from behind the curtain and placed a small chair on the stage. Auntie Collida looked at Riggles and said, "Sit, please!"

"NO!" Riggles shouted, gritting his teeth together. "You don't scare me!"

Auntie Collida passed the smoking coal near Riggles. She spoke again more firmly, "Sit, please!" This time, a face definitely formed in the smoke, and as Auntie

Collida spoke the words it moved its own wispy mouth in unison. Riggles leapt into the chair.

"I wants no one in the audience to worry!" Auntie Collida said. "While I plans to drive out all the wickets and the rudelies from this boy, I plan, as always, to leave just a little wicket behind, as no little boy is any fun at all unless he has just a little wicket in him!

"Tell me, Riggles, why do you think you are here today?" Auntie Collida asked.

"Well, my ma says I have to go to school. But I ain't goin' to no school! It's stupid!" Riggles barked.

Auntie Collida placed the smoking bowls on the floor next to Riggles. She removed the locket from around her neck and held it up for the boy to see. "Can't see the value of school?" She began to swing the locket back and forth. "Watch the locket, Riggles, watch it closely. It is a magic locket, to be sure. Do you knows what I haves inside this locket?"

Riggles began to look sleepy, and he shook his head no.

"Inside this locket is the shriveled eye of Karloff, the great Eskimo warlord! It was passed down to me through the generations, so that I might call on Karloff to chase the wickets! To chase the rudlies!"

Auntie Collida continued to swing the locket back and forth, and Riggles continued to get sleepier and sleepier. Smoke rose from the bowls on the floor and snaked around Riggles's legs. "Oh great Karloff, I calls on you to drive out the wickets which makes this boy hates schooling so much. It's okay to hates schooling a little, everybody does and that's understandable, but make him not hates it so much!" Auntie Collida chanted.

Suddenly, Riggles eyes bolted wide open, and his tongue stuck out the side of his mouth. "Oh great Karloff," Auntie Collida continued, "drive out the rudelies from this boy so that he will always go to school and make friends and do his work!" Auntie Collida lifted her eye patch and looked straight at Riggles with her white, cloudy eye. The volume of her voice rose as she completed her spell. "Oh great Karloff, look through my old and fading eye! I calls upon you! By the power of Karloff! By the power of all the voodoo priestesses! By the power of the cayenne, the jalapeno, and the gorgonzola! Drive out them wickets! Drive out them rudelies!"

Auntie Collida waved her fingers over Riggles and screamed, "Be gone!"

Suddenly, Riggles slumped forward. For a moment all was silent. Then the boy sat up and looked around the room at the audience. "Hello," he said.

"Riggles, how are you feeling?" Auntie Collida asked.

"I'm fine, ma'am," Riggles answered politely.

"Do you have anything to say to your mother?" Auntie Collida asked.

Riggles stood up and walked to the edge of the stage. He straightened out his shirt and said, "Mother, I finally see the value of an education!" He smiled and jumped off the stage into the waiting arms of his mother.

"Who else out there needs the services of Auntie Collida?" Auntie Collida asked the audience.

"This is silliness," Plumley whispered to Utten. "This is all a fake!"

"I don't think so," Utten replied. "I've seen a lot of magic before, and this looks like the real thing!"

"Pollywog snot!" Plumley said. "I'm leaving!" Plumley slipped out through the doors with such speed that Utten barely had time to flap off his shoulder.

Later that day the crowds dispersed and the circus set sail for Killickity Harbor on the other side of the ocean. Utten went with Auntie Collida and Frehley back to their spot next to Kashmir. Auntie Collida, exhausted from her performance, flopped down into a hay pile, and Utten perched on her knee. "Could you get us some tea, Frehley? I'm very tired."

"Yes, grandmother," Frehley said, and began to pour the water for the tea.

Utten immediately began to fire questions at Auntie

Collida. "Where did you learn such magic? Is Karloff's eye really in the locket? Why did you wear the eye patch? Do your spells always work?"

"Easy, Utten, easy!" Auntie Collida said. "One question at a time, please! I'm an old woman, you know."

"Sorry," Utten said. "This is all so exciting!"

"I don't know where I learned my magic," Auntie Collida explained. "It just seemed that as I got older, I had a special gift with children. Most of the show is for effect. I don't really talk like that, but it makes me more believable to the crowd for some reason. I do the chant, and something about me makes children want to be nicer."

"So it's not really magic?" Utten asked, a little disappointed.

"I don't think it's really magic, Utten. All children are good in their hearts to begin with, so I don't think I really change anybody. I'm not sure myself what happens. But I enjoy doing it, and people enjoy watching it. Sometimes I think that parents just imagine that their kids have the wickets and rudelies, and when I'm done they imagine that the wickets and the rudelies are gone. I don't know for sure." Frehley handed Auntie Collida a cup of hot tea. "Thank you, dear." Auntie Collida took a sip of the tea, and it soothed her. "Wonderful tea!" she exclaimed.

Frehley sat herself down in the hay next to her grandmother. "Oh my!" she said, feeling her fat belly. "That was a strong one!"

"A strong what?" Utten said. He flew over and landed on Frehley's knee.

"Here, Utten. Feel right here." Utten turned back into his normal form, and Frehley took his tiny hand and placed it on her belly. Almost immediately, Utten felt a tiny thump against the wall of her stomach.

"Do you feel all right?" Utten said, pulling his hand away.

"I feel fine!" Frehley laughed, holding her belly. "Oh! There's another one!"

"Is it gas?" Utten asked, very concerned.

"No, of course not," said Frehley. "It's a baby!"

Auntie Collida laughed out loud. "Frehley has a baby in her belly, Utten! I thought you knew that!"

Utten squawked and without thinking slipped into his bird form. His feathers became ruffled, and he fell off Frehley's knee. "Excuse me, but I think I have to go now," he warbled. "Yes, as a matter of fact, I'm sure of it!" Utten tried to fly, but he was so upset that he turned his wings back into arms. Puzzled, Frehley and Auntie Collida watched as he ran off through the old casino half in his bird form and half in his normal form, trying to fly but only flapping his arms. "Maybe I'll see you folks later!" he called back.

As soon as he got out of the casino, Utten realized that he wasn't flying, and turned himself completely into his bird form. He flew off immediately to Captain Hobart.

The Captain was intently studying a radar screen in the control room, his eyes creased with worry. Utten landed on the console next to the radar, accidentally clicking on the ship's alarm siren. Its shrill howl ran through the ship for a half second before Captain Hobart shut it off. He immediately picked up the intercom system. "This is your Captain. Don't worry folks! That was just a siren test courtesy of our new friend, Utten. So long as I have your attention, I want everyone to be aware that we may be experiencing some stormy weather tonight. I would like everyone to stay below decks. Thank you, Captain Hobart out."

"Sorry," Utten said when Captain Hobart clicked the intercom off. "But something terrible has happened and I wanted you to know about it right away!"

"What's the matter, Utten? Is somebody hurt?" Captain Hobart said, very concerned.

"You're not going to believe this!" Utten squawked. "Mistress Frehley has a baby in her belly!"

"I know all about that, Utten," Captain Hobart said, laughing. "Isn't it wonderful?"

Utten froze, unable to believe his ears. Even Captain Hobart was in on the horrible baby swallowing by Mistress Frehley! Utten squawked again, flew two nervous circles in the air, and darted away to find Corker and Plumley. He found Plumley near the sports deck watching the storm roll in. "Plumley, we have to get off of this ship! It's full of crazy people!"

Plumley calmly looked at Utten. "What are you talking about?"

"Follow me!" Utten shouted, and took off in the direction of the casino. Along the way they bumped into Corker, and Utten urged her to come along as well. "As the ship's guard dog, it is your duty to attend to this matter!" he informed her, then led them both back to the old casino.

Frehley and Auntie Collida were still sitting on the hay pile, and they smiled when Utten returned. "I thought you'd be back," Auntie Collida said.

Utten perched on Corker's head and pointed his wing at Frehley's stomach. "Mistress Frehley has a baby in her belly! She swallowed it whole and it's still kicking inside her!"

The room exploded with laughter. Frehley held her belly and rolled over onto her side. Auntie Collida's head swung back and her laughter shot straight up into the air. Even Corker dropped to the ground and rolled over on her back, releasing chortled barks.

"What's the matter with you people?" Utten demanded, flapping in the air over Corker. "Have you all lost your minds?"

"She didn't swallow the baby, Utten. She's pregnant!" Auntie Collida spat between bouts of laughter.

"Pregnant?" Utten said, completely confused.

As the laughter in the room began to abate, the group heard something that they never expected to hear—Plumley was also laughing. It was a quiet, snickering kind of laugh, so quiet that they hadn't noticed it at first. But now that they were beginning to compose themselves, they couldn't miss it. Plumley sat on the floor of the old casino, completely tickled.

"Don't you know what it means to be pregnant?" he asked Utten.

Utten's pale belly turned slightly pink. "No," he said.

"Oh my," Auntie Collida whispered. "We've embarrassed him. We're sorry Utten, we just assumed that you would know. Don't female . . . female 'Uttens' get pregnant?"

"Female Uttens? Who ever heard of a female Utten?" Utten replied.

"Utten, where do you come from? How were you born?" Frehley asked, suddenly very interested.

Realizing that everyone was staring at him, Utten looked down at the floor. "I don't know. I've just always been Utten. I was never born. I just always have been."

"Don't you grow old? Won't you die?" Auntie Collida said.

"No," Utten answered. "I'll always just be Utten."

The room fell very silent. No one knew exactly what to say. Finally, Auntie Collida broke the silence. "This is going to take some explaining. Utten, will you take a walk with me?"

"Sure," Utten said, leaping at the opportunity to leave. It was very rare that Utten felt self-conscious, and he wasn't used to the feelings.

Utten and Auntie Collida walked out through the old casino and down the steps to the very bottom of the ship. Auntie Collida planned a very long walk, for she knew it would take a long time to explain things to Utten. As they walked, the ship began to sway as the storm rolled in.

"Utten, do you understand the idea of birth, and the idea of death?" she asked.

"Sort of, but not exactly. I never quite got the details of it. There were too many unanswered questions. For example, if someone gets born, what were they before they were born? Also, when somebody dies, where do they go off to? It doesn't make any sense."

"It doesn't make any sense. And those of us who live and die spend our whole lives asking those questions. There are no answers to those questions, either. There is only one rule, everything that is born must one day die. Some die sooner, and some die later, but everything must die."

"What about you? Doesn't that frighten you?" Utten asked.

"No. I've lived a good long life, and I've lived more years than most get to live. I've had a good life. I have wonderful children, and wonderful grandchildren. Soon, if I stay around long enough, I'll have a great-grandchild. All my life I have been surrounded by marvelous people. But I don't have much time left. Death doesn't frighten me, though. It's all part of the process. Actually, just between you and me, I'm kind of excited to see what's on the other side!"

Utten then asked the really hard question. "How did the baby get inside of Mistress Frehley?" Auntie Collida did her best to answer the question completely. There were parts that she tried to skim over, but Utten wouldn't let her. He wanted all the details. A few of the details made his belly turn bright red, and one in particular made all the spots on his back converge into one big blotch, but he recovered. In the end, he understood things fairly well. At least as well as an Utten could.

"Kashmir is pregnant, too, you know. Both she and Frehley are due at any time now," Auntie Collida explained.

"But, who is the father of Frehley's baby?" Utten asked.

"Her husband, Utten," Auntie Collida said. "Captain Jonathon T. Hobart!"

Their walk came full circle, and Utten and Auntie Collida found themselves standing in front of the little group once again. Utten walked right up to Frehley. "I'm sorry for my silliness. It's all been explained to me now, and I think I understand." Utten lay his head against

Frehley's body. "Ooooooooh!" he said. "This is fascinating!" He spread out his arms and grabbed hold of Frehley's belly. "Wow!" he exclaimed. "I could listen to this all day!" He released his hold on Frehley and ran over to attach himself to Kashmir's belly. "Hey! I can hear something in here, too!"

Auntie Collida walked over to Plumley. "Now, about you," she said. "I think I have my energy back." A low rumble of thunder rattled the night around the ship.

"What are you talking about? Get away from me!" Plumley said.

Auntie Collida reached into her pocket and pulled out the locket. She let the chain drop and gently swung the locket back and forth. "If ever there was a boy in need of having some wickets and rudelies driven out, you're him. You have a withered heart, young Plumley."

Plumley wanted to run away, but he couldn't take his eyes off the locket. All he could see was its shining silver. All he could hear was the sound of Auntie Collida's voice mixed with the sound of the wind which ran in wailing circles around the boat. Utten ceased his baby listening to watch Auntie Collida.

"Once again I call upon the shriveled eye of Karloff, the great Eskimo warlord! To chase the wickets, to chase the rudelies from this boy called Plumley!"

Plumley felt himself get very sleepy, and suddenly it felt as if the room had no up and no down. "Oh great Karloff,

I call on you to drive out the wickets which make this boy so miserable!" Auntie Collida chanted. "Oh great Karloff, purge the ghosts which haunt this young man!" The ship began to rock back and forth as the waves grew in size.

"Go get 'im, Auntie Collida!" Utten cheered.

Just like Riggles's before him, Plumley's eyes bolted wide open, and his tongue stuck out the side of his mouth. "Oh great Karloff," Auntie Collida continued, "drive out the rudelies from this boy so that he will have peace in his heart!"

Auntie Collida raised her voice as she began the final incantations which would make the spell take hold of Plumley. Outside, the sky ripped open, and the rain began to fall. "Oh great Karloff, look through my old and fading eye! I call upon you! By the power of Karloff! By the power of all the voodoo priestesses! By the power of the cayenne, the jalapeno, and the gorgonzola! Drive out them wickets! Drive out them rudelies!"

Auntie Collida waved her fingers over Plumley and began to scream the final words which would seal the spell . . .

But her voice was drowned out by the sounding of the ship's alarm siren.

No Day and No Night

10

THE HUSH BOGS

Captain Hobart's voice came over the intercom and woke Plumley from his trance. "Everyone please remain calm! We are experiencing some rough weather, and it looks like it's going to get rougher. I want everyone to find a safe, secure place and hold on tight!"

Auntie Collida and Frehley immediately took Kashmir over to a corner of the old casino and made her lie down. They sat down close to her belly and held onto her sturdy legs for support. "Utten, please go tell Captain Hobart that I'm okay!" Frehley asked. Utten flapped off to the control room of the ship with Corker and Plumley close behind. When they found him, Captain Hobart was holding onto the steering column with all his might trying to keep the ship on a straight path through the storm.

"I think it's a hurricane, Utten," Captain Hobart explained. "It seemed to come up from nowhere!"

Plumley looked out at the front of the ship. Rain and seawater drenched the bow, and the sky was a swirling mass of gray and black clouds. The boat pitched, and Plumley and Corker slid sideways into one of the walls.

"Plumley, please take Corker down to our hay pile and get the bucket out. If this storm gets any worse, I might need it!" Utten shouted over the roar of the storm.

"You'd abandon us with the bucket?" Plumley shouted accusingly.

"Certainly not!" Utten shouted back. "There's no time to explain! Just please go!"

Knowing that it would be safer down by the hay pile, Plumley and Corker left the control room. Utten landed on Captain Hobart's shoulder. "Should we abandon the ship?" Utten asked.

"We'd never survive in the life boats, Utten. The only chance is to try and keep her afloat." As he said this, a heavy wave struck the side of the boat, and she leaned over towards her starboard side. "I didn't want to panic everybody, Utten, but I don't think we're going to make it!"

Utten turned back into his normal form and stood on the console next to Captain Hobart. He grabbed at the wheel and pulled with the captain against the force of the storm, but he too could tell that they were fighting a losing battle. Together, they could just barely maintain control, and the storm was clearly growing in strength.

Utten and Captain Hobart didn't have to fight much longer. An enormous wave struck the side of the boat, crashing through the glass into the control room and throwing both of them against the far wall. The wheel began to spin, and the ship fell mercy to the whims of the storm. She listed onto her starboard side, and soon water began to pour over the starboard decks.

"Captain! Captain!" Utten yelled, hopping around in the salty water. Captain Hobart did not respond. The blow had knocked him unconscious.

"Wake up, Captain, the ship is sinking! You have to wake up!"

Captain Hobart was out cold. The ship continued to lean onto her starboard side. Soon she would tip over, and then it would not be long before she sank to the bottom. There was nothing Utten, nor Captain Hobart, nor anybody else could do about it.

Too small to pull Captain Hobart into the safety of the outer hall, Utten grabbed a rope from under one of the control panels and secured the captain to a hand rail as best he could. "Hang on, Captain," Utten said. "We may be out of this sooner than you think!" Then he disappeared out the door and down the hallway.

When Utten found Plumley and Corker, Plumley had curled up in a ball in the hay pile. Corker held the bucket by its handle in her mouth. She dropped it to the ground, and Utten immediately disappeared inside. He reappeared a moment later carrying his hammer and anvil, which he placed on the slanted floor next to Corker. He disappeared inside again.

The ship lurched again, and the bucket almost tipped over, but Corker caught the edge and held it steady. The tiny anvil rolled over and bumped into the wall. When it struck the wall, a tiny spark appeared, and it immediately flew down inside the bucket. When she saw the tiny spark, Corker remembered her trip through time and a chill ran down her back.

"Hey, get out of here, I don't have time for this!" Utten shouted at the spark. He was quiet for a moment, then he shouted out to Corker. "I know it's here some-where, Corker, but I can't seem to get my hands on it!" Corker heard a number of loud of crashes from inside the bucket, then a sound like a warm wax baseball hitting a stop sign. "Here it is!" Utten yelled. He climbed out of the bucket. In his hand he held a tiny crystal.

Plumley sat up in the hay pile. "What's going on?"

"I'll explain later!" Utten shouted. "But brace your-self. This is going to be a rough ride." He righted the anvil and grabbed his hammer. He held the crystal with one hand to the anvil, and with his other hand he brought down the hammer with all his might. A large spark shot out and ricocheted against the wall, circling around near Utten as if trying to get its bearings.

"There's no time to lose! Get going!" Utten shouted, and the tiny spark sped away leaving a tail like a comet behind it.

Utten struck the crystal again, and another large spark appeared. It too flew off into the ship. Another hammer strike, and then another spark. And then another. And another. And another. Utten struck the crystal at least a hundred times by Corker's count.

Corker had no idea where all the sparks were going. She hoped that they were somehow taking over control of the ship and steering it safely through the storm, but the floor beneath her continued to shift as the ship listed. Water began to pour into the hall nearby. Finally, Utten struck the hammer into the crystal one last time. A last tiny spark appeared. "Check the ship!" Utten commanded. "Make sure everyone is accounted for!"

The tiny comet flew off. "Okay, guys. I want you to gather around the bucket. Plumley, you put one arm around Corker and hold her tight. Corker, you grab the bucket by the handle. Plumley, be ready to grab hold of me when I tell you to."

"Utten, what's going on?" Plumley demanded. As he said it, the ship tipped further on her side, and then finally capsized. The three of them rolled down the wall as the ceiling suddenly became the floor.

"There's not much time left!" Utten said. "I hope I got everybody! Grab hold of each other!"

The spark which had been told to check the ship returned, shimmering lightly in front of Utten. "Okay," Utten shouted. "Everybody is okay! Now it's our turn!"

Corker didn't like what Utten was suggesting, but she knew there was really no room for an argument. Utten righted the anvil one last time. He laid the crystal upon its surface, pulled his hand away, and brought the hammer down with a crack. The sound of that hammer was so powerful that Plumley wasn't sure where the hammer crack ended and the storm's thunder began.

The crystal shattered. Its shards spread out across the anvil like powdery streaks of broken glass. For a moment, nothing happened. Then each powdery piece of glass turned into a burning spark, each spark brighter than the ones that Utten had sent through the ship. They rose up away from the anvil in a swarm and spread out around Utten, Plumley, and Corker.

"It's beautiful!" Plumley exclaimed.

"Please hold on!" Utten warned, shouting as loud as he could. "Hold on or we'll lose each other."

Corker moaned. The sparks began to gather close to her fur, then divide and spread over her. The last thing she wanted to do was to travel through time again. Corker didn't understand that traveling through time would have seemed pleasant compared to what was about to happen to her and Utten and Plumley.

The clouds of sparks continued to grow, slowly

enveloping the group. Soon, all three were nothing more than figures of brilliant light. Then they were gone.

The sparks that Utten sent out were not time sparks. In fact, Utten didn't have the power to create time travel sparks; it was the time travel *sparks* that occasionally found *him*. The sparks that Utten created with his anvil were similar, though, to the sparks that had sent him and Corker through time. If Utten were to try to describe it to you, he would probably say that the sparks he created with his anvil were like cousins to the time sparks. They were cousins that he had learned to control through magic.

The sparks he had created didn't send people through time, but they did send people somewhere. And they were perfectly suited to this emergency. Each spark that Utten created with the strike of his hammer went out into the ship and found a person or a small group of people and transported them somewhere. But the magic was unpredictable—Utten didn't know exactly where everyone was going to be transported. He didn't have the magical power to sent people to specific places. He just reasoned that anyplace was better than a sinking ship, so he sent out an army of sparks to transport everybody somewhere.

Consequently, Rolo ended up on a tropical beach in Fiji, which is not such a bad place to end up. His spark was even kind enough the let him take his motorcycle with him. Maxwell the one-armed lion tamer ended up riding a subway in Brooklyn, New York. At first he worried because he had heard that New York had a high crime rate, but then he saw that his spark had been wise enough to send the lions along with him.

Gipper the chimpanzee ended up on an avocado farm in California that was on the brink of bankruptcy. He made fast friends with the farmhands, and his energy and enthusiasm during the harvest helped save the farm from the creditors.

The Jumping Orlando Brothers ended up at a news briefing at the White House in Washington, D.C. and the daring gymnastics they demonstrated as they tried to escape from the secret service caught the eye of the President himself. Eventually, the secret service figured out that they were harmless, and the boys were hired to perform at the White House's Independence Day Barbecue.

Kashmir the elephant wound up on the doorstep of a woman named Breada who lives in County Laois, Ireland. The elephant thrilled her son Alan, but did not thrill her husband Jim, who had to go into town and buy a new shovel. Later that week, he had to help deliver Kashmir's baby girl.

Auntie Collida and Frehley ended up in Boston, Massachusetts, having tea at an outdoor café.

Ironically, Captain Hobart ended up on another ship, an aircraft carrier called the Enterprise. Within a week the crew of the Enterprise brought him into Boston Harbor, and he was reunited with his wife just in time to help her bring their son into the world.

Utten saved everybody on the ship. Everyone ended up somewhere, even if it wasn't exactly where they wanted to be. Unfortunately, in order to do so, he had to make a sacrifice. All magic has a balance, and saving the lives on the ship held quite a high price.

Plumley felt like his body had been pulled into pieces and tossed around on the ground. He moaned and opened his eyes. He and Corker lay nose to nose on the ground. "Ugh!" he groaned as he sat up. "You have dog breath."

Corker opened up her eyes. She sat up and looked Plumley straight in the face. What normally would have come out as barks and whines came out clear as a bell to Plumley. "I'm a dog, you cranky old coot. What's your excuse?"

Plumley fell over backwards, splashing into something wet. "You . . . you . . . you spoke!" he stammered.

"I've been speaking since the moment you met me. You just haven't been able to understand me," Corker explained. "And let me tell you something, it hasn't been easy listening to your whining, your complaining, and your snippy little comments, knowing that there was no way to respond in a language you would understand. I've had it up to here—"

Plumley lifted his hand and pointed at her. "You're speaking! Dogs don't talk!"

"Of course dogs talk. We talk all the time!"

"Stop it!" Plumley cried. "This is absurd!"

Utten flapped around on the ground, once again trying to maintain a consistent form. He finally got one that was manageable, though not quite normal. All his parts were in the right place with the exception of one bird claw, which stuck straight out of his forehead.

"Hold on here, hold on!" Utten said, his forehead talon waving. "Everybody get a hold of themselves!"

Frightened, Plumley shut his mouth and stared at Corker. Then he noticed his surroundings. "This is a nightmare. I'm having a nightmare," he whispered.

The three of them had landed in some kind of swamp. Tall bare cedar trees stretched up towards the sky from the wet ground, the bark flaking from their half rotten trunks. Overhead, deep purple clouds drifted by silently on their way to nowhere. Three paths led off in different directions, and down one of them Plumley thought he could make out a dim glow of light. Plumley couldn't tell what time of day it was. In fact, it didn't seem that the word "day" applied at all. It wasn't day, but it certainly wasn't night either. For some reason, neither of those words seemed to have any meaning.

The bog smelled, but it wasn't the normal unpleasant smell that one would associate with a swamp. This smell was more synthetic, less natural, like the smell of a closet where chemicals are stored.

What was most unpleasant about the swamp was its stillness. Nothing moved, not even the patches of fog that Plumley could spot through the trees. Nothing seemed to even breathe. They heard no sound apart from the sounds that the trio themselves were making, and that frightened Plumley most of all. It made him want to remain very quiet, just in case there was something out there that might be listening for them.

"Where are we, Utten?" Plumley asked.

"Let me give you the good news first," Utten prefaced. "Everyone who was on the ship survived. Those sparks we created transported everybody to another spot on earth where they'd be safer."

"What's the bad news?" Plumley asked. He was listening to Utten, but he was also listening to the swamp for any kind of noise.

"The other good news is that we're not on the ship. We would have died there. The ship ended up on the bottom of the ocean," Utten said.

"So what's the bad news?" Plumley asked again.

"I think I know what the bad news is," Corker said. "The bad news is that all magic has a balance. There's a little give, and a little take. In order to give all those people their lives, we had to make a sacrifice. Am I right?"

"Right," Utten said calmly.

"Well, where on earth are we?" Plumley asked, his voice growing a little angry. He liked the feel of his anger. It was familiar to him, and it helped him forget his fear.

"We're not on earth," Utten confessed. "We're someplace . . . else."

Plumley splashed through a puddle so that he could stand next to Utten. "Listen, you'd better start telling me what's going on, and you'd better start telling me right now! I've had just about enough of this!"

"Easy, Plumley, easy," Utten said. Corker trotted a few yards up one of the paths to see what she could find. She trotted back and checked out the other paths. As she investigated, Utten explained further. "There's more places than just earth, Plumley. Some are good, and some are bad. This is like . . . well, I guess you might say it's another dimension. It's a place that you can't get to from earth unless you use magic. Time has no meaning here. The laws of your world have no meaning here. That's why you can understand Corker, though you couldn't understand her before. Things are different here."

"Then pull out that anvil and get sparking, you little blue frog, because I want to go home right now!" Plumley shouted.

"It's not that easy. I wish it were!" Utten shouted back. "Everyone on that ship was saved, but in order for my magic to save them, we had to make a sacrifice. Being here creates the balance in magic. I can't just whip out my anvil again and ask magic to unbalance itself. We're stuck here, possibly forever. So you'd better get used to the idea. And you'd better stick with me and Corker, because we're going to need each other just to survive!"

Plumley paced around the little crossroads between the paths. "I'd have been better off if I'd never listened to you and that silly dog, Utten," Plumley said. "I'd be better off if I just relied on myself. I'd be back at school right now. I might have to do yard work and laundry work and kitchen work, but I'd be home safe and sound. Sticking by you two is what's gotten me into trouble. Are all your adventures like this one? Because this one doesn't seem to have a happy end at all."

"This one isn't over yet, Plumley," Corker pointed out. "Let's stop arguing and figure out what we're going to do."

"I know what I'm going to do," Plumley said. "I'm going to get out of here, with or without your help." Plumley looked down all of the three paths and chose the one that had the dim light off in the distance. "There's got to be someone or something around here that can get me home. From now on, I'm on my own."

Plumley walked away from them down the path.

"Wait, Plumley!" Utten shouted. "You have to be careful! You don't know what's out there!" Plumley didn't even turn around.

Plumley didn't have to walk for long before he found something. The path ended at a structure. It was shaped like a house, only smaller. Its walls were stone. Its roof was slate. The path led right up to its door. A light flickered inside. Corker and Utten came up the path behind Plumley.

"Here we go," Plumley said defiantly. "I'll bet there's someone in here that can be of more help than you two."

"Wait!" Utten warned. "Plumley, don't go in there! You don't understand. This place is full of bad magic!"

"Bad magic?" scoffed Plumley. His anger made him feel brave. "If your magic is good magic, Utten, I think I'll try my luck with the bad!" He stepped inside the structure. Corker moved to follow him, but Utten held her back.

"We shouldn't go in there," Utten said. "I'm not sure, but from what I sense, very few who go in ever come back out again."

Plumley found himself standing inside the only room of the mausoleum. A thin layer of light, dusty soil covered the entryway, probably tracked in by others from the bog. There was only a single window set into the far wall. Thick ivy covered the walls of the room, and tiny creatures moved around underneath the leaves. From the ceiling, Plumley could hear the low chirping sounds of creatures suspended in the shadows.

In front of Plumley stood a large desk, and behind it sat a peculiar figure unlike anything Plumley had ever seen before. Though furred in the manner of an unpleasant rodent, it dressed in the clothes of a man. It had tiny eyes, and tiny ears, a tiny nose, and a tiny mouth. It even had tiny hands. Strangely, though, other parts of its body were inordinately huge. It had enormous arms, a huge head, and extremely wide shoulders. It wore a vest which pinched the huge body, almost as if the vest itself was just barely binding the body together. A pair of enormous, thick-lensed glasses perched on the tiny nose and magnified its miniscule eyes, making them appear huge. The figure had long, pointed fingernails. Its clothes and the first finger on its right hand were smeared with ink.

The figure hunched over an enormous book. Across the top of the desk there sat an inkwell and hundreds of tiny hourglasses. A few snails slimed their way around in between the objects. The figure leaned forward and dipped its inky finger into the black inkwell. It poised the finger over the book.

"I am Moal. What is your name?" it said without looking up.

Though unnerved by Moal, Plumley tried not to let it show. "I require some assistance," he said, his voice shaking a little. "Can you tell me—"

"I am waiting for your name," Moal said coolly.

"But I simply want—" Plumley began.

Moal's enormous arm slammed his tiny fist down on the desk. "I don't care! You must register first! Don't you understand? At this point all questions are irrelevant!"

"But—"

"Name!" Moal shouted.

"But—"

"Name!"

"Listen—"

"I don't care! You're being extremely rude!" Moal roared. He still had not looked up.

"It's in my nature!" Plumley shouted back, a bit annoyed.

"Not any more it's not!" Moal roared. "Now give me your name!" The animals in the ceiling began to shriek as they heard Moal's anger rise.

"Plumley!" Plumley finally shouted, succumbing to Moal's stubbornness.

Moal suddenly became calm. "Plumley? Plumley, let me see . . . Plumley." With his left hand, Moal flipped through the pages of his book. "Oh yes, Plumley. Mr. Plumley. Old Man Plumley, as they say. Hello, Mr. Plumley. Yes, you're right here." Moal scanned the edge of his desk, looking over the many hourglasses. "Oh, but Mr. Plumley, according to this, you're early. There must be some mistake. No one is ever early."

"Old Man Plumley?" Plumley asked. "I don't know what you're talking about. I just need some information."

"How could you be here early?" Moal continued, not listening to Plumley. "Oh well, I guess it doesn't really matter. I don't care. It's not like you had a lot of time left."

"Time left? What are you talking about?" Plumley asked. "Look, I just need to know how to get out of here!"

Moal chuckled a little. "You can't get out of here, Old Man Plumley. Once you're here, you're here to stay." Moal looked up at Plumley for the first time since Plumley entered the mausoleum. His tiny jaw fell open. "Why, you're only just a boy! We've never had a boy before. There certainly is a mix-up somewhere." Moal shuffled down off his stool and came around the desk to get a better look at Plumley. His huge upper body was only barely supported by tiny, thin legs. "Yes, you definitely are a boy. There is no doubt about that. Well, it doesn't matter to me. It's all the same to me. I don't care. A soul is a soul is a soul, that's what I say!"

Plumley felt goose pimples on the back of his neck. Something very strange was going on, and it was beginning to frighten him. He was beginning to wish that he had listened to Utten.

"What do you mean, a soul is a soul is a soul?" Plumley asked.

Moal chuckled again. "Don't you realize where you are, boy? You're in the Hush Bogs. Nobody ever leaves here. They only come here for one reason."

"What reason is that?" Plumley asked.

Moal walked over to the large window in the wall behind his desk. "Come here, boy. Come here and look."

Plumley approached the window and looked out. From the back wall of the stone mausoleum, the bogs gradually sloped away. Plumley could see far out through the cypress trees. The view, however, didn't look that much different than the view he had walking up to the front of the mausoleum.

"I don't see anything," Plumley confessed.

"Keep watching boy, you'll see them," Moal urged.

Gradually, Plumley could make out a shape in the trees. It moved very slowly. Then he spotted another, and then another. Some looked a lot like people. Others looked just like indistinct human shapes. If Plumley didn't know any better, he would have sworn that they were ghosts.

"What are they?" he asked.

"They're souls, Mr. Plumley," Moal said proudly. "They're the souls of forgotten people. While they lived, some were mean, some were nasty, some were just down-right grumpy. But all of them lived their lives in such a way that no one wanted to be near them. Those who knew them found them miserable to be around. When they died, they came here, and they came here for one reason only."

Plumley swallowed, trying to get rid of the ball of fear that had gathered in his throat. "What reason is that?"

"They came here because when they died . . . nobody cared," Moal hissed.

Moal stepped away from the window and resumed his perch on his stool. "Let me see, Plumley . . . Plumley . . . oh, here it is again . . . P . . . L . . . U . . . M . . . L . . . E—"

"Wait!" Plumley shouted. "There must be some mistake! Look at me! I'm just a boy!"

Moal looked up calmly from his book. "Yes, I'm sure that there is some mistake. According to my records, you're not due yet. You're due soon, to be sure, but you're not due yet. And according to my records, you're supposed to be an old man, not a little boy. But that doesn't matter to me. I don't care. All I know is that your name is in my book."

"How can I be due soon if I'm just a boy?" Plumley sputtered. Maybe he could find a way out using logic.

Moal held up his inky fingernail and pointed at the

hourglasses on his desk. "See these, Mr. Plumley? Take a close look at them." Plumley leaned in. Each hourglass kept track of a separate time. The insides of the hourglasses weren't filled with sand, though. They were filled with tiny mites. In the upper chambers, the mites scrambled over each other, each trying to get as far away from the hole as possible. Plumley looked closely at their streams. As the mites fell through the tiny hole in the hourglass, they grabbed hold of another and tried to climb back up the stream to the hourglass's upper chamber. Some of them made it, forcing their way back up through the hole, but most fell straight to the bottom. Plumley realized that theirs was a pointless struggle. No matter how good a climber each mite was, eventually they would all fall through the hole.

"See this one here?" Moal asked, pointing with his black nail.

Plumley followed the nail. The hourglass it pointed to had a name inscribed on the bottom. It read, "PLUMLEY." What Moal said was true. There were not a lot of mites left in the hourglass's upper chamber.

Plumley gasped and stepped back. "That's not possible! It's simply not possible!"

"You see this one here?" Moal asked, pointing to an hourglass which still had a lot of mites left in the upper chamber. "This man is still fairly young. He might have time to change, and if he does I will be forced sadly to remove his name from my ledger. But he probably won't change. They seldom do.

"According to my notes in the ledger, Old Man Plumley, towards the end you tried to make friends. First you tried with a dog, and you had moderate success. Then you met a little blue thing, who liked you very much. But by then it was too late. By then, the ink in my ledger was dry, and once dry there is no way to rewrite it!"

Plumley's mind reeled. He tried to take all this information in, but his mind couldn't grasp it all. It didn't make any sense to him. How could Moal's ledger say that he was an old man? Then he remembered what Utten had said. *"You might say it's another dimension. Time has no meaning here. The laws of your world have no meaning here."*

"You can't mean this!" Plumley cried. "I won't let this happen!"

Moal answered him very calmly. "You may do what you want. I don't care. But know this, Old Man Plumley. When the mites in your hourglass run out, you'll be here forever, and there's no changing that. Your efforts are as futile as those of the mites, Mr. Plumley." Moal turned the ledger around and offered the inkwell to Plumley. "Why don't you just sign in now?"

Plumley became frantic. He reached out and grabbed his hourglass. "I won't let this happen!" he shouted.

"Please put that back," Moal said calmly.

"No!" shouted Plumley. He backed towards the door. "No! It's mine! It's my life, and you can't have it!"

"It doesn't matter where you are when the mites run out. Once they're gone, they're gone." Moal leaned over his ledger again. "You may run, if you wish. I don't care. You'll be back."

"No, I won't!" Plumley shouted. He darted out the door of the mausoleum. "Run!" he screamed at Corker and Utten.

Moal got off his stool and watched Plumley, Corker, and Utten disappear into the bogs. He then returned to his stool and pulled out a blank piece of yellowed paper from the side of his desk. He dipped his fingernail in his inkwell and wrote the following note:

> My friends:
>
> There are some travelers coming your way through the swamp. One is a young boy. Another is a dog. Last, but certainly not least, is a blue creature, whose magic you must be careful of. I am not sure which path they have taken, but it doesn't really matter, does it? All the paths lead to the same place, more or less. Bring the boy to me. Bring the blue man to me. Do whatever you please with the mutt.
>
> Sincerely,
> Moal

Moal folded up the piece of paper and placed it in an envelope. He plucked one of the snails from the edge of the desk and let it run along the edge of the envelope.

Moal sealed the envelope with snail slime, then held it up over his head. "Come down, one of you!" he called up. Tiny chirping voices chattered, fearfully arguing over whose turn it was to fly down and pluck the letter from Moal's hand.

"It can be any one of you. I don't care. But I will punish you all if one of you does not step forward now," Moal said coldly. A single bat dropped from the ceiling. It hovered nervously in the air a few feet from Moal. Suddenly it darted forward, grabbed the envelope, and retreated to a safe distance away from him.

"Deliver that note to Skoll and Haite," Moal commanded. "Do not dally." Moal waved his arm, dismissing the creature. The bat flew out the door of the mausoleum into the Hush Bogs.

CAN YOU SEE HIM?

11

A Soul Comes Calling

"Anyplace is better than here!" Plumley shouted as he followed closely on Corker's heels. Corker ran without purpose or direction, the bucket dangling from her mouth. Whenever the path split off, she made a quick decision. Utten flapped along behind them in the rear, constantly checking over his shoulder to see if anything might be chasing them.

When Plumley was convinced that they had traveled far enough he called for Corker to stop. He leaned over and placed his hands on his knees, trying to regain his breath. Utten landed on the ground in front of him.

"What happened in there?" Utten asked. "You lit out of there like you'd seen a ghost!"

"I saw many," Plumley wheezed, quietly slipping the hourglass into his pocket. "And now I have questions."

Plumley sat down on the ground to rest. "First, who is Old Man Plumley?" Corker's ears perked up. She looked over at Utten, waiting for him to decide what they should say next.

Utten flew over and perched on Plumley's knee. "That's a pretty complex question," Utten began, but Plumley interrupted him.

"He's me, isn't he? There was a creature in there—a horrible creature named Moal. He called me Old Man Plumley. He said that my life was almost over. He said that I was doomed to stay here forever," Plumley said, still out of breath.

Utten was quiet for a long time. Finally, deciding that honesty was the best policy, he said, "Old Man Plumley is the meanest man who ever lived. He is wicked. His yard is covered with prickers and weeds that smell like garlic. The house is always dark inside, even during the day, so they say."

Plumley's jaw dropped. "Is that true?" he asked.

"That's the way he was described to me," Utten said.

Corker joined in. "The truth is that Old Man Plumley is just a lonely, cranky old man. Not really mean. He just wanted to be left alone all his life."

"When he got older," Utten continued, "he finally decided that he wanted a friend, so he adopted a dog named Corker from the local shelter."

Corker picked up the tale again. "Then, one day, a little blue man broke into his house. The little blue man had been dared to break into the house of the meanest, creepiest man in town."

"To the little blue man's surprise, Plumley was not as nasty as people had made him out to be," Utten said, and he started to smile. He enjoyed telling the story with Corker.

"Plumley and the little blue man became friends, but Plumley was getting too old to keep up with the energy of his new friend. Knowing that the blue man was magic, Plumley asked the blue man to travel through time, to find himself as a boy, and to take the boy on an adventure."

Utten picked up the story again. "Old Man Plumley had hoped that having an adventure might do the boy some good, and that if young Plumley and the blue man had a great adventure together, then maybe young Plumley wouldn't grow up to be a cranky, lonely old man."

"That was the plan," Corker said. "But so far, your crankiness has been far greater than either of us anticipated. I wish I knew what you were so angry about."

"That's the truth of it," Utten concluded. "I think that somehow our time paths have gotten crossed. Remember how I said that time has no meaning here? Maybe Moal's book is on our time, mine and Corker's. According to our time, you *are* a very old man."

Plumley sat and listened to the whole story, and when it was finished, he remained quiet for a very long time. Finally, he took the hourglass out of his pocket and looked at the mites inside. "I don't believe you," he said. "I don't believe that I grow up to be the meanest man in town. I'm not mean—I just like for people to leave me alone. There may be some truth to the story, but it can't all be true."

"Why would we lie to you now?" Corker asked. "We have nothing to lose now!"

"I don't know, I just know that what you say doesn't make any sense," Plumley said. "Besides, if you were supposed to come back through time and have a happy adventure with me, you've certainly botched the job, both of you. This has been more of a nightmare than a fun adventure. And now I'm trapped in this place, maybe forever."

Plumley held up the hourglass and watched the falling mites. "Moal said that this hourglass marked the time I had left to live. Well, I'm going to fix this situation right now, and I'm going to do it without the help of either of you. I'm going to do it on my own, without anybody's help." With one swift motion, Plumley flipped the hourglass over. "Wait a minute!" he gasped. "That's not possible! This can't be happening!"

The mites didn't reverse their direction. They continued to fall into the same chamber, only this time they fell upwards instead of downwards.

Utten looked carefully at the hourglass. "As I told you before, the laws of your universe don't apply here. Time has no real meaning here."

Plumley fell back into the dirt. "What do I do now?"

"The question is, what do *we* do now? We're stuck here, just the same as you, Plumley," Utten said.

"I for one would like to get back to my friend, my own Plumley. I wasn't supposed to come on this trip in the first place," Corker said. Remembering that it was his fault that Corker was there at all, Utten flew over and landed next to her. She leaned her head down and said, "It's okay Utten, I don't blame you."

"Well, I do," Utten confessed. "And I'll find us a way out! I promise! I'll get everybody back home, safe and sound."

"How?" Plumley asked.

Utten turned back into his normal form. "I'm not sure yet, but it'll come to me!"

"I think we're all very tired," Corker said. "Why don't we rest for a while and then try to find our way out of here?"

"I'm not tired," Plumley said, though he was lying.

Corker lifted up her nose and sniffed at the air. She looked off into the bogs. "Well, you're going to rest anyway. Fatigue will only make us all cranky, and we certainly don't need that. Lie down and rest. I'll keep a watch out."

Plumley didn't feel like arguing with her. He placed his back against one of the cedar trees, turned over on his side, and tried to get comfortable. He continued to clutch the hourglass, and the mites continued their descent. Utten came over next to him and curled up on the ground in front of him. Corker sat vigil over the two of them.

For a while, nobody said anything. Plumley lay there trying to rest but found himself wondering where the paths of the bogs led to. He wondered why there seemed to be no day and no night. He wondered what might happen if one of those lost souls drifted down the path and found them there sleeping. He began to wonder what would happen if he couldn't get home before the hourglass ran out. He began to shiver, not because he was cold, but because he was afraid.

"Are you all right?" Utten asked him.

"It's nothing," Plumley said. "I was just thinking . . . I was just thinking about sylberpodders. I'm beginning to think that maybe they're real."

Utten stood up and climbed onto Plumley's shoulder. "Don't you worry, Plumley! You sleep tight! If there are any sylberpodders about, I'll get them!" He pretended a sylberpodder was flying nearby, and he chopped at it with the side of his hand. "And I'll get the choates and yinkers, too!" That was enough for Plumley. He relaxed, and sleep overcame him.

Once Plumley settled, Utten sat down on his shoulder and began to mull over their situation. He was the only one of the group who had ever traveled into another dimension before. The other dimensions he had been to had always been easy to get out of. This one puzzled him. Still, he had to find a way for them to get out.

Corker lifted her nose again. She pulled the air of the bogs into her nostrils and digested its scents. Her keen senses told her that something was definitely out there. She had sensed it before, and now it was even stronger. There was something or someone out there in the bogs.

That something was close by. That something was watching them.

When Plumley awoke some time later, he had no way of knowing how long he had been sleeping. Utten dozed on the ground in front of him. Corker stood still as a statue, staring into the bogs. Plumley rubbed his eyes and stretched his back.

"Good morning," Corker said.

"It's not morning. There's no morning in this place," Plumley said grumpily.

"Good morning anyway, you poop," Corker said.

Plumley sat up, noticing that Corker was staring at something in the woods. "What's the matter?" Plumley asked. On the ground, Utten began to stir.

"There's someone, or something, watching us," Corker

said plainly. "He's hard to see, but he is there. I'm not sure your eyes will be able to pick him up."

Taking that as a challenge, Plumley stared off into the bogs trying to spot what Corker had spotted. "What does it look like?" he asked.

"It looks like a person, but he's only half there. Can you see him?" Corker said, still not breaking her stare.

"No, but it sounds like one of Moal's ghosts. I don't think one of them would hurt us. He's probably just drifting by," Plumley suggested.

Corker remained rigid. "No," she said. "He's been staring at me for over two hours now."

Utten climbed up Corker's back and peered out over her head. He spotted the figure right away, and it sent a chilled ripple of feathers down his back. "Oh my," he whispered. "It is watching us."

Plumley saw the feathers appear on Utten's back, and it caused goose bumps to appear on his own flesh. "Let's get out of here," he said.

"Let me try this first," Corker said. She stood, tensed the sharp muscles of her back, and howled a terse warning at the figure in the bogs. "There he goes. He's gone."

Silently, Utten thought to himself that if he had heard such a howl directed at him, he would have headed in the other direction as well. Once again, his gentle friend Corker had surprised him with her hidden ferocity.

"I want to leave anyway," Plumley said hurriedly.

Though he had slept for quite a while, he still felt tired. He was also hungry, and there wasn't anything nearby that looked even remotely edible.

"I agree," Utten said. "Let's find our way out of here."

"Okay," Corker said, finally looking away from the cedar trees. "But which path do we take?"

"Any path," Plumley answered. He picked up the bucket. "Any path at all."

They soon found out that taking any path would not get them very far. None of the paths led in a straight line; instead they curved and wound around the puddles and the large cedar trees. They found that they couldn't walk for more than a hundred yards without their route branching into two or three paths. Not knowing which way to go, they simply guessed. Soon they found themselves right back where they started.

"Isn't this the spot where we slept?" Plumley asked.

"I can't tell!" Utten shouted. "It all looks the same to me!"

Corker sniffed the ground. "It is," she said. "I can smell Plumley on this patch of ground here."

"Are you saying that I stink?" Plumley said indignantly.

"No, just that I can smell—" Corker retorted.

"I'll have you know that I am very hygienic for a boy my age!"

"There's no use arguing!" Utten shouted, quieting them both. "Let's just keep moving!"

They tried again, making their way through the network of paths. They felt that they were doing more weaving than walking. Soon, they saw Moal's mausoleum up ahead on the path.

"Turn back!" Plumley shouted. He turned around and trotted away down the path.

Once again they found their way back to the place they had rested, then once again at Moal's mausoleum. They walked in circles for hours, then Corker finally said, "He's back. He's behind us."

Away down the path they saw the drifting shape of a man. He was there, but he also was not.

"I don't like this," Plumley said. "Let's move faster."

They picked up their pace and started again into the bogs. Corker sniffed out their previous trails and took them down paths that did not hold their scent. Still, they ended up criss-crossing their own scent again and again. They were traveling in circles, and now a figure was following them. In fact, he seemed to be getting closer and closer to them, slowly closing the distance. They picked up their pace again, but the figure kept closing.

When he got close enough, Plumley took a good look at him. He had an ancient white face, and he didn't seem to be dressed in anything at all except rags made of mist. He had legs but no feet, and his ankles looked like torn tissues flapping in the breeze. No part of him touched the ground. He simply drifted in the air. As he followed, he kept watching them. He never looked away, not even for an instant. He never blinked. He simply watched and followed. Soon, he got close enough to hear them talking about him. That is, if he could hear, or if he even cared.

Finally Corker stopped. "We can't keep this pace up," she protested. "Our paths are too crisscrossed. We're moving too fast for me to keep up with the scent."

"We have to keep moving, that thing is right behind us!" Plumley barked. He moved up the path away from Corker and Utten, but he became afraid that something terrible might be up ahead as well. "We have to do *something*!"

"Look, he's stopped!" Utten said.

The figure had indeed stopped. He kept watching, but he hovered in the path some way back. Corker barked at him again, and he retreated slightly, but then came forward to hold his position again.

"What does he want?" Plumley asked.

Nobody did anything. Plumley and Utten stood rock still, and the figure simply hovered a short way down the path. After a moment, Corker took a few steps towards the figure. The hair raised on her back, she lowered her head towards the ground, and keeping her eyes on the gray shape hovering down the path, she let out a howl so threatening that both Utten and Plumley shivered. The figure, however, did not shiver, and he did not step back. In fact, he waited just a few seconds, then took a slow step forward.

Corker growled low and tensed her hind legs as if about to strike at their follower. She kept her head low and the fur on her back raised. "He's not backing off, boys," she whispered between growls. "I'm not sure what to do next."

"We run," Plumley suggested, his voice shaking. "We keep running!"

"We can't outrun him forever," Corker reminded him, not taking her eyes off the figure. "We're lost. We'll never lose him here. And he doesn't seem to be tiring like we are. Eventually, we will have to rest. Eventually, we'll have to face him."

Plumley looked towards the gray figure, then up the winding path ahead of them. They were being chased by a ghost, and they were headed nowhere.

"If he comes, I'll go for him," Corker explained. "You guys take off running. Maybe I can hold him here long enough for you to get a safe distance away."

The figure took another step forward. Corker's hind legs shifted tensely in the dirt.

"I have an idea," Utten finally said. He turned into his normal form and walked down the path towards the figure.

"You're crazy! Come back here!" Plumley shouted.

"I know what I'm doing," Utten said, then added more quietly, "I think." Utten plodded down the path towards the figure. On the outside, he tried to remain as calm and cool as possible, and from the figure's point of view, he did appear confident. From behind, Corker and Plumley clearly saw the little bumps on Utten's back as his feathers threatened to poke out. Corker allowed her body to relax slightly, but remained ready to strike if necessary.

The figure did not back away from Utten at all, and Utten stood right below it on the ground. He looked up, cleared this throat to ward off any involuntary squawks, and said in as friendly a voice as possible, "Hello, my name is Utten. I live in a bucket. I travel the world living a life of high adventure. I'm magic, and when I want to, I can turn myself into a bird."

Utten waited for the figure to respond, but it did absolutely nothing. It simply stared at him with wide hollow eyes. The gray wisps which made up his lower body flapped gently as if a light breeze were passing.

Utten decided to try again. "What's your name?" he asked very politely.

A broad smile spread across the figure's face, and he seemed to glow a bit.

"What's your name?" Utten asked again.

"Do you really want to know?" the figure asked timidly.

"Yes!" Utten said excitedly.

"Really?" he asked again, and Utten nodded.

"Joe! My name is Joe. Nobody has asked me my name for centuries," he beamed, and his smile broadened. "Who are you people? Why have you come here?"

Sensing there was no danger, Corker relaxed. She trotted up to Joe and Utten. She sniffed at the figure. He had no scent.

"We're here only by accident. We're trying to find the way out of the bogs," Corker said.

"And who are you?" Joe asked her.

"My name is Corker," she said. And though she had heard Joe say it quite clearly, she asked anyway. "What did you say your name was? I couldn't quite hear you from back there."

Joe's smile got even wider. "Joe! My name is Joe! And I can show you the way out of the bogs, if you like." Joe drifted on past them up the path. He went right by Plumley, who was frozen in his tracks. Joe waved happily at Plumley. "Hello, my name is Joe," he smiled, expecting that Plumley would want to know.

"What are you doing here?" Utten asked as they followed along behind Joe. The path came to a fork, but Joe did not hesitate in choosing a direction.

"Oh, I came to Moal many years ago, and I have been wandering here ever since. You're the first people I've seen in all that time," Joe explained.

"What about the other gho—I mean, other folks? I saw a lot of them through Moal's window," Plumley asked.

"If there are others I've never seen them," Joe explained with a sigh, changing direction at an intersection of paths. "In fact, I'd decided that I must be the only one here. I thought to myself, 'Joe, you were probably the meanest guy alive when you were on earth. And you're the only one in all of history mean enough to be confined here.' That's a lot to weigh on a guy's mind! I've had eons to think about it. I always said that if I ever saw another person again, I'd change my ways. I'd be nice to them. Finally you come along, and I have the opportunity to show you the way out!"

Plumley humphed. "Lucky for you we happened along!" he said crossly. He was so nasty about it that Corker reached out and nipped him lightly on the behind. "Hey!" he yelled, jumping.

"Why were you hiding in the woods so long?" Corker asked Joe, still glaring at Plumley.

"I wasn't sure of you. I was afraid you might be monsters or devils. I've found that it's better not to talk to them at all. Many of them are extremely tricky, and those that aren't tricky are vicious." Plumley stopped his scoffing when he heard Joe mention monsters and devils. He didn't like the idea of having to walk the bogs with them around.

Joe took another few turns, and finally the path began to straighten out a little. "I've followed these trails for so many years, I could do this with my eyes closed." The path began to slope upwards. The ground became less moist, and there were fewer cedar trees. Joe stopped walking. "If you follow this path, it will take you out of the bogs."

"Where will it go?" Plumley asked. "We want to get out this realm completely, not just get out of the bogs."

"For that you will have to find Methuselah," Joe replied.

"Who's Methuselah?" Plumley grumbled, not happy that Joe was adding more complications to their escape.

"If you follow this path, it will lead to a mountain. Climb the mountain, and you will find Methuselah. But I doubt she will let you leave. She lets no one leave," Joe said.

"Thank you for the information. Would you like to come with us?" Utten asked.

"No," Joe sighed. "It's safer here in the bogs. Please be careful out there. Moal is just a gatekeeper for this place. There are other devils about."

"Are you sure?" Utten said. Even in the short time he had known him, Utten had grown to like Joe. He found his story fascinating. He didn't like the idea of leaving Joe behind in Moal's Hush Bogs.

"Don't worry, Utten," Joe said. "I'll be fine. You

asked me my name, remember? That alone will keep a smile on my face for decades." Joe drifted away back down the path they had walked up. "I will have to take a waft by Moal's mausoleum so that he can see my smile. I'm sure that it will ruin his century. And maybe I'll start talking to myself in the trees, just to add a little noise to the Hush Bogs. Who knows, maybe some invisible soul will answer!" Joe drifted away, and just before he got out of earshot, Utten thought he heard Joe begin to whistle.

"What a neat guy," Utten said as Joe disappeared in the distance. The three of them continued their trek up the path and out of the bogs.

"Do you think he meant what he said? I mean about the devils and monsters?" Plumley asked.

"I don't think we should worry, Plumley," Corker said. "We've still got each other, whether you like it or not." Though she tried to be reassuring, secretly Corker still worried. When they had stopped so that Plumley and Utten could sleep, she had definitely smelled something in the air. When she spied Joe peeping at them through the cedar trees, she hoped that it was him she smelled. When she had finally gotten close to him, she learned that Joe had absolutely no scent that she could detect.

That could mean only one thing. There was still something else out there.

NEIGHBORLY, ONE MIGHT SAY

12

THE PICNIC LUNCH

"Who do you think Methuselah is?" Plumley asked as they hiked up the path away from the bogs. The farther they got from the bogs, the drier the land got. The drier the land got, the less cedar trees they saw. The fewer cedar trees they saw, the more pine trees there seemed to be.

"I have no idea. She doesn't sound like she'll be any more help than Moal was," Utten commented.

Corker felt a bit more optimistic about Methuselah. "If she were a monster of some kind, I think Joe would have said so. Remember, he said to try and *avoid* the monsters, but to *find* Methuselah. I'm not sure what she is, but I don't think she'll do us any harm. She may not do us good, but I don't think she'll do us harm," she reasoned. She fell silent for a moment, then added, "She's our best hope, I think."

The pines around them became thicker. In fact, the branches grew so thick that it would have been impossible for any of them to walk away from the path. It was almost as if they were walking through a tunnel with walls of thick, prickly pine branches.

Plumley reached into his pocket and removed the hourglass. The mites continued to fall. He tried to flip them over again, even though he knew what the result would be. The mites still traveled in the same direction. He stopped and tapped the hourglass on one of the pine branches, but it didn't disrupt the mites at all. They still struggled helplessly to avoid falling through the hole in the hourglass. Utten watched Plumley fiddle futilely with the hourglass. He could sense the magic of the hourglass, and he knew that nothing Plumley did would reverse the flow of the mites.

"If it gets too close to the end, I'm going to smash this thing wide open," Plumley declared, and stuffed the hourglass back into his pocket. Though he knew that even smashing the hourglass wouldn't help, Utten said nothing. That news would only frustrate Plumley.

For a while, they walked in silence. Plumley swung the bucket in an arc pointlessly. Finally, it was Plumley who spoke. "So, according to what you said, this Old Man Plumley adopted you from a shelter?" he asked Corker.

"Yes," Corker said, ignoring the fact that Plumley

used the words "Old Man Plumley" as if he were talking about a cartoon character.

"Why were you in the shelter?" Plumley asked.

Utten landed on Corker's back and turned into his normal form. He straddled the back of Corker's neck. "Do you mind?" he asked. "My wings are getting tired."

"Not at all," Corker said. "When I was a pup, I was taken from my litter and sold to some folks that had a son about seven years old. The boy wanted to play this game that he called 'fetch the stick.' Fetching the stick meant that the boy would throw the stick as far as he could, and then he would stand there and expect me to run and bring it back to him. My feeling was that if the boy was going to throw the stick away then the boy could very well go and get it himself. The boy didn't like that. Neither did his parents. Finally they decided that it was too much trouble to feed me and such if I wasn't even willing to go and fetch the stick. So they left me outside most of the time, and often forgot to feed me. Eventually I started to bark a lot so that they would take notice of me. They didn't like the barking, so they took me to the shelter."

Utten noticed that up ahead the trees seemed to clear a little, right at the top of the long hill that they were climbing.

"Why didn't you want to play fetch the stick? Most dogs like fetch the stick," Plumley challenged her.

"Actually, most dogs will tire of fetch the stick after a while. Only the dumbest of dogs will play it forever. And most humans tire of fetch the stick, too, long before the dogs do. This boy didn't. You see, I'm part Plott."

"What?" Plumley interrupted.

"Plott. A type of dog bred for hunting. We were bred to run and hunt and learn. I would have loved to run around in the woods with the boy. I would have loved to chase bugs down by the stream. But a dog can only play fetch the stick for so long. I didn't want to play at all. So they sent me to the shelter. By that time I was pretty thin from the lack of food, and I didn't like people much."

"Didn't like people much, huh?" Plumley asked, a smile crossing his face.

"Then the Old Man came along. He liked me because I was shy. He took me home. He was too old to play fetch the stick, but he let me run around in the woods all I wanted to. His house was old and run down, and there were plenty of things inside and out for me to investigate. We got along well," Corker said.

"Ah ha!" cried Plumley triumphantly. "There's your mistake! I knew this story was full of pollywog snot when I first heard it, and now I'm sure. You just offered the proof!"

"The truth exists, Plumley, regardless of whether or not you choose to believe in it," Utten answered.

"Yes, the truth does! And I have found the truth! Your story cannot possibly be true!" Plumley shouted. He almost had a spring in his step, and he swung the bucket with smug pride.

"Why do you say that?" Corker asked. She looked up ahead, and she also saw that they were coming to a clearing in the woods.

"You said that I would live in an old, run down house, didn't you?" Plumley asked.

"Yes, very old, and very run down," Utten said. "I saw it myself."

Plumley stopped walking and placed his hands on his hips. The bucket dangled from his fist at his beltline. Clearly, he was savoring whatever victory he felt he had found. "I won't live in a run down old house. When I get older, I stand to inherit quite a large sum of money, and I won't have to live in an old house! I will live in a mansion." Plumley basked in his revelation. He had found this one hole in the fabric of Utten and Corker's story, and the flaw gave him strength. Perhaps the other stories, including Moal's, held flaws as well.

"Where is your money now?" Utten asked.

"My uncle is holding it for me. When I'm eighteen, I'm going to be a rich man!" Plumley said, and he resumed walking. "So you can stop telling me those silly stories, because now I know they're not true."

Corker thought hard about what Plumley had said, turning his story over and over in her mind. Finally, something clicked in her brain. She figured out the mystery that had been plaguing her since she and Utten had first come through time. "I have one question Plumley," she said. "What's the first thing you plan to do with the money when you get it?"

"I've been thinking about that for quite a while now. I know exactly what I'm going to do," Plumley boasted. "The first thing I'll do is take my money and buy that old boarding school right out from underneath old Liggit. Then I'll kick them all out. Every football-playing, pea-shooting, mud-smearing one of them!"

Corker stopped walking and hung her head. It was all clear to her now. The pieces of Plumley's life fell into place.

"And I won't live a lonely life! I'll have a lot of money, and I'll have big parties at my new house. I'll invite all my friends, too! And I'll invite big people—mayors, congressmen, senators! I'll dance the tango in Liggit's office!" Plumley beamed as he ran through his dream in his head. "So you and Moal can take all your stories about Old Man Plumley and keep them to yourselves, because I know it's all bunk!"

Corker didn't respond. She knew that there would be no big parties with all of Plumley's friends because Plumley didn't have any friends. He would buy out the school, send everyone away, and then immediately begin the process of growing old alone.

"Of course, that's assuming that I find my way out this place you two have dragged me to," Plumley added, then stopped dead in his tracks.

They had reached the top of the hill, and the landscape changed radically on the other side. The path turned into an old dirt road which stretched off into the distance for miles. Far away in the distance, a mountain of rock rose out of the flat plain like a giant stone cathedral thrust up out of the earth. Its walls rose straight into the sky for what looked like a mile. Its top appeared fairly flat, though spiked spires adorned its edges.

The country road stretched between them and the mountain. On either side lay what appeared to be miles and miles of farmland that had long ago been abandoned to turn to pale straw and dust. Barbed wire fences lined both sides of the road, closing off the gray fields on either side. A few hundred yards up the road a decaying windmill twisted listlessly in the passive breeze. In front of the windmill, a scarecrow lay tangled in the barbed wire fence. Two crows, one on either shoulder, pecked at his stuffing.

"We've got a long way to go," Utten said, looking off at the stone mountain in the distance. They approached the scarecrow, and Corker eyed it warily.

"I wish we had something to eat," Plumley said. "I'm hungry. I don't think I can make it all the way there without food."

Corker stopped and looked around. Something had whispered. It seemed to come from the scarecrow, though she didn't believe it could have. The scarecrow was in a terrible state, even by scarecrow standards. Its clothes were badly torn by the barbed wire, and it had little stuffing left. One of its arms was just a sleeve, and its head hung awkwardly, barely even connected to its body. She could not tell if its clothes were black because black was their original color or because they had mildewed to that state. The crows hung close to the decrepit thing's head, pecking at its loosely connected neck.

"Did you say something?" she asked it.

The scarecrow lifted its head, causing Corker to instinctively step back. Its eyes were merely two buttons, and one dangled from a loose string. "Why yes, I did," it said. "I was just commenting to my friends here that it would be nice—a nice thing to do—neighborly, one might say—if we could provide you with a little something—maybe lunch to help you on your way?" The two crows took to the air and flew off out of sight.

"That would be nice," Utten said warily.

Corker stepped forward and smelled the scarecrow—mildew and wet leaves. It certainly was not the creature she had detected earlier.

"They'll bring you something—they're brothers, you know—they're very resourceful—if you'll just stop to rest for a bit—engage me in conversation for a while?" the scarecrow offered.

"Maybe we should keep going," Plumley suggested. "This makes me nervous."

The scarecrow cocked his head and looked at Plumley. "Why, there's nothing to fear—at least from me—I'm just an old scarecrow—not in very good condition, I must say—and being tangled as I am I can't be all that dangerous to you. Besides, there is a long walk ahead of you."

Plumley looked at the stone mountain in the distance. In the time they had been talking to the scarecrow, the road had appeared to get even longer. The distance they had to travel seemed greater. Taking a rest seemed almost necessary.

"Maybe, for a bit," Plumley said quietly, and sat down in the dirt a safe distance from the scarecrow. Corker sat down as well, equally suspicious.

"So tell me—just for the sake of conversation," the scarecrow said. "Why are you going to the mountain?"

"Who said we're going to the mountain?" Utten said, noticing that the breeze was causing tiny leaves to fall from the scarecrow's middle.

"The road only goes two places," the scarecrow reasoned. "One, of course, is to the Hush Bogs—you must already know that, for you came from there—and the other goes to the mountain. So it is only logical that you are going to the mountain—an easy conclusion even for an old dense scarecrow like me."

"We're going to see Methuselah. We're hoping that she'll send us back home," Plumley said. In the distance, he spotted a tiny red shape flying towards them through the air.

The scarecrow laughed. "Send you home—but haven't you tried clicking your heels together three times—or is it four now-a-days—this inflation is murder!" The scarecrow found this extremely funny, and his laughter caused more leaves to fall out of his middle.

Plumley watched as the red shape got closer. "Do you know anything about Methuselah?" Utten asked, hoping to find out some information.

"Not much," the scarecrow confessed. "I don't get off the fence much—as you can imagine."

Corker, whose eyes were sharper than the others, could see the red shape more clearly. The crows were flying back, carrying a laden red blanket between them. The crows flew closer and placed the blanket on the road right in front of the three travelers.

"Here we are—fine work, boys," the scarecrow said. With their talons the crows opened the blanket up. Inside was an entire picnic feast, including many different kinds of sandwiches, some apples and pears, a bowl full of potato salad, a bag of corn chips, some bottles of soda, and some chocolate cake. Along with the food they also saw a pair of binoculars, a pipe, a deck of cards, and an old, yellowed hard-covered book.

Utten stepped forward to examine the blanket. He detected no magic at all. "It's the real thing," he reassured Plumley and Corker, and took a huge bite out of one of the apples. The crows hopped around the blanket next to him pecking at crumbs. Plumley picked up the sandwich closest to him and ate nervously. Corker ate the potato salad right out of the bowl.

"Of course it's the real thing," the scarecrow mused. "It wouldn't be nice—or neighborly, and we are being neighborly—to bring you anything else, would it?" The scarecrow began to shift his leg. Slowly, he twisted it around until it was free of the barbed wire. He began to remove his other leg.

Plumley looked nervously at Corker and Utten. Corker sat on her haunches, prepared to leap if necessary. The scarecrow twisted his neck to free his head, and more leaves fell from his middle. He freed one of his arms and attempted to stand. The other arm tore off and dangled from the barbs on the fence.

"Nasty fence," the scarecrow said, and with his good arm he freed the other and attached it back to his shoulder.

"It really does have a wicked disposition." The scarecrow stepped forward. He moved very slowly and calmly as he sat on the blanket with them. "Let's see—peanut butter and jelly—oh, peanuts give me a rash—baloney, egg salad—I can't stand egg salad. Once again, nothing I like—how I hate picnic food." The scarecrow chuckled. He seemed to genuinely enjoy watching them picnic by the fence.

By the time Utten noticed that the bucket was missing, it was already too late. It had been right next to the picnic blanket when they sat down, but while they had been eating the crows had silently lifted it off the ground and carried it away into the distance.

"My bucket!" Utten shouted.

"Oh, pay them no mind," the scarecrow smiled. "They're only doing you a favor—that nasty bucket seemed so heavy—to have to carry it all that way would have been so tiring—they're so helpful, those two—I don't know what I'd do without them."

"But, but I need that bucket!" Utten shouted. He thought of slipping into his bird form and taking off after them, but the idea of leaving his friends alone with the scarecrow made him go cold inside.

The scarecrow picked up the binoculars and peered through them into the distance. "There they go—such good boys. It'll be there, waiting for you—heavy bucket, too much to carry all that way," he mused, then chuckled to himself again.

Corker watched the crows carry the bucket. They disappeared into the rocks near the base of the mountain. Part of her felt relieved; the crows could have carried the bucket back to Moal, which would have put the trio in a very awkward position. But they did exactly what the scarecrow said, carrying the bucket forward on a path that they were taking anyway. Still, Utten was not convinced. "Corker, most of my magic is in that bucket," he whispered to her.

The scarecrow picked up the cards and began to shuffle. "Anyone for Crazy Eights? I do love a game. I love all games. But it's so rare that I find someone to play with."

"I'm sorry, but we don't have any time for games," Plumley said. For Plumley, the words actually sounded very polite. Plumley pulled the hourglass from his pocket and examined the descent of his mites.

"Even though I have provided this feast for you—you were very hungry, remember—and my friends and I brought you this food—you wouldn't have time for one little game?" the scarecrow asked. Before anyone could answer, he changed his tone completely and added, "Oh, listen to me—of course you need to be on your way—no time for games—I understand completely." The scarecrow placed the deck of cards down on the blanket. "Such a pretty dog—such a pretty coat—layers of color so nice," he said, leaning over to pet Corker. She didn't even notice, her eyes still locked on the spot near the mountain where she had seen the crows disappear.

Corker yelped in pain and leapt away, her tail between her legs. The scarecrow looked at her, surprised. "I only wanted to pet you," he explained. "You have such pretty fur."

Corker cowered away from the scarecrow. "Move away from the blanket, boys!" she warned. "His touch— it's like fire and ice mixed together! It stings! It felt like death itself touched me! Move away now!"

Utten and Plumley scrambled away from the blanket. "What do you want from us?" Plumley yelled.

The scarecrow slowly stood up, and as he did his body seemed to flood with strength. His clothes, while still tattered, did not look quite so frail. Though leaves continued to drift off of him, he appeared to have more than enough stuffing to fill out his clothing. His neck appeared to be securely attached to his broad shoulders.

"The question is not what do *I* want—the question has never been that—the real question is, what do *you* want?" the scarecrow shouted at them. He spread his arms out wide. He clenched one glove into a solid fist, and when he did it looked as if a giant mirror appeared behind him. Suddenly, instead of there being one road leading to the stone mountain, there were two roads, and two stone mountains. He clenched his fist again, and there were four roads and four mountains. He clenched it yet again, and there were eight.

The scarecrow spoke again, his voice as tense as stretched wire. "Only one of those roads will lead to the mountain that you want—the others will lead nowhere at all—and I might—just might—tell you which one! That is, if you are willing to be nice—neighborly as they say," the scarecrow said, then lowered his hands to his sides. His voice suddenly grew calm again. "So, how about a game? Crazy Eights, maybe—or something else—I like all games!"

YOU DIDN'T PLAY FAIR

13

FULL OF LEAVES INSIDE

Corker, Utten, and Plumley sat in terrified silence as the scarecrow continued. "I will play any game at all— just name the game—name any game that I can't beat you at, and I'll show you the road to take. What could be more simple? It's really quite a friendly offer—don't you think—it'll give us the chance to get to know each other better!"

"Just let us be on our way!" Utten demanded, being sure to stay far out of the reach of the scarecrow.

The scarecrow immediately flopped down on the blanket. The two crows returned from the mountain and flew over to perch on his shoulders. The scarecrow began to whisper to them so low that the others couldn't hear.

Utten, Plumley, and Corker huddled together on the

other side of the road. "My, this certainly is a pickle," Utten said. "He had those crows steal my bucket on purpose! He must know how much magic I keep there."

"We can't just take our chances and choose a road. But I wish we could. I don't like this creature," Corker said. She reached around and chewed lightly at the sore spot where the scarecrow had touched her.

"This is surely one of the devils that Joe warned us about," Plumley added. "But we can't just choose a path. There's so little chance that we'll choose the right one."

The scarecrow ran his finger through an egg salad sandwich, then flicked the egg over the barbed wire fence. "I would like to play with the dog first—such a pretty coat she has—I have made up my mind about it. I think the dog should choose the first game—what are you best at? I bet you I'm better!"

"He wants me first!" Corker said, her voice wavering a little.

"Calm down!" Plumley said harshly. "I'm sure there's a way out of this. Maybe he just really wants to play."

Utten laid a hand on Corker's paw. "It'll be all right. He told us to name a game. What kinds of things are you good at?"

"Well, there's, let's see . . ." Corker thought. "I can run pretty well. I can also sniff quite proficiently. I can track, and I can chase. These are all things that I'm pretty confident of."

"I think you should choose running," Utten suggested. "He's just a broken down old scarecrow. He can't possible run as fast as you."

"Okay," Corker said. Her side still stung where the scarecrow had touched her, but she was willing to place her trust in Utten. "Running it is."

Utten approached the scarecrow, who was feeding corn chips to his crows. "How about a race?" Utten suggested. "Corker would be willing to race you."

The scarecrow stood up and brushed himself off. "A race? I love a good race." He picked up an apple and held it up in the air. Immediately one of the crows grabbed it and took flight. "Take this back up the road—just a little ways—and place it right in the middle," the scarecrow commanded. The crow flew off down the road and placed the apple, then returned to perch on the fence beside his brother.

Corker walked over and stood by the scarecrow, carefully watching lest he reach down to touch her again. "And so we race," the scarecrow said. "First one to grab the apple wins. If you win, I show you the right road. If I win, we all play some more. Clear?" Corker nodded her head and scratched at the ground with her hind legs, ready to sprint whenever she got the signal.

"And perhaps—if he was feeling neighborly—the little

blue man might give us the runner's marks?" the scarecrow suggested. He leaned over and stood in position next to Corker.

"Ready?" Utten asked, and held his hand up. "On your mark! Get set! Go!" Utten threw his hand down.

Corker took off like a shot. Utten had never realized that she could run so fast. As he marveled at her speed, he didn't notice that the scarecrow didn't even move.

"Oh dear," the scarecrow worried. "These shoes—I'm afraid these shoes are not the best running shoes—it certainly won't be a fair race." He looked up the road. Corker was already half way to the apple. The scarecrow sighed. "Oh well, they will just have to do!"

The scarecrow bolted from his mark.

"My word," Plumley said. He had never seen any-thing move so fast and so effortlessly. As he ran, the scarecrow began to sing, though neither Plumley nor Utten could hear the words. Within a second, the scare-crow had passed Corker. He plucked the apple up easily, then slowly jogged back.

"You won't be on your way anytime soon—I don't think—if that's the best you have to offer," the scarecrow taunted. He placed the apple back in the exact same spot he had picked it up and flopped down on the blanket. The crows flew over and perched on his shoulders again. Corker ran up, panting. "Who's next?" the scarecrow asked.

Plumley, Corker, and Utten huddled again. "How could he move so fast?" Plumley asked. "I've never seen anything like it!"

"He's full of leaves and straw. He's light as a feather," Corker panted. "That's what he was singing to me as he passed me on the road. Running to him is effortless."

"Maybe we should have gone with sniffing," Plumley suggested. He didn't intend be mean, but it certainly came out sounding that way. The group shared an uncomfortable moment of silence as Plumley's blame settled on Corker.

"We underestimated him," Utten suggested. "He has legs, and he can run better than we thought. But he doesn't have wings! He certainly can't fly! And *he* probably doesn't know that I can turn into a bird."

"Good idea!" Corker said, "Challenge him to a flying contest!" The three of them broke their huddle.

"I have a game I'd like to play!" Utten shouted.

"Are you sure I can't beat you at it—I'm very good at things," the scarecrow warned. "Why, that last little contest was no contest at all."

Corker growled, and the fur on her back raised. "Utten, beat this sack of leaves so that we can get on our way."

Utten stepped up to the blanket. "My game is called flying. Whoever can get the highest into the air wins," Utten said confidently.

The scarecrow cocked his head. "You can fly?"

"That's the contest, take it or leave it," Utten replied, ignoring the scarecrow's question.

The scarecrow stood himself up again and dusted off some crumbs. "Flying you say—I've never tried, but I'm sure I could manage it somehow—how about we perch there—on the fence—like my friends are. Whoever gets highest, you say—oh I like this game—very creative—I can't wait to see what happens!"

Utten climbed the fence and stood on the barbed wire. The scarecrow did the same, balancing precariously by holding one of the posts. "Are we ready?" the scarecrow asked, teetering awkwardly on the thin wire.

"Not quite yet," Utten yelled, and a broad smile creased his face. He held out one arm, and feathers dropped into place below it. Then he changed the other. Feathers covered his back and belly, his beak protruded from his mouth, and his talons gripped the wire. He squawked once at the crows, who flitted away from him and landed on the fence on the other side of the scarecrow.

"Tricky, tricky," the scarecrow smiled, gripping the post tighter as he struggled to keep his balance. "You are obviously at an advantage here—I may not be able to win this one—let's go over the rules once more, shall we?"

"Whoever gets higher wins. That's the contest," Utten said.

"Such rules, such rules," the scarecrow mused. "I shall just have to do my best!" He let go of the post and stood on the wire with perfect balance. Utten saw that the scarecrow's awkwardness on the wire was merely an act, and for a moment he was intimidated.

"Ready, set, go!" Utten shouted, eager to get the contest over.

The scarecrow held his arms out wide. Very quietly, he began to sing, "I'm light as a feather, I'm full of leaves inside . . ." The two crows flapped their wings and rose in the air. With their talons, they grabbed the scarecrow by either shoulder and lifted him into the air. "I can fly on the breeze, there's nothing inside of me . . ." the scarecrow continued to sing as the crows lifted him off the ground.

"Not fair!" Plumley shouted. "That's cheating!"

"Fly, Utten!" Corker barked. "You can fly better than those two crows!"

But Utten couldn't fly. He flapped his wings, but he couldn't get off the wire. The barbs of the wire had wrapped around his talons, fastening him to the fence. "I can't get free!" Utten cried, exasperated. "They won't let me go!"

"Cheat! Cheat!" Plumley yelled into the air, but the scarecrow did not even acknowledge him.

"I'm light as a feather, I can fly on the breeze . . ." The scarecrow sang his silly, random song as he and the crows flew in light, slow circles just above Plumley's head.

Utten struggled against the wire, but the barbs held him tightly. Finally, the crows let the scarecrow down. "It seems I won that one—unfortunate about the barbed wire—quite nasty, isn't it? I had no idea that it would hold you down like that—funny, I didn't have to fly high at all, did I?" the scarecrow taunted.

"You cheated!" Plumley yelled. He stepped right up to the scarecrow, close enough that the scarecrow could have reached out and touched him easily. "You didn't play fair!"

"Fair play?" the scarecrow laughed. "As if he didn't try to hide the fact that he was a bird! There was only one rule—whoever gets higher wins—I specifically asked that the rules be restated before the game was played. And I got higher than the poor blue bird—he unfortunately underestimated the foul abilities of the wire fence—nasty fence, not friendly at all. I see nothing for you to be so upset about, boy—one would think that you'd be hard at work coming up with the next game—it is your turn, isn't it?" The scarecrow flopped down on the blanket again, and the crows again sat with him.

The barbed wire released Utten, and the three travelers huddled again. Utten turned back into his normal form.

"It's not your fault, Utten," Corker said reassuringly.

"By the way," the scarecrow taunted. "I'm getting rather tired—let's make this the last game—I do need my beauty rest. If you win, I'll show you the right road to take—if you lose, you can go back and visit Moal again."

They had to succeed this time. There was no way around it. They had to beat the scarecrow, or they would never get to Methuselah.

"What game do you want to play, Plumley?" Utten asked.

"What are you best at?" Corker added.

Plumley ignored them, concentrating his thoughts. Inside, he fumed over the fact that the scarecrow had cheated them.

Utten hunched over into a boxing stance and threw some punches into the air. "How about chess?" he suggested. "You've been playing chess a lot. I bet you could beat him!"

"What about a chess board?" Corker asked.

"We could make one! Or those crows could fetch one!" Utten said, throwing a sharp right cross at his invisible boxing opponent.

Plumley didn't answer them. When he spoke, he seemed to be speaking to himself alone. "I'll put an end to this right now," he murmured. "This is all pollywog snot anyway, and I'm sick of being afraid." He rose to face the scarecrow, which had pulled a piece of string from the blanket and was playing tug of war with one of the crows. When he saw Plumley approach, he gave his end to the other crow so that the two could fight each other.

"Do we have a game—I hope it's a simple game—I'm very tired. Please go easy on me," the scarecrow said falsely.

"I would like to go over the rules for choosing the game once more. Shall we?" Plumley asked.

"Certainly!" the scarecrow said, and he began to stand up.

"You won't have to stand for this game," Plumley informed him. "You can just sit your little straw bottom back down right where you were."

The scarecrow hesitated. He didn't like the tone of Plumley's voice. He enjoyed hearing a voice edged with fear, but Plumley's voice held no fear. The scarecrow sat back down, pretending not to notice Plumley's attitude.

"What a relief to know that I can sit through this game!" the scarecrow said as he settled. "Now the rules . . . you name any game that I can't beat you at, and I'll let you pass along the road. If I beat you in the game that you choose—keep in mind I have let you folks choose every game so far—I have been very neighborly about it—if I beat you, you either go back to see Moal—or I suppose you could take your chances with the roads— though I can't imagine anyone taking—"

"In that case, I have a game," Plumley interrupted. The scarecrow went to rise again, but Plumley sat down on the blanket next to him. Plumley reached over the two battling crows and picked up the deck of cards. He removed them and began to shuffle.

"Oh, I love cards," the scarecrow sighed, settling back down. "And it's been so long since I played—I am surely a bit rusty—you will clearly have the advantage. A smart boy like—"

"Shut up," Plumley snapped sharply. He began to lay cards down in front of him in piles. He lay down seven piles. The first pile had one card, the second had two, and so on up to the seventh pile which had seven. Plumley turned over the top card on each pile. Corker and Utten watched intently, eager to figure out what Plumley's plan was. Even the crows stopped playing tug of war and hopped over to watch the card game.

"In this game, the player can lay a club or a spade on a heart or a diamond or vice versa. But all the cards have to be in numerical order going down. Then, up top," Plumley said as he laid an ace of spades above his other piles, "you try to stack all the cards in order by suit. All the hearts go on hearts, all the spades go on spades, and so on."

Utten began to see Plumley's plan. "Go get him, Plumley!" he shouted. Corker concentrated, trying to figure out the rules of the game.

Using the cards in his hand, Plumley began to stack cards in order by number. He got the ace of spades and the ace of hearts up above. "You win the game by getting all your cards in the suit piles above. Does this make any sense to you?"

"Certainly—it's very clear, I think—I shall watch you very closely," the scarecrow replied, though he sounded a bit perplexed. "What is the name of this game?"

"Solitaire," Plumley said plainly. He laid out all the cards in his hand. When he was done, he had only eight cards in his piles above.

"Oh my," Plumley sighed. "I only got eight cards out of fifty-two. I didn't win."

The scarecrow beamed. "That means that once again, I am the winner!"

"No, as a matter of fact, it does not," Plumley said. He rose and brushed himself off. "And I would appreciate it if you would show us the correct path to find Methuselah."

The scarecrow stood up and loomed over Plumley. "What are you talking about? Such logic! You lost the game—I thought you were a smart boy!"

"True, I lost at solitaire," Plumley confessed. "But you said that I had to name a game that you couldn't beat me at. You can't beat me at solitaire because you can't play me at solitaire. It's a game for only one player.

When I lose, I get beaten by no one except the cards. Now, if you will show us the way to the mountain . . ."

The scarecrow fumed. "You tricked me!" With the same hand he had used to shock Corker, he reached out his leather glove towards Plumley, stopping just inches from Plumley's face. The boy stood his ground.

Holding his hand right next to Plumley's cheek, the scarecrow clenched his fist, and four of the roads disappeared. His clenched it twice more, and there was only the single road laid out before them. He opened his fist and held his fingers right next to Plumley's cheek for a moment. He waved the fingers slightly, staring at the boy with his blank, button eyes as he considered whether or not to drag one burning finger across Plumley's cheek before allowing him to leave. Plumley remained absolutely still, half out of terror and half out of anger towards this demon. He did not dare to even breathe until the scarecrow finally pulled his hand away.

The scarecrow turned and walked over to the barbed wire fence. He crawled in between the wires, lacing himself in the same tangled pattern that the group had found him in when they first walked down the road. Stuffing disappeared from his arm, tears reappeared in his clothes, and his head swung half-connected to his neck. His illusion of weakness, frailty, and decay was restored for the next passerby.

"Go on," he said. "Go to the mountain. You'll never make it. There's worse than me out there, you know. There's much worse than me waiting for you." The crows took their positions on the scarecrow's shoulders, and they began to whisper quietly together.

Utten, Plumley, and Corker wasted no time getting away from the scarecrow. Once they were a safe distance away, Utten spoke.

"Great job, Plumley! You really showed him!"

"Someone had to," Plumley said coldly.

Utten ceased his praise, and for a while, nobody spoke.

"He's right, you know. There is something else out there," Corker finally said. "When we rested in the bogs, I caught the scent of something close by. I wasn't sure what it was. I was hoping that it was Joe, but he had no scent at all. Then I was hoping that it was the scarecrow, but he only smelled like leaves. There's something else out there, and we're going to have to face it sooner or later."

"What is it? Do you know?" Utten asked.

Corker hesitated. "It's an animal of some kind, maybe two actually. And they're waiting for the best time to attack."

Utten shuddered. He had hoped that they simply had a long walk ahead of them.

Plumley walked a few paces ahead of Corker and

Utten. He was going to find a way to get home, even if he had to do it all by himself. His anger, his fear, and his determination to get home had so blinded him, however, that he didn't realize he had forgotten his hourglass on the picnic blanket in the road.

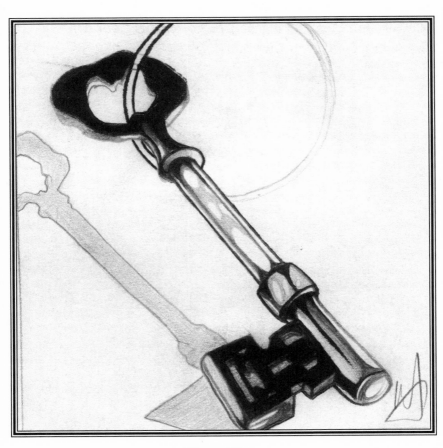

THE KEY

14

BETWEEN THEM AND THE SKY

It wasn't a mountain in the traditional sense. It looked more like one single enormous rock thrust up out of the ground. For as far as the eye could see the flat, dusty land around it stretched away into the distance. In fact, the only visible structures were the barbed wire fence along the old dirt road and the old broken down windmill, which now seemed so far behind them that it was barely noticeable on the horizon.

Now that they stood at its base, the mountain seemed to be the only significant structure in this entire dimension. At its base, piled boulders created a nest of rubble around the mountain. From that rubble, rock walls rose straight up into the sky for over a mile. Up top, the walls of rock ended in jagged spires that tore at passing clouds.

"We're going to climb that thing?" Utten asked.

"I'm going to do whatever it takes to find Methuselah and get myself home," Plumley said.

The road ahead led directly into the rubble at the base of the mountain. The barbed wire fence came to an abrupt end, the last few feet of wire corkscrewing aimlessly off into the air. In its place, large jagged rocks formed the new walls. As if taking a cue from the twisting, bobbing barbed wire, their route curled around the boulders.

Corker felt anxiety rise in her belly. If something came at them from in front, the only escape route was back the way they came, towards the scarecrow. If something came from behind, they would be forced to run farther up the trail into the unknown.

Actually, they had even fewer options than that. Going back to the scarecrow was not an option. If something tried to block their path, they would have to fight. There was no other choice.

Corker stopped dead on the path. The scent had come back to her.

Corker saw a dark object move through the rocks up ahead. "Boys," she said. "Be careful. I think we're about to meet trouble."

For a while the smell and the shape disappeared, and the party began to move forward again. Then, suddenly, the scent hit Corker again. It was definitely an animal of some kind. But something about the scent was strange.

The dark shape dodged through the rocks up ahead of them and then disappeared again. Utten turned into his bird form and went aloft to have a look, but he could not spot anything. Whatever the creature was, it moved quickly to conceal itself.

"I can't see anything," he confessed to Corker. "Whatever it is, it's fast."

Suddenly, the scent hit Corker hard. The creature was very, very close by. "It's here," she said to Utten. "It's right here somewhere." They looked all around, but the rocks appeared empty.

Then Plumley felt a drop of liquid land on his shoulder. He looked up. "Oh no," he cried.

Approximately twenty feet over their heads, a long rock jutted out, forming a jagged platform over the pathway. An enormous wolf stood on the platform. His mouth hung open slightly, and a second drop of drool fell from his lower jaw and hit the dusty ground next to Plumley.

Instantly the hair on Corker's back spiked, and she began to growl. The wolf looked down at her, then at Utten, and finally at Plumley. "So you're the Old Man," it hissed. It leapt from the platform, fell twenty feet through the air, and landed in the middle of Corker, Utten, and Plumley, who each pulled away from it in separate directions.

He stood a good six inches taller than Corker, and though lanky for his size, he was clearly wider than she was as well. His black and gray coat held a slightly oily sheen. A burst of dingy yellow fur adorned his chest. On his head, a curl of yellow fur stretched back from each eye, giving him the illusion of horns. His body was slim, his legs strong, and he stood with the cockiness of youth. He flashed his sharp teeth at Plumley, and Plumley backed away.

He addressed the boy. "Old Man, my name is Skoll. I'll be your escort back to Moal's Hush Bogs."

"I'm not going back to Moal's Hush Bogs, not ever," Plumley said defiantly, his voice quaking. "You can't make me!"

Skoll scratched with his forepaw in the dust. "We'll see about that," he hissed. He leapt at Plumley, jaws open, reaching for the boy's throat.

Corker caught him in midair. Her own jaws closed around Skoll's neck, but she could only hold him for a moment. The two of them fell into the dust together, then broke apart.

Corker stood up quickly and backed away from Skoll. "Move away, you two!" Corker screamed, "this may get bloody!" Utten and Plumley moved as close to the rocks as they could to avoid the fray.

Skoll got up very slowly. "What do you think you're

doing, you runt?" he hissed at Corker. "You can't possibly hope to best me!"

"I can do more than hope," Corker howled back. "I can drag your greasy fur around like a rag doll!"

Skoll leapt again, this time directly at Corker. She reared up, and Skoll's forepaws struck her in the center of her chest. Surprised at the force of his blow, she fell over backwards in the dust, the wind kicked out of her. "There were instructions, you know," Skoll laughed. "The boy goes back. The little blue man goes back. But I can do whatever I please with you, mutt! I am bigger than you, and I've got twice your strength. What can you possibly hope to accomplish from this?"

Corker didn't answer him. She leapt at him again, but this time didn't aim for the throat. Her jaws closed on the soft fleshy portion of Skoll's nose, and he squealed.

"You wanted a fight, that much I can tell!" Corker yelled when she released him. "So quit squawking like a pigeon and fight me."

"Get him, Corker!" Utten yelled, though he knew that Skoll held the advantage.

Again they tangled. Using his immense size, Skoll easily pinned Corker to the ground, but she reached around with her jaws and gripped Skoll by the hind leg, throwing his balance off. She rolled over on top of him and again reached for his throat. Skoll placed his hind legs against her belly and thrust, throwing her away and scratching into the skin of her stomach. Corker felt the pain, but engaged him quickly again.

Skoll's jaws flashed, and Corker yelped as she felt him tear at her ear.

"That's for the nose," Skoll barked, then fell on her again.

They rolled over and over in the dust, kicking each other, biting when they could. When next they broke, both were beginning to pant.

"There's more to you than I expected," Skoll admitted. "But it still won't be enough."

"You're less than I expected," Corker lied. "Let's finish this!"

Skoll lunged, but Corker fell back and caught his weight. She pressed with her hind legs, and using her back for leverage she tossed Skoll through the air. He landed on his side, and Corker immediately lunged on top of him. She grabbed his hind leg in her jaws and twisted, and Skoll howled. He kicked her off and backed away.

"This has been fun," he said, limping. "But it's time I ended you." Again he lunged upon her, and Corker crumpled under his weight. This time, he used his hind legs to pin her body down, and his heavy jaws closed on her throat.

Corker felt her throat close and her breath cut off.

She tried to kick out, but Skoll held her with his hind legs. As she struggled against his jaws, Skoll let a sound escape his throat that was half giggle and half growl.

Corker continued to struggle, but she could not breathe. She felt her world going dark.

"Corker, get up!" Utten urged her.

Corker looked over at them. If she went out, Plumley and Utten would have no defense against Skoll. She fought the blackness that was creeping in on her brain.

Sweeping with her foreleg, Corker scratched Skoll across his already wounded nose. The pain she inflicted was just enough to cause Skoll to loosen his grip, and she shifted, causing Skoll to fall over on his side. She climbed on top of him, pinned his forelegs with her hind ones, and wrapped her jaws around his muzzle. Some of her teeth sunk into the wounded nose.

Skoll whined, but Corker held his jaw shut. He felt his own airways begin to close. He kicked wildly with his legs, but he couldn't get enough leverage to kick Corker off of him.

Corker focused on his muzzle. Whatever happened, she must not let go. She had already wounded it, and she realized that it was his only weak point. She sucked deeply into her own lungs, then bore down with her jaws pressing Skoll's snout into the dirt.

Skoll's breathing became short, and his legs stopped

kicking. Without air to breathe, his energy ebbed. As his body calmed, Corker pressed harder on his snout. She shook her jaws back and forth slightly, and Skoll whined meekly at the pain.

Finally, Skoll let out the long whine that meant, "I submit." Corker released her hold and stepped back. Her energy spent, she nearly fell backwards into the dust.

"She won," Utten yelled, bursting into his bird form and flying over to her. Even Plumley was excited, and ran over and wrapped his arms around her.

"No," she said. "No, something's wrong." She collapsed into Plumley's arms.

"What's wrong?" Utten asked. "You won! You bested him! He has to let us pass!"

"No," Corker panted. "It's not him! His scent is similar, but there was someone else! I'm sure of it! It's not him!"

Skoll rolled over in the dirt. "Mama," he whined softly. "Mama . . . Mama . . ."

A second dark shape appeared overhead. Utten looked up. "No!" he shouted. "It's not fair!"

The other wolf leapt from the rock platform and landed next to Skoll. She looked similar to Skoll, but she was much, much larger. She stood at least a foot taller than Skoll, and where Skoll had the sleek slimness of youth, she carried the bulky muscle of experience. She sniffed at Skoll, then raised her head. Across the top of her dome, streaks of yellow fur similar to Skoll's marked long horns. But under those horns, her eyes glowed red.

"My name is Haite," she growled. "Who did this to my boy? Step forward, or I will kill you all."

Corker pulled herself from Plumley's arms and limped forward. Above her, the towering wolf roared, and Plumley and Utten both cowered from her.

"Do not fight her, boys," Corker warned. "She'll kill you both." She stood before the immense creature, and then did the only thing possible. Her options spent, she laid on the ground, rolled over on her back, and whined in submission.

Haite spun around and kicked Corker with her hind legs. "Get up, runt," Haite commanded. Corker rolled over in the dust and righted herself. "Get moving up the path," Haite said, nodding her head at Plumley and Utten. She snapped her jaws at Corker, and Corker jumped into line with the boys.

Skoll and Haite followed behind them like prison guards ushering in new arrivals. Haite moved with the lumbering stride of a great ox, but Skoll walked with the anxious, quick energy of a wild jackyl. Together, they led Plumley, Utten, and the limping Corker up the winding path through the rocks, all the way up to the edge where the rubble fell away and the mountain's stone walls rose straight up to spiked peaks more than a mile in the air. Here, the path split. Off to the left, Plumley saw the path lead to a wide, round indentation in the rock, a column which stretched the entire height of the mountain. Inside the column, row upon row of zigzagging, climbing steps led all the way up to the top of the stone mountain.

Skoll leaned over and hissed in Plumley's ear. "It'll do you no good to eyeball it, Old Man. You'll never be climbing those steps." Skoll directed Plumley and the others up the right split of the path, which led up to a small cave in the side of the mountain.

Brittle bones littered the dusty floor of the cave. A rusted steel cage sat in the middle of the floor. A heavy rope led from the top of the cage up through a pulley in the ceiling and then down to the floor again. The bars of the cage were lined with rusted mesh to keep tiny Utten from squeezing through. Near the back wall, Utten's bucket lay on its side in the dirt. The crows had delivered it straight to Skoll and Haite.

Skoll and Haite ushered the three into the cage. Just as Corker stepped into the cage, Haite lashed out with her jaws, clamping on Corker's hind left leg and yanking it out from underneath her. Corker yelped, then scrambled to her feet and leapt for the safety of the cage. Behind her, the steel door shut, and Haite clamped the lock shut with her muzzle.

Skoll gathered the loose end of the rope in his teeth and hoisted the cage off the ground. Haite grabbed another section of rope and pulled as well, and working one after the other they managed to hoist the cage high up off the floor of the cave. Skoll wrapped the end of the rope around a jutting rock, leaving the swaying cage suspended high above the dry, dusty floor.

"Welcome," Haite hissed menacingly, looking up at the cage. "Welcome to our home, though I don't think you're going to enjoy your stay much. Especially you, runt." Haite looked directly at Corker and lifted her lip, exposing a row of razor teeth. "I don't think you're going to like it at all.

"A little while ago, we received a letter from an associate of ours, a fat freaky thing by the name of Moal. He instructed us to capture you and to return you to him in the Hush Bogs. All that is, except *Corky*." Haite spoke Corker's name as if she were speaking the name of a spoiled child. "*Corky* gets to stay with us. We get to do whatever we please with *Corky*."

Utten pressed his face against the rusted mesh. "The name is Corcoran!" Utten said, his belly turning light purple.

"It really doesn't matter," Haite hissed. "She's lucky I don't call her lunch!"

Skoll laughed. "Yeah!" he shouted up. An annoyed look crept over Haite's face, and she nipped Skoll lightly at the ear. "Ouch!" Skoll yelped, and jumped away from her.

"Shut up, boy!" Haite growled. "You've nothing to gloat about! She bested you!" Skoll retreated to a corner of the cave, his tail tucked between his legs and his head low. "But don't worry boy, we'll get another chance at her. And I doubt she'll be so lucky this time.

"I'm off to meet with Moal," Haite informed them. "We have a few things to negotiate before I turn you over to him. I expect you won't be comfortable while I'm gone," Haite said. She nodded at Skoll, who emerged from his hiding place. "Under no circumstances are you to let them out of there, boy. Do you understand? Just watch them. Watch the blue one for tricks of magic. And don't do anything stupid. Is that clear?"

Skoll nodded his head. "Perfectly, Mama. Perfectly clear."

Haite took one last look up at the cage. The faces of her captives looked down at her, their rusted prison swaying lightly back and forth. Utten pounded at the bars of the cage. "You let us out of here! Let us out now or else!"

Haite smirked. Confident that the lock and rope were secure, she lumbered slowly out of the cave and down the path.

SKOLL

15

THE SECOND BATTLE

Skoll paced around the perimeter of the cave, looking up at the cage every few steps. Finally he lay down in the dust. He faced away from the cage but watched it nervously out of the corner of his eye.

"Remember, Skoll, don't do anything stupid. Do you think you can keep from being stupid until mama gets back?" Corker said, deliberately taunting the wolf.

"You shut up!" Skoll warned. "You may have bested me, you runt, but there'll be another round. Of that you can be sure. There'll be another round. And this time you won't be lucky."

"I made you cry for your Mommy, Skoll. Luckily she was there to bail you out, or we'd be up at the top of the mountain right now," Corker reminded him. Skoll didn't answer.

"What does it mean, you 'bested' him?" Plumley asked. "Why don't you just say that you beat him?"

As Corker explained things to Plumley, she deliberately raised her voice so that Skoll could hear her. "Besting is a lot like beating someone, only better. When one wolf or one dog bests another, they force them to submit. They force them to GIVE UP! They force them to admit that their opponent is STRONGER, more WORTHY!"

Skoll rolled over in the dust and pretended not to listen to her. Corker made her jab a little sharper. "In this case," she added, "I made my opponent not only submit, but also cry for his Mommy." Skoll tried his best to pretend that he hadn't heard Corker, but he inadvertently let an angry snort escape from his muzzle.

"Being bested means you acknowledge that you lost in a fair fight. You acknowledge the superiority of your opponent," Corker explained.

"But what prevents the opponent from simply attacking once you release your hold? Why not attack again after being bested?" Plumley asked. Utten shuddered when he heard Plumley's suggestion. Even he knew what would happen if someone attacked again after being bested.

"You can attack again after being bested, but it's not wise. If you attack again after being bested, you're making a declaration. You're declaring that the fight is to the death," Corker explained. "And that's close to suicide, because you've already admitted that your opponent is stronger than you are. Who would want to fight to the death with someone who was a better fighter than they were?"

"Who makes up these rules?" Plumley asked.

"They're just the rules," Corker explained. "They always have been, and they always will be."

Skoll shifted on his dirt bed. "You can't beat Mama," he said, then chuckled.

"No, but I can beat you, can't I?" Corker said. Skoll didn't answer. "You watch," Corker whispered to Utten. "We're not finished yet."

Plumley began to investigate the cage. He checked all over for weak spots, but there seemed to be none. Though rusty, the bars were an inch thick and were welded into the steel ceiling. There were no screws or bolts to unscrew. The door hinge and lock were as solid as the bars. Seeing no way to break out, Plumley collapsed in the corner. "It's impossible," he said.

Corker sat on her hind legs and stared down at Skoll. Though he didn't look directly at her, she knew that he could see her out of the corner of his eyes. The muscles of his back twitched nervously. He didn't like her eyes on him.

"I should have listened to myself in the beginning. This is hopeless," Plumley said. He looked down at Utten, who was backing away from the mesh.

"It's not hopeless yet," Utten said. He ran straight into the mesh, then bounced backward onto the floor of the cage, dazed. "Ooooooh!" he whined. "That hurt!"

"If I had just stuck to what I knew. If I just hadn't listened to you!" Plumley said. "I'd be home right now washing dishes in the dining hall. People would be making fun of me, and Liggit would be making my life miserable, but at least I'd have a life."

"You still do have a life!" Utten said. "We're not done yet!"

"I really don't mean to be cruel, but I should never have listened to you. When I try to rely on other people to help me, I end up in more trouble. Like running away with you. Like getting on that silly boat. When I rely on myself, I get along fine. Our encounter with the scarecrow proved it. I'm better off when I'm by myself.

"The truth is, I like you, Utten. And I like Corker, too. But I'm not putting my hopes on anyone anymore. Never again." Plumley sank back against the bars of the cage and closed his eyes.

Corker continued to stare down at Skoll, who continued to shift nervously in the dust. After a long silence, Corker said very simply, "Oh. So there it is."

Utten's brow furrowed with confusion, but Corker turned to him and winked. She looked back down at Skoll. "It was simpler than I thought."

For a long time, Skoll said nothing. Corker waited

patiently, her eyes never leaving him, never allowing him to relax. Finally, he could stand it no longer, and he spoke. "What's simpler than you thought?"

"Oh, nothing," Corker said, still staring.

Utten decided to join in the game. "Oh, of course, I see it, too! That is pretty simple." He had no idea what he was talking about, but he didn't care. Corker was up to something, and Utten wanted to help her see her plan through.

Skoll sat up in the dust. "No, really, what? What's simple?"

"You wouldn't understand," Corker condescended.

"Yes, I would!" Skoll blurted. "You're trying to trick me. I can tell!"

"Okay," Corker said plainly, then lay down on the floor of the cage. She turned her face away from the bars so that Skoll couldn't see her. A big smile graced her muzzle. "Just watch," she whispered to Utten.

For a few minutes, Skoll said nothing; he just stared up at the suspended cage. "Really. What do you see?" he said finally.

Corker sat up again and looked down at him. "I can see how to break out of this cage." Hearing this, Plumley sat up. "It's very simple, once you look at it," Corker continued. "It's like a puzzle. You've heard of puzzles before haven't you, Skoll? They're the kinds of things that smart people can figure out."

"I'm not stupid!" Skoll spat.

Corker shook her head. "I'm afraid even your Mother doesn't think that's true, Skoll. I distinctly heard her call you stupid."

"I heard it, too," Utten chimed in.

"Yeah, me too," Plumley added.

"So I guess the verdict is in," Corker said. "We've figured out how to get out of the cage because we're smart. You wouldn't be able to figure it out because you're not. Smart people are good at puzzles, but you are not."

"Which do you mean? I'm not smart, or I'm not good at puzzles?" Skoll asked.

"They go together," Corker explained condescendingly. Then she lay down on the floor of the cage again. Patiently she waited. She knew what was coming. It was only a matter of time. When finally it came, the words hitting her ears were as sweet as the most precious honey.

"I could figure out how to get out of that stupid cage," Skoll barked.

Corker sat up. She answered him without a trace of emotion in her voice. "Could not," she said.

"Could too!" Skoll yelled.

"Could not," Corker said calmly, shaking her head.

"Could too!" Skoll barked.

"Could not," Corker repeated.

"Could too!" Skoll screamed, foam beginning to form at the edge of his mouth.

"Prove it!" Corker barked at him.

Skoll stopped and thought for a moment. Somewhere in the back of his mind, a voice was telling him that he was about to do something very stupid. The voice told him that he should just lie down and ignore everything that Corker had to say.

Skoll was about to listen to that voice when Corker said, "Let's face it, Skoll. The way I bested you on the path, well, it just proves my superiority. So why don't you just forget about this whole cage thing and lie back down and wait for Mama to come home. You're really not much without her at your side, remember?"

Skoll flew into a rage. He ran around the cave below the cage. Finally, he could stand it no longer, and he untied the rope and lowered the cage to the ground. From behind a nearby rock he pulled a rusty key. Holding the key straight in his teeth, he headed for the lock. He was almost to the lock when he stopped.

The little voice in the back of his head was speaking to him again, and this time he decided that he should listen. He dropped the key to the ground. "One of you has to stay in the cage," Skoll demanded, pleased with himself.

Utten's hand shot up into the air. "I volunteer!" he shouted as loud as he could. Satisfied, Skoll picked up the key and opened the lock. Corker and Plumley stepped out, and Skoll stepped inside with Utten. Plumley closed the lock and removed the key.

"Just pull on that rope over there," Skoll instructed them.

"Thank you, I think we can figure it out," Corker interrupted him. She and Plumley pulled on the rope and hoisted it back up to the ceiling. Corker sat on the ground underneath the cage. Meanwhile, Utten slipped to the back of the cage. Plumley grabbed the bucket and stood underneath. Skoll examined the door of the cage, his eyes roving in desperation.

"What do you think?" Corker called up to Skoll.

"Give me a minute!" Skoll barked back.

Skoll was so intent on figuring out the secret of the cage that he didn't notice the tiny squishy noise from behind him. He didn't even spot Plumley holding up the bucket beneath the cage. He didn't see Utten in his blob form squeezing through the mesh. Only when the thin blue goo had gathered in the bucket did Skoll realize what had happened.

"Hey!" Skoll barked. "Come back up here!"

Corker smiled up at him. "See, Skoll? I told you I saw how to get out of the cage. And I told you it was rather simple as well." Utten turned back to his normal form, and the three of them walked out of the cave, ignoring the howling protests of Skoll.

"My hourglass," Plumley shouted as they reached the stone steps leading up to the top of the mountain. "I can't find my hourglass!" He checked all of his pockets, but he didn't have it. He ran back towards the cave with Skoll.

"Plumley, come back!" Corker yelled. "We don't have time for this!"

Plumley ignored her, running into the cave and checking the ground around the cage. Above him the caged Skoll shouted and cursed and spat at him. Plumley couldn't find the hourglass. He returned to the path.

"Where do you remember having it last?" Utten asked.

"Let's see," Plumley thought frantically. "I had it in the bogs, and I had it on the dirt road. No, wait, I didn't! I checked it while we were having lunch with the scarecrow. I had it in my hand, and then the scarecrow touched Corker with his glove! I remember jumping away . . . I must have dropped it!"

"Forget it, Plumley!" Corker insisted. "You don't need it!"

Plumley began to run away down the path. "No," he cried. "I need it! I need to get it back!"

Corker took off after him. "Plumley, forget about it! Please, just climb with us!"

"But I need it!" Plumley snapped. He continued to run away down the path. Corker grabbed his pant leg in her teeth, but he ripped it away.

"Please, Plumley," Corker begged. "Haite will be coming back! If she catches us, that'll be the end!"

Plumley kept walking. "I need it!" he insisted.

Corker blocked his path and bared her teeth. "I won't let you do this," she warned.

Plumley's voice grew soft. "Corker, I need to get that hourglass back. It's important to me. It's my life in there."

The edge of fear in his voice made Corker realize that she would never convince Plumley to leave the hourglass behind. "Let me get it for you," she suggested.

"No! Absolutely not!" Plumley huffed.

"Please, Plumley," she begged. "I'm faster than you. I can be there and back much faster than you can. Please."

Plumley refused to be moved. "No! I'm going to do it myself!"

Corker calmed herself down and made one more appeal. "Plumley, please trust me. You can put your faith in me."

Plumley hesitated. He knew that Corker could get there and back much more quickly than he could, even with her injuries from the fight. His lips began to form the word 'no' anyway—then Corker said, "I won't let you down."

"Okay," he nodded, and headed back up the path towards Utten.

"You and Utten climb as fast as you can!" Corker

said. "I'll be back before you know it!" She took off down the path as fast as she could, knowing full well that she was heading straight towards Haite.

Utten turned into his bird form and began to fly up the steps. Plumley paused on the first step and watched Corker disappear into the rocks. "Come on, Plumley, there's no time to lose!" Utten called.

Haite noticed the difference in Moal's Hush Bogs immediately. It wasn't hushed in the least. As a matter of fact, it was filled with what sounded like chirping. She lumbered into the stone entryway of the mausoleum. Moal perched behind his ledger. His hair was tangled, and a few of the buttons on his vest had popped. A large splash of ink stained his front.

"I am Moal," Moal said, not looking up. "What is your name?"

"It's me, you fool," Haite hissed, her voice jolting the disheveled Moal. "What's going on out there?"

"It's been going on since those three left!" Moal explained, his voice sounding like that of a madman. "It started with one. Just one! He started whistling for no reason! Then another heard him, and she started whistling! It spread like a virus! Soon they were all whistling!"

From out in the Hush Bogs, a voice called out, "Marco!" With a thundering roar, a thousand souls answered the call of "Marco" with a resounding "Polo!" They sounded like a crowd at a football stadium shouting in unison. Their clamor shook Moal from his stool, and he fell to the floor of the mausoleum

"Oh no, here they go again!" Moal whined, picking himself up off the floor. "They won't stop playing that game! They love it! It's a nightmare, I tell you, a nightmare! Those three ruined my Hush Bogs!"

Haite smiled. She didn't care much for Moal, and anything that made him miserable brought her joy. She didn't want to give him any good news, but she had no choice. "I've got them," she said.

"Where are they? Bring them in!" Moal demanded. Outside, the game of Marco Polo continued. Moal popped another button on his vest.

"Not so fast, Moal. I want to renegotiate," Haite said, sitting down with a thud on the rocks.

Moal's tiny jaw muscles tightened. "Renegotiate what? Just bring them to me!"

"These weren't just some wandering souls that we rounded up for you this time, Moal. These people are special. They're living. I think they demand a higher price."

Outside, the game of Marco Polo grew louder. The person who was "it" had located another player, and the whole crowd of souls erupted in laughter. Moal winced at their joy. "What did you have in mind?" he asked.

"We're sick and tired of roaming around that barren mountain trying to keep your souls from reaching Methuselah. We want some freedom," Haite explained. "We know you can arrange it. We want access to the world of the living. There, we could have some real fun."

Moal thought about it for a moment. If he granted Haite and Skoll access to the world of the living, they wouldn't be around to help him as much. More of his souls might reach Methuselah. Then again, he still had the scarecrow to help him.

Outside, the rules of the Marco Polo game broke down, and all of the souls began to laugh and to scream 'Marco' and 'Polo' at once. They sounded like thousands of gleeful children.

"Fine. I'll arrange the access for you and Skoll," Moal agreed. "But you must do something for me. You must destroy the little blue man for what he did to the Hush Bogs. Once he is dead, I want you to bring his body back to me. Maybe I can use his residual magic to restore the Hush Bogs to silence."

"Shall we kill the boy?" Haite asked, getting up and moving her hulking frame towards the doorway.

"No, certainly not!" Moal laughed. "That boy must stay here with me until the hourglass runs out. Then, his soul will be mine forever."

"Whatever you say," Haite said over her shoulder. She started back through the bogs.

Corker reached the windmill in no time. The blanket was still laid out, and one of the crows pecked at the remnants of the food. When he saw her approach, he hopped away and perched on the scarecrow's shoulder. They began their whispering.

Corker quickly spotted the hourglass on the blanket. She grabbed it in her teeth and started back for the stone mountain. Behind her, she thought she heard the scarecrow speak, but she didn't wait around to hear what he had to say. She ran as swiftly as her legs would carry her, praying that Haite was not following behind her.

When she reached the cover of the rubble at the base of the stone mountain, she stopped to look back over her shoulder. Far off in the distance, she saw the huge black wolf emerge over the hill and race down the dirt road towards her.

Corker continued down the path that wound through the boulders all the way to Haite and Skoll's cave. By the time she hit the stone steps that led to the top of the mountain, she was quite out of breath. Again she checked behind her. Down towards the entrance to the cave, Haite stood staring up at her. Anger burned in the red eyes under her yellow horned streaks. She disappeared inside the cave.

Corker ran for her life up the steps. She had made it about halfway up when she saw both Skoll and Haite emerge from the cave and head for the stairwell. She realized that she and Utten and Plumley would have only seconds to convince Methuselah to allow them passage back home before Skoll and Haite made it to the top of the mountain.

Though Corker's legs were already screaming for rest, she pushed herself even faster. The burn in her hind muscles turned to pain which got sharper and sharper with each step she bounded. Her legs ready to collapse under her, her lungs on fire, she finally burst out onto the top of the stone mountain. Behind her, she heard the scraping of Skoll and Haite's claws as they charged up the steps.

Only Plumley and Utten waited for her. The top of the mountain was solid rock and barren of life. A few peaks touched the clouds off to her right, and to her left a ring of withered trees struggled for life in a patch of dry soil. Methuselah, whatever she might be, was nowhere in sight.

"Where is she?" Corker yelled, dropping the hourglass. "Where is Methuselah?"

"There's nothing here!" Plumley said. "We've checked

all over! There's nothing! And that's the only way down!"

Corker looked back down the steps. Haite and Skoll were almost to the top. She picked up the hourglass and returned it to Plumley. "What are we going to do?" she asked.

The three of them backed away from the stairwell towards the trees. They watched in horror as Skoll and Haite burst forth onto the top of the stone mountain.

Haite's eyes seemed to smoke. Foam dripped from her fangs. "Guard the stairs, boy," she screamed at Skoll. "No one leaves here!"

Haite paced back and forth in front of Plumley, Utten, and Corker. With each pass she got closer, and the three of them backed farther and farther away from her. "The plans have changed a little," she informed them. "It seems rather ironic that it is we who will get access to the world of the living, not you!"

Plumley, Corker, and Utten had backed themselves into the ring of trees. Once inside, they had nowhere else to go. The far side of the ring bordered on the edge of the stone mountain and the one mile drop to the rocks below.

"But before we go anywhere," Haite continued, "I'm going to take this runt apart piece by piece." Haite leaped forward, her jaws wide. She snapped them shut in the air in front of Corker, who backed into the center of the ring.

"We'll help you, Corker," Utten shouted, but Corker motioned towards the safe edge of the circle of trees.

"If the blue man even tries to use his magic, eat him," Haite shouted at Skoll.

"Please, boys," Corker begged. "Get away! Get to safety!"

Standing in front of Haite face to face, Corker could not help but feel tiny by comparison. Haite stood a foot taller than Corker, and her girth was solid muscle. She hunched in front of Corker, her teeth bared and dripping, her ears laid back against her skull. Her red eyes narrowed to slits as she watched Corker for any sign of movement.

Corker braced herself. She crouched down. The hair on her back spiked, and her ears laid back. From deep inside her, she issued a howl so fierce that it gave Haite pause, but not for very long. Haite leapt, but Corker stepped aside, avoiding the larger animal's attack.

They began to pace around in a circle, each eyeing the other carefully for any sign of attack. Finally, Corker took the initiative. She lunged in low, trying to get her jaws at one of Haite's hind legs. Haite dodged sideways, then spun around and clamped her immense jaws on the back of Corker's neck. Corker felt Haite's immense weight lean on top of her, and instantly her legs buckled as she was driven to the ground. Haite held her there, pressing with her shoulders and squeezing with her jaws, while Corker remained pinned and helpless in the dust.

"Get up, Corker!" Plumley yelled. "You can do it!"

Though Haite had Corker pinned, the hold was not enough to make her submit. Haite released her hold on Corker and backed away a few steps.

"There's no hope for you," Haite taunted. "This is already over!"

Corker leapt at Haite again. As Haite countered, Corker relaxed and rolled, allowing Haite to pin her to the ground on her back. Trapped under Haite's forepaws, she reached up with her hind legs and drove them into Haite's stomach, using all her leverage to scrape her nails into the larger animal's soft belly. Haite howled and jumped away. Corker's swipes had broken her skin, and Haite was bleeding.

"Clever," Haite admitted, "but still not enough." She lunged at Corker, and the two of them rolled over in the dirt. This time the attack went to Haite, who kicked at Corker's side, buckling one of her ribs. Corker got up off the ground and trotted towards the edge of the circle, hoping to get herself some time. Her side ached where her rib had cracked, and it made it difficult for her to breathe.

Haite didn't give her a chance to recover. She attacked Corker from behind, sinking her powerful jaws into Corker's shoulder and pushing her again to the ground. Haite leapt off, then circled around to Corker's other side and snapped at the other leg. Corker fell to the ground.

"You have no hope of besting me!" Haite screamed at

Corker. She attacked again, this time snapping her jaws at Corker's hind legs. Corker rolled over out of the way.

Corker knew her only hope was to stay out of Haite's way. As the smaller dog, she had the benefit of agility. But she could only dodge so long. Eventually, Haite would strike with a blow that Corker could not get up from.

That blow came sooner than Corker expected. As she tried to get to her feet, Haite rammed her in her side like a bull, sending her through the air to land in the dust a few feet away. In no time, Haite was on top of Corker, holding her down with her forepaws. "Now, we end this," Haite hissed. She leaned down and clamped her muzzle over Corker's neck from the side and squeezed. Corker felt Haite's teeth pressing against her throat, and her already taxed lungs lost their supply of oxygen.

She wriggled. She tried to kick out. Haite was simply too powerful an opponent. A cold cloud began to seep into Corker's brain. Almost as if someone were pouring ink into her eyes, her sight went black. The world became as quiet as death, and her muscles stopped answering her call to fight back.

Corker whined her submission.

Haite stepped off of her. Corker lay silently on the ground. The onslaught finally over, she breathed refreshing air into her lungs and tried to clear her head.

"Skoll!" Haite called out. "Hobble the boy. Bite his ankle so he can't run."

Skoll approached Utten and Plumley. Utten's feathers popped out and ruffled uncontrollably. "Stay away, you overgrown poodle!" he yelled.

"Utten, turn into your bird form and fly!" Plumley suggested.

Haite chimed in. "If the blue man tries to fly, or if he uses his magic in any way, go for the boy's throat."

"Yes, Mama," Skoll said, saliva dripping from his fangs. He approached them very cautiously, wary of Utten's magic. Skoll growled. Utten tried to growl back, but it came out as a squawk.

"You thought it was funny, locking me in the cage, didn't you?" Skoll asked Utten.

"Pretty funny, yes," Utten admitted nervously.

Skoll snapped with his jaws, and Utten and Plumley jumped backwards. Skoll backed them against one of the stone spires. He leaned in close and smiled, baring all of his yellow, pointed teeth. "This is going to hurt, little man," he giggled.

From behind him, Skoll heard a light crack of bone. His mother howled. He turned. Corker had Haite by the hind leg and was twisting with her jaws. Haite bucked and tried to pull away, but Corker held fast. When Haite finally did break Corker's hold, the damage had been done. Haite had been hobbled.

"Corker, no!" Plumley shouted, but it was far too late. Corker and Haite were now fighting to the death.

Another howl, this one of rage, issued from Haite's throat. She turned on Corker, limping. "To the death?" Haite asked. Corker answered with a howl of her own. The two of them ran at each other.

Corker, her energy renewed, got the better of Haite on the first attack. She leaped onto the wolf's back and bit hard on the top of Haite's skull. Haite shook her off like a rag doll, but Corker had succeeded in cutting Haite's fur above one of her horns. Haite spun around and snapped at Corker again, but Corker dodged her jaws, which came together with such a snap it jolted Haite's whole skull.

Corker bit at her hind quarters again, this time trying to weaken the other leg, but Haite spun away before she got hold. The two of them rolled over onto each other in the dust.

Utten turned into his bird form and perched on Plumley's shoulder. "Corker's not going to make it, is she Utten?" Plumley asked him.

"It's not over yet," Utten said, but in his voice Plumley heard no trace of hope.

Again and again Corker attacked Haite, and again and again Haite countered her. Soon, it became clear that Haite was merely toying with Corker, trying to tire her out before she dealt the fatal blow. With each full attack of Corker's, Haite made a minor counter attack. She nipped at Corker's ear. She clawed lightly at Corker's back. She bit Corker's tail. Each little attack was enough to cause pain and to remind Corker that Haite was in complete control.

Finally, Haite decided she had had enough. She lunged at Corker, knocking her over into the dust onto her back. She reached down with her jaws and sank them deep into Corker's belly. Corker howled like a terrified, wounded puppy.

This time, there would be no submission. Even if Corker called submission, Haite would have no obligation to honor it. This time, Corker felt her life slipping away. But this time, Haite had also become far too overconfident. She had left herself open.

Corker reached up with her jaw and grabbed Haite tightly around the neck. She squeezed, clamping down her hold. Startled, Haite tried to back away from her, but she only succeeded in dragging Corker across the dust with her. Corker reached around with her own hind legs and kicked at Haite's only strong hind leg, and the larger animal fell to the ground.

Haite kicked and clawed, but she couldn't gain back her footing. Corker held on, focusing every last bit of the energy in her body on keeping her jaws clamped like a vice.

Soon, Haite's kicks began to get weak. After a few moments, Corker felt her draw in one last breath, and then the kicking stopped. Corker held tight on Haite's throat even after she felt Haite die.

There were no cheers from Plumley and Utten, who were terrified by what they had seen. They walked over to the animals on the ground.

Corker's eyes were closed, and her breathing came in broken, wheezing gasps. Plumley picked her up and carried her away from the body of Haite.

Skoll was gone.

Plumley cradled Corker in his arms, and he knew without asking Utten that she was dying.

Suddenly, Haite's body disappeared. One moment it was there, and the next it was gone. It noiselessly faded away right before their eyes.

Then the trees spoke.

THE LAST FEW MITES

16

The Trial of Old Man Plumley

The voices came at them from the ring of trees. Each word was lobbed from a different tree in the ring, and each tree had its own distinct voice. Some were old voices, others were young. Some were male, others were female. Some even seemed to have accents. Their words came together to form complete sentences and complete thoughts regardless of their individual, odd vocal pieces.

"I am Methuselah. Why do you come to me?" she asked.

Plumley heard her, but he didn't answer. He was too concerned with Corker to care who or what was speaking.

"I am Utten," declared Utten. He wasn't sure where to address his voice, so he walked around within the circle. It seemed to him to be the most polite way to speak.

"I live in a bucket. I'm magic, and when I want to I can turn myself into a bird. What are you?" he asked.

"My seed first took root thousands of years ago, and it has been growing through time and space ever since. Even now, my roots reach to the soil in the World of the Living and beyond. Why have you come before me?"

Plumley lifted his head, and his angry eyes rolled from tree to tree. "Why didn't you help us? Those wolves wanted to kill us all!"

"I do not interfere in the lives of other beings. Whether the dog or the wolf won the battle, nothing would change much. Today, the dog held victory over the wolf. But it might have been different. The wolf might have been victorious over the dog. Either way, our roots would remain the same." Methuselah paused, then repeated her question. "Why do you come before me?"

"We are here by accident," Utten explained. "In truth, this entire situation is my fault." Utten told Methuselah the entire story, beginning at Old Man Plumley's house, back through time to Liggit's boarding school, then on to the boat and the storm. He explained how they ended up in Moal's Hush Bogs, and how they found their way out to the stone mountain. "All we want is to go home, and we are hoping that you can help us!"

Methuselah remained silent for a moment before speaking. "I need time to consider this request. I must check precedent through recorded time. You will have my answer soon." With that, Methuselah went quiet.

Utten returned to Plumley's side. Plumley still clutched Corker, who was unconscious. "If we get her back home, I can call a doctor. But we have to go soon," Plumley said desperately.

"She'd never survive the trip," Utten said. "She's not going to make it. I don't even need my magic to know that."

"No!" Plumley shouted. "She can't die! It's not fair!"

In his arms, Corker stirred. She opened her eyes. When she spoke, her words were barely audible. "Did I do it?" she asked.

"Yes!" Plumley told her. "You beat her!"

"And Skoll?" Corker asked.

"Scampered off like a spooked rabbit!" Utten shouted.

"Good," she said. "Will Methuselah let you through?"

"She's considering the request," Utten said.

"If she grants you passage, you will go, both of you," Corker said. "I know that I won't make it, and I'm not going to die for nothing. You must go through before Skoll returns."

"He won't be back," Utten suggested. "You scared him off."

"No," Corker corrected him. "He'll run for guidance to the smartest person he knows, and that's Moal. He'll return, and when he does he'll bring Moal with him. If you get the chance, you must go."

"I . . . we won't leave you," Plumley said. "You've given your life for us. We won't go!"

"I didn't do it for you," Corker said. "If you do get home, one day you will grow to become my master. I did it for him. I did it for the Old Man, who despite his faults is still a fine person inside. Even with all your anger, you still have his potential inside you, Plumley. With any luck, you will realize it sooner this time around." Corker's eyes closed, and her breathing grew light. Her time was short.

Suddenly, Methuselah's many voices rang out again. "I have reached a verdict," she informed them. Plumley and Utten looked up. "The boy will be granted passage back to the World of the Living. The dog will remain here. The blue man will remain here."

"What?" Plumley asked. "Why?"

"Your presence here is unnecessary, Plumley," Methuselah explained. "In fact, it endangers the natural flow of time. Therefore, it is logical that you be returned. The dog, however, is nearly dead. There is no reason to send her back. I will dispose of her as I did the wolf. The blue man is not of the World of the Living. His existence there is no more or less necessary to the process of life than it would be here. There is no reason to send him back. Therefore he will stay."

Plumley laid Corker down on the ground and stood in the circle. "I won't leave without them!" he shouted to Methuselah.

"Then you will stay," Methuselah said plainly.

"Wait!" Utten shouted. "He has to go! It's what we've been fighting for all this time!"

Plumley walked to the outer circle of the Methuselah's ring and looked over the edge of the stone mountain. Down below, he saw the dirt road stretching back towards the bogs. He knew that eventually, Moal and Skoll would be heading down that road towards them. Because Moal did not have the grace and speed of a wolf, they would come slowly, but they would come.

"I won't go," Plumley said. "I won't abandon them here. She's given her life to save mine, and I can't abandon her like this." He walked away from the edge and sat next to Corker.

"Don't you remember, Plumley?" Utten said. "You said that you wished you had gone it alone! You said that you weren't going to rely on anyone anymore!"

"That was before!" Plumley explained. "You don't understand, Utten. This is the first time anyone's ever proven to me that I could trust them. She proved it to me with her life. I can't leave her!"

"You have to go!" Utten said.

Plumley took the hourglass from his pocket and placed it in front of Utten. "You take this, Utten. When Moal comes, you fly away with it. Don't let him get it, whatever you do. But I'm going to stay right here. Even if Skoll decides to kill me, I'm going to stay right here!" Plumley walked over to Corker, picked her up, and cradled her in his arms.

"You'd do that? You'd stay even if Skoll came back to kill you?" Utten asked.

"Yes," Plumley replied.

Utten stood the hourglass on its base and watched the mites fall. There was very little time left before the mites ran out, maybe a few hours at most.

"You'd give your life rather than abandon her?" Utten asked.

"Yes!" Plumley shouted.

Utten sat down in the dust. He looked at Corker, then at Plumley, then back at Corker.

"What is it, Utten?" Plumley asked.

Utten chose his words cautiously. "All magic has a balance to it, Plumley. There's some give, but there's also some take. Everything balances out."

"What are you talking about?" Plumley said.

Utten stared at Corker and didn't say anything for a long time. "There's a way to save her," he finally said. "But it's not safe. It's not safe at all. You might both die. And either way, it will be extremely painful for you."

"What do I have to do?" Plumley asked.

"The first thing you have to do is mean what you say. If you don't mean what you say, the spell will kill her instantly. You have to believe it in your heart," Utten warned.

Plumley looked down at Corker, who continued to fade in his arms. "I mean it," he said. "And I'm willing to do whatever it takes."

Utten climbed into the bucket and pulled out the hammer and the anvil. He crawled back inside and disappeared for a long time. When he finally came out again, he was carrying a dull, rusty coin. He placed it on the anvil and began to hammer it into shape. "Lay her down on the ground," Utten instructed Plumley. "Then you lie down too. Try to remain calm, and breathe slow." Utten hammered at the coin, checking it over and over for dents. It took him quite a while, but there was no room for error this time.

Utten placed the coin in Plumley's hand. "This is a simple spell, really. It will balance the energy between you and Corker. That means that she'll get some of your strength to help her to recover. But it also means that you'll take some of her injuries inside your own body. Do you understand?"

"Yes," Plumley said. "Please do it, before it's too late."

Utten raised his hammer, then brought it down on the bare anvil. A clap of thunder rang from the anvil, over the edge of the stone mountain, and across the valley. A tiny spark appeared. It flew over Plumley, circling twice. Then it passed over Corker. It flew into Corker's mouth and down her throat. Corker's whole body bucked as the spark traveled inside her. She seemed to almost rise up off the ground. Then the spark flew from the center of her chest. It had gained in size. It passed over the top of Plumley, then dove into his chest.

Plumley groaned suddenly as the spark discharged its energy in his body. Plumley had underestimated just how painful this experience would be. The muscles of his face tightened and he turned red. Tears streamed from his eyes. He felt his insides bruise just as if he had been the one who had been kicked by Haite. Utten swung the hammer again, and thunder again spilled across the plains. A second spark passed through Corker and into Plumley. Corker began to breathe regularly. Plumley closed his eyes and fought back against the pain which spread through him again.

The third spark was the last. It took one more piece of Corker's pain into Plumley's body, and then Utten lay the hammer down. Corker opened her eyes and looked at Plumley. "Is he okay?" she asked, her voice stronger than before.

"Both of you need to rest. I'll keep watch," Utten

said. He dared not tell her that their hopes for survival were not good. Even if they both survived, they would not be well before Skoll returned with Moal.

Corker closed her eyes and slept.

Utten turned into his bird form and flew over the stone mountain. He saw no sign that Moal or Skoll were approaching. He flew back down and perched on the top of Plumley's hourglass to keep watch over his sleeping friends.

Moal's body was not built for climbing long flights of stairs. In fact, it wasn't built for much physical activity at all. Moal's body was best suited for sitting and writing and growing more and more disproportionate with each passing eon. Climbing the stairwells in the side of the stone mountain stressed Moal, and its difficulty was compounded by the fact that he had to haul his ledger up the stairs with him. He tried to keep up with Skoll, who was absolutely convinced that Moal would avenge his mother's death and was bounding the steps two at a time in his excitement.

When he reached the top, Moal's enormous chest wheezed like a broken accordion. Because his skin was accustomed to the moist air of the bogs, the walk to the dry dusty mountain had parched him and made him itchy all over. These facts combined to make Moal an extremely unhappy clerk.

The ledger stuffed under his arm, his free hand scratching at his back, he walked with Skoll into the ring of trees and stood over Utten, Plumley, and Corker. Plumley and Corker were still asleep. Moal blinked down at them through his giant glasses.

"Little blue man," Moal asked, "your name is Utten, isn't it?"

"That's my name," Utten said, watching Skoll carefully.

"Utten," Moal said. "Utten. Well, Utten, this game is over. You're all coming back with me."

"Methuselah has already granted Plumley passage home. And now that Corker will survive," Utten said, watching Skoll carefully for any reaction, "I believe that she will go too."

"I don't care," Moal said. He opened up his ledger, and licking his inky finger flipped through the pages to the one which kept Plumley's record. He held the open ledger high over his head. "I challenge your ruling, Methuselah. I lay claim to the boy."

Meanwhile, Skoll edged closer and closer to the sleeping Corker. Utten watched carefully. "I've had just about enough of you," Utten said. He picked up his hammer and let it fall absently on the anvil. It gave off a miniscule plink, and a tiny spark, barely perceptible to the naked eye, rose from the anvil. The spark hovered in front of Skoll, who backed away from it, his tail between his legs. Slowly the spark followed after him.

Methuselah's voice rang out. "On what grounds do you challenge my ruling, Moal?" she asked.

"On the grounds that the boy belongs in the Hush Bogs with me. I have the documents to prove it," Moal replied.

"Then I will reopen my hearing regarding the boy," Methuselah said.

"Wait!" Utten shouted, jumping up. "You already said that he could go through! You already ruled!"

"The boy chose to stay. New evidence has been presented, and it is my duty to hear it in its entirety," Methuselah answered.

Utten bristled. He turned into his bird form and perched on one of Methuselah's many branches. "But that's not fair! Plumley isn't well! He can't even defend himself!" Down below, Skoll had backed out of the ring of trees, the tiny spark keeping slow pursuit.

"That is of no consequence," Methuselah said. "The facts will be the facts, regardless of whether the boy is awake or asleep. I will hear your evidence, Moal."

Moal paused and smiled. This was the first thing that had gone his way since the souls of the Hush Bogs started tormenting him with their singing and their playing. Now he had his chance to get back at those who had caused his torment.

"As you well know, Methuselah, this ledger keeps the record of souls who will one day end up in my Hush Bogs. It marks the date of their birth. It also marks the date of their death. In between, it lists the accomplishments, or lack of, that they achieve in their lives. I enter it as exhibit number one," Moal said dramatically. "I have this ledger open to a page which proves that Plumley lived a very long, very bitter life of seclusion. He was feared by all those around him because of his sheer nastiness. Towards the end, the rumors about him grew to almost supernatural proportions."

"That's not accurate!" Utten shouted.

"Explain," Methuselah insisted. Utten flew over next to Plumley and Corker and retrieved the hourglass. On the other side of the mountain top, Skoll gave out a little yelp as the tiny flea spark leaped on him and dug into his fur. Skoll began to scratch at it.

"This hourglass—" Utten began.

"Might I remind my colleague, Mr. Utten, that that hourglass is stolen property? Stolen from my Hush Bogs!" Moal blurted.

"Conceded, Mr. Moal," Utten said. "And since this hourglass is the property of your Hush Bogs, surely you can inform Methuselah what it was designed to measure."

Moal bristled. He hadn't expected Utten to use such official language. "I keep one for each of my souls while they are in the World of the Living," Moal explained. "It keeps track of their lives. When the mites run out, it means that their lives have ended, and then they come before me."

"And you will note," Utten said, placing the hourglass on the ground in front of Moal, "that the mites in the hourglass have not yet run out, have they?"

"They are almost gone, yes," Moal said.

"But not quite?" Utten asked.

"Yes! Fine! Time has not run out yet!" Moal barked, his giant eyeglasses slipping off his nose and hitting him on the upper lip.

"Then I would appreciate it if my esteemed colleague, Mr. Moal, would not refer to Mr. Plumley in the past tense. Old Man Plumley is not quite dead yet."

Moal fumed as Utten resumed his perch on one of Methuselah's upper branches. "I am pleased that Mr. Utten has brought the hourglass into evidence," he said sarcastically, "and I would like to present it as exhibit number two." Moal picked up the hourglass and held it up to the trees. "As you can plainly see, this hourglass has very little time left. It simply would not make sense to send the boy back when he clearly would be returning here in a very short time. You see—"

"But I am sure that my colleague Mr. Moal realizes

that the hourglass was designed to measure the life of a very old man." Utten said, unable to resist the urge to interrupt his opponent. "Here on this mountain top we have a young boy. Would you care to explain that, Mr. Moal?" Utten suggested.

Moal spat out his words angrily. "I suggest that *you* explain it, Mr. Utten. I suggest that that is not a young boy over there, but that it is in fact the Old Man himself, and that through some trickery of magic you have given him the form of a boy. In proof of that fact I offer into evidence the boy's current condition. That 'boy' is not well; in fact, he may be dying as we speak. Even now the hourglass is running out. I suggest that this hourglass is marking a demise that we can watch with our own eyes!"

Moal walked over and stood over Plumley's sleeping form. "This is magic, I tell you! This is the Old Man, and he is dying as we speak!"

"That's not true!" Utten yelled. "That's simply not true!"

"I will render my verdict based on evidence, Utten," Methuselah said. "Moal's argument is plausible, and it is supported by facts. Can you offer evidence to the contrary?"

Utten searched his mind for any bit of evidence which could offer a different story, but he could find none. It was true, Plumley was not well. He might even be dying because he was willing to save Corker. And it did seem like more than just a coincidence that he was ailing at exactly the same time that the hourglass was running out. "I can offer no evidence to prove my story."

Moal beamed. He slammed his ledger shut. "Methuselah, I am just about ready to rest my case. But before I do, let me add one emotional plea."

"Emotion is irrelevant to the facts, Moal," Methuselah commented.

"I realize that. But you see, these three have destroyed the Hush Bogs. When they left, they infected my population with careless friendliness. You should hear my souls down there now. They whistle, they play games. They will not shut up! The Hush Bogs are no longer hushed, and quite honestly, it is beginning to drive me insane! I believe that some of my souls have actually regressed and become children again. Just a few hours ago I looked out the window of the bogs, and I swear that some of them have become visible to each other. My dear Methuselah, at times I have seen sunshine! I believe that I am entitled to some kind of compensation. Perhaps, if the blue man was turned over to me, I could use his magic to restore the Hush Bogs to their rightful order."

"I'd never help you out!" Utten said.

"I don't expect you would," Moal hissed. "That's why I would sap the magic out of you and distribute it myself! If you survived the process, I might just turn you into one of my prized bats!"

All was quiet on the mountain top for a moment. From the other side of the mountain, they could hear the low howling of Skoll as he itched at the tiny flea spark. Skoll began to run around in circles to try to get away from the flea.

"Utten, do you have anything to add?" Methuselah asked.

Utten didn't have anything to add. Moal had presented a better argument, that much was true. If Utten didn't say anything, then surely Methuselah would side with Moal. He thought carefully, trying desperately to gather together pieces of an argument that he could use against Moal.

"It doesn't matter," Utten said finally. "It doesn't matter at all."

Moal raised his eyebrows, hearing what he thought was a concession speech from Utten.

"Maybe that is a young boy over there who is clinging to life. And maybe it is an old man. But what does it matter? We cannot ignore one important fact. The reason that Plumley is ailing is because he risked his life to save that of his friend. Does that behavior fit the description of the Old Man listed in Moal's ledger? I don't think so. If it is the Old Man over there, then Moal has not taken into account that he has changed his life so dramatically with this single sacrifice that he no longer belongs in the Hush Bogs. And if it is the boy over there, and he is not allowed to go home, then we destroy the potential that is inside him, the potential that the boy has to live a good life.

"I believe that is what Moal fears. He is not afraid that this is really the Old Man turned young by magic; he is afraid that this truly is Plumley as a young boy! And by allowing him to go home, Moal is forced to gamble, because if the boy goes home then he has the potential to change the course of his life and write a new story." Utten fluttered into the air and circled around Moal, who frowned and pretended to ignore him.

"Plumley has the potential to live a new life, and to rewrite the ink of Moal's ledger! That's a risk that Moal can't take!" Utten explained, then landed on the ground next to Moal and turned back into his normal form. "It doesn't matter whether this is Old Man Plumley, or Plumley the young boy. He has demonstrated by his actions that he is no longer the man listed in the ledger. So he must be allowed to go home!"

Methuselah's voice did not change its even pace. "I need time to consider this request. I must check precedent through recorded time. You will have my answer soon," she said.

Moal stood awkwardly in the center of the ring of trees. Utten walked over to sit with Corker and Plumley. Skoll, whose tormenter was driving him into a frenzy, ran to the stairwell and down from the mountain top, his flea spark in close pursuit.

Hours seemed to pass. Moal stood in the center of the ring of trees, waiting for the verdict with his ledger stuffed under one enormous arm. Meanwhile, Utten watched as both Plumley and Corker grew stronger and stronger.

Finally, Methuselah spoke again. "I will grant passage for both Plumley and the dog," she said plainly.

Moal began to shout in protest, but Methuselah cut him off. "I weighed the evidence very carefully, Moal. The decision is final. It is important that the boy be allowed to return and to write his own future."

Another button popped from the vest of Moal. "But . . . but . . . my bogs! My Hush Bogs! At least give me the blue man, so that I can restore it to order!"

Utten, Plumley, and Corker began to fade from view. As he felt himself begin to pass through the dimensional walls with his friends, Utten waved goodbye to Moal.

"Bring him back," Moal insisted. "At least bring the blue man back!"

"Keeping Utten here would allow you to change the Hush Bogs back to what you would like it to be. But the Hush Bogs, like all things, must grow and evolve. Therefore, it is in the best interest of all things that the blue man return with his friends so that he will be out of your reach. Change is the one constant throughout time,

Moal, and finally it has come to the Hush Bogs. I suggest you go back and make the best of it."

Methuselah fell silent. Utten, Plumley, and Corker had faded away. Even the bucket was gone. Moal stood alone on the stone mountain. Above him, the spires of Methuselah's mountain sliced at passing clouds. Moal spied Plumley's hourglass in the sand at his feet. He picked it up off the ground and examined it.

Inside the hourglass, gravity reversed, and the mites began to climb upward.

IN LIGGIT'S GARDEN

17

THE FINAL PASSING

Dawn arrived at the Liverstanes Boarding School for Boys. The students still slept in their beds, and Liggit had only just risen. A few minutes remained before Liggit rang first bell to call the boys from their beds.

In the bushes near the football field, Utten kept a close watch over Corker and Plumley. Methulusa's transport had been relatively gentle, much more gentle than Utten had expected. She placed them gingerly in the woods near the school during the night, and their trip had been so peaceful that neither Corker nor Plumley had stirred.

Plumley woke first. He blinked his eyes and looked around. He sat up, and when he did the soreness of his ribs jabbed at him. He winced and lay back down, deciding that he would be better off if he took things slowly. Utten climbed up on top of Plumley and stood on his chest, pleased to see him stir.

"Good morning, Plumley!" Utten shouted.

"Good morning, Utten," Plumley said wearily. "Is Corker all right?"

"She's fine. I think you'll both be very sore for a couple of weeks, but other than that you'll be okay!" Utten said gleefully. Corker opened her eyes, and Utten hopped off Plumley and lay his hand on her forehead. "Take it easy, you're still pretty sore! One step at a time."

Plumley eased himself into a sitting position. "We're home!" he said. "How did we get here?"

"Moal came back while you were asleep! He tried to convince Methuselah to turn you over to him, so we had a trial, and I put a whoopin' on him!" Utten said proudly, his belly turning slightly purple. "You should have seen it! I was awesome!"

Plumley peered out through the bushes. Through the windows of the headmaster's office, he saw Liggit slipping his long thin arms into the sleeves of his black suit. "I'm really home!" Plumley said. "Safe and sound!"

"Safe, sound, and sore!" Utten shouted, throwing a triumphant fist up into the air.

"Corker, I'm home!" Plumley said.

Corker barked at him.

"Oh no . . ." Plumley said softly. "I can't hear her any-more . . ."

"She said 'Congratulations,'" Utten explained.

Plumley paused for a moment. "She did, didn't she?" he said. "Corker, say something else!"

"Like what?" she asked. It came out only as barks, and yet Plumley answered her.

"Like anything, you know—hey! I can almost understand you! It's all barks, but I can still hear you . . . sort of," Plumley beamed. "And there was something else. While we were passing through from the stone mountain. I was asleep, but I remember something, or someone."

"We met someone going the other way," Utten said.

"I don't remember a thing," Corker confessed.

"There was someone, though wasn't there?" Plumley said, still trying to remember. "It was Auntie Collida! But *she* wasn't going to Moal's Hush Bogs, was she?"

"No," Utten said. "But she was moving on. She was very excited about it, and also very pleased to see us, even though you were asleep. She and I talked for quite some time, and while we talked she passed some magic over you and Corker to help you heal faster. Then she said goodbye and moved along!"

"Wow!" Plumley said. "Does that make you sad?"

"Not really," Utten said. "I'll miss her, but I'm very happy for her. And maybe someday I'll see her again! Who knows?"

Plumley stood up and stretched. Now that he was

moving around, he felt stronger, though he was still very sore in some areas. Liggit rang first bell, and Liverstanes began to rise. The bustling of boys getting ready for breakfast drifted down on them from the upstairs windows.

"So what's next?" Utten asked. "Shall we head up river to the frozen tundra, or go apple picking down south?"

"I think that it's time I went back inside there," Plumley said. "We had a good adventure, but at some point I have to get back to my real life."

"Are you sure?" Utten asked. "I know a secret valley in Mexico where there are so many eels, you only have to dip your feet in the water to get a great foot massage!" The image of her feet stuck in eel-infested waters nauseated Corker, and she forced herself up on wobbly feet just to shake the picture from her head.

"No," Plumley said. "I think it's time you and Corker got back to your own time, and I got back to my life. How are you going to get back, anyway?"

"Well, all we have to do is find Utten!" Utten declared.

"Find Utten?" Plumley said. "But you are Utten!"

"Think of it this way, Plumley. What were you doing one week ago at this very second?" Utten asked.

Plumley scratched his head. "I guess I was getting out of bed and brushing my teeth." Plumley said.

"Right!" Utten said. "And if you were to go back in time right now to that exact moment, you could go upstairs and say hello to yourself, right?"

"Sure," Plumley said. "I guess so!"

"That's all I have to do! I find Utten, and we shake hands, and then off I go, to wherever I want. When Utten and I get together, our magic is very powerful!" Utten explained. "Are you ready to go, Corker?"

"I think I'm going to stay," Corker said. "You go back and check on the Old Man. I'll stay here for awhile."

"But where will you live?" Utten protested. "You can't enroll in the school!"

"I'll find a way," Corker said. "I'll stay in the woods." She walked over and sat next to Plumley, who scratched her head.

"If you think it's best," Utten said, and Corker nodded. "But what are you going to do about Liggit?" he asked Plumley.

"Don't worry about Liggit, I'll take care of him," Plumley said. "You just get yourself home."

Utten looked around the little clearing in the bushes. He knew he was forgetting something, but he couldn't think of what it was. Then it came to him—the bucket. He didn't know how to take the bucket back through time with him. He could try to take it with him, but he might end up going through time without it, and then the other Utten would have two buckets. One bucket was more than a single Utten could handle; he couldn't imagine trying to tend to two!

Corker saw his indecision, and picked the bucket up by its handle. "Don't worry," she said, placing the bucket next to Plumley. "It'll be right here when you get back to your own time. We'll take good care of it."

"All right!" Utten said. As he hated long good-byes, he immediately turned into his bird form and took to the air. "So long," he called, circling over their heads twice before taking off in the direction of the creek. "We sure had a great adventure!"

"Goodbye, Utten," Plumley said sadly. He took comfort knowing that he would see Utten at some time in the future, even if it would be a long way off.

Scratching Corker behind her ears, Plumley said, "It's time I went in there. I'll come out to see you later this afternoon. We can explore the woods together, if you like!" Plumley said. Corker watched him leave the bushes and walk up towards the school.

Through his window, Liggit saw Plumley coming, and he left his office and walked with brisk, stiff legs out to meet him across the field.

"Mr. Plumley! It's about time you returned!" Liggit fumed. "Do you realize how long you have been gone? I have a list of punishments that should last you the rest of your tenure here at Liverstanes!"

Plumley simply looked up at Liggit and smiled a

deep, broad grin. "Hello, Headmaster Liggit," he said. "It's a pleasure to see you. How are you this morning?"

It didn't take Utten long to find the other Utten. As he had guessed, the other Utten was exploring the mighty Quoquannaug River. When Utten flitted down and landed on the rim of the bucket, the other Utten was expertly maneuvering through some pretty tough rapids. "Hello, Utten," Utten said. He was careful to keep himself in his bird form so that he wouldn't get himself confused with the other Utten.

"Hello, Utten!" the other Utten said. "Having an adventure through time?"

"An incredible adventure!" the bird Utten said. "I'd tell you all about it, but it would ruin the surprise!"

The other Utten held out his hand, and the bird Utten reached forward with his wing. "Let's get you back home!" the other Utten said. When Utten's wing touched the other Utten's hand, a shower of sparks leapt out and covered the bird Utten.

"So long, Utten!" Utten said, not sure himself which Utten had said it to whom. The sparks surrounded the little blue bird, and when the process was complete, Utten found himself sitting on the floor of a library. Next to him, Old Man Plumley dozed in his easy chair. The spell he and the other Utten had cast had worked perfectly, and it had delivered Utten directly to Old Man Plumley.

Mixed up again from the trip, Utten turned himself into his blob form before trying to become normal again. When he had righted himself, he climbed up onto the chair next to Plumley.

Plumley stirred. "Utten, is that you?" he asked. Though his voice had grown old and his face had wrinkled, in the man sitting before him Utten could still see the boy he had met. "I've waited so long for you to come back." Plumley seemed extremely tired, more tired than Utten had ever seen him. Still, he smiled at the sight of his returned friend.

Utten looked around him. They were in the library of the old house. Plumley wore almost the exact same clothes as before. In fact, it looked like nothing much had changed. The room looked a little bit cleaner, but apart from that, Old Man Plumley was still Old Man Plumley.

"Wait a minute!" Utten said. "I thought things would be different. I thought that since I went back through time and we had that adventure, that your life would have changed. But you're still the same!"

Plumley smiled wearily. "Don't you worry, Utten. I don't think Moal is going to get me. Why don't you tell me the story?"

"What story?" Utten asked.

"The story about you and me and Captain Hobart's Travelling Ocean Circus and Moal's Hush Bogs and Skoll and Haite and Methuselah," Plumley said.

"But you already know that story," Utten said. "You lived it!"

"I know," Plumley said, closing his eyes and tilting his head back. "But it's been so long. I'd love to hear it."

Utten climbed up on Plumley's shoulder and began to tell the story. He started at Cranston's twaddleyard, and told him all about the mean old man who lived all alone at the bend of the river. He told Plumley how he and the Old Man had become friends, and about how he had turned the old man into a baby by accident. He told him about the chess pieces and how they had made him and Corker go back through time. Back in time he met young Plumley, who was being hounded by Headmaster Liggit.

"Liggit," Plumley repeated the name and smiled when Utten mentioned the old headmaster.

Utten told him about how he and Plumley and Corker had escaped to Captain Hobart's Traveling Ocean Circus. There they met Auntie Collida, who almost drove the wickets and the rudelies out of the grumpy boy.

"The eye of Karloff," Plumley smiled, remembering with his eyes closed. He could picture it all perfectly.

Utten told him about the great storm that came up, and how he had to transport everyone off the ship. But in return for saving the others, they were banished to Moal's Hush Bogs.

Utten told him about Joe, the wandering spirit, and how Joe had ruined the Hush Bogs for Moal. He reminded Plumley how he had outsmarted the scarecrow whose glove held the touch of death, and how they were captured by two evil wolves.

Plumley chuckled as Utten reminded him how Corker outsmarted Skoll. "She was a smart dog," Plumley said.

Utten told about the final dog fight up on top of the stone mountain, and how he had risked his life to save Corker's. He reminded Plumley how close to death he had come, and told with great relish how he had outmaneuvered Moal in the trial, winning all three of them transport back to the land of the living.

When Utten finished his story, he saw that Plumley had drifted off. He swung at the air with his right hand. "Don't worry, Plumley," he yelled. "If there are any sylberpodders about, I'll get them!" He pretended that a sylberpodder was right in front of him, and he . . .

Utten stopped. Plumley wasn't asleep. It took Utten a moment to realize it, but then he knew. Plumley had passed, and he had no reason to fear sylberpodders anymore, or choates or yinkers for that matter.

Utten walked down Plumley's arm, and because he didn't know what to do, he curled up in the palm of Plumley's hand. He thought about their great adventure together. He thought about how Plumley had resisted his friendship for so long before finally realizing that he could trust people. And he worried that all their struggles had been for nothing. Plumley still grew up to be the Old Man, who closed down the school and lived all alone.

Someone entered the room. Utten looked up. It was a dog, a rather beautiful dog, with fur that looked like marbled wood . . .

"Corker!" Utten yelled. "Is that you?"

The dog looked up at Plumley, and recognizing his passing, lay her head on her master's lap. "No," she said. "My name is Penny. I'm Corker's great-great granddaughter. I've been waiting for you for some time, Utten."

Penny lifted her head from Plumley's lap. "Let's leave him alone," she said. "Come with me. I've got a story to tell you." Utten climbed onto her shoulders, and with a final look at Plumley, she turned to walk out of the library.

"My grandmother told me this story, and it was told to her by her grandmother, Corker. She made me promise that if you ever returned, I would tell the story to you," Penny began. "Corker found this out from Plumley years after you left them. When Plumley was very young, too young to even remember it, his parents died in an accident. His greedy relatives took everything from their house. They didn't even leave him a picture of them, and

Plumley lived his entire life not knowing what his parents even looked like. As an orphan, he became the responsibility of the state, which shuffled him from place to place as they tried to find a relative who was willing to take him. Wherever Plumley went, be it a foster home or an orphanage, he tried to make friends, but as soon as he made friends the state would move him around again. He never had time to become truly close to anyone.

"Meanwhile, insurance companies argued over the accident that had happened to Plumley's parents. They finally decided on a sum of money to compensate Plumley, who suddenly became a very rich young boy. Soon after the money was settled, an uncle stepped forward to claim the boy. Plumley thought he was finally going to go live in a stable home. He spent two weeks at his uncle's house, but never saw him. His uncle was off vacationing, and he sent Plumley to boarding school at Liverstanes while he was away. He was only interested in the boy's money."

Penny opened the door to the library, then pulled it tightly shut with her muzzle behind her. As she walked down the hallway towards the main stairwell, Plumley heard some noise coming from inside the house.

"At Liverstanes Plumley was afraid to make friends, and the other kids made fun of him because they thought he was stuck up. Also, Liggit hated him, and made his life miserable. Strangely, though, after his adventure with you, Plumley was always very pleasant to Liggit. Whenever he saw him, he greeted him happily and asked him how he was. No matter how angry Liggit got, Plumley continued to be kind to him. When Plumley got older, he took what was left of his money and bought Liverstanes out from under Liggit. That's when things began to change. Even Corker didn't expect what happened next."

Down the hall, Utten could hear the sound of activity. He heard many voices, and loud thumps and bangings, and laughing. Even a little singing.

"Plumley closed down the school and sent all the boys home. But he kept Liggit on. Liggit wasn't the headmaster anymore; there wasn't even a school for Liggit to be headmaster of. So Plumley hired Liggit to be his gardener. Liggit was an awful gardener. Everything he touched died. But still Plumley kept him on. In the mornings, he would say, 'Good morning, Mr. Liggit.' Liggit would usually answer with a grunt. And at the end of the day, Plumley would say pleasantly, 'Nice work today, Mr. Liggit' and Liggit would grunt again."

Penny began to walk down the stairs, and Utten could see where all the noise was coming from. The house was filled with children. Boy and girls of all ages ran from room to room, or read books in the corners, or climbed on the banisters, or played ball indoors. Several nurses tended to their needs and tried to keep them from breaking the furniture. What used to be an old, creepy house struck Utten as a very lively, very fun place to be.

Penny continued her story. "Corker never understood why Plumley was so kind to Liggit after Liggit had been so cruel to him. One day she asked him. He replied, 'I will be his friend whether he likes it or not. When I was in Moal's mausoleum in the Hush Bogs, and I read over the names on the hourglasses, I saw Liggit's name on an hourglass very close to mine!' As mean and nasty as Liggit was, Plumley couldn't let him end up in the bogs."

"The bogs actually turned out to be a pretty fun place in the end," Utten said.

Penny nodded and continued. "Liggit stayed here until the day he died. Towards the end, he even got the hang of gardening. We have lovely gardens today!"

Utten couldn't believe Penny's story, nor could he believe the incredible amount of activity in the house. It seemed that the walls of the house might bust at any minute from the energy of all the children!

Penny trotted down the stairs and out onto the front porch. There, hanging over the entryway, hung a sign which read:

UNCLE PLUMLEY'S ORPHANAGE
FOR BOYS AND GIRLS

"Plumley created a new place here. He opened up his doors to all kids who had no other place to go. He created a place where kids wouldn't be shuffled around, where they would be safe, and where they could have fun."

Utten looked up at the sign, relieved to find out that Plumley's life *had* changed. "But will the orphanage be shut down now that . . . now that . . ." Utten asked, not sure which words to use to describe Plumley's passing. Penny knew what he was talking about.

"Plumley has been running the orphanage for generations. Some of the first children to live here now help to run it. It will live on for good long time, and Plumley's generosity will continue to help kids for a long, long time," Penny explained.

Penny walked across the field to the exact spot in the bushes where Utten, Plumley, and Corker had sat so many years ago. The branches had grown a lot since then, but Utten still recognized the spot. She ducked down and entered the bushes, then stopped in a little clearing and let Utten down off her neck. She scratched at the earth, and cleared away the soil from a plank of wood. She lifted the wood, which covered a small hiding place in the ground. She reached in with her muzzle, pulled out Utten's bucket, and set it on the ground next to him.

"My bucket!" Utten shouted, climbing up and sitting on its rim. "They told me they'd take care of it!"

"It may be a little rusty, and it probably won't start," Penny warned him.

"It was always like that!" Utten explained.

"It was a pleasure to meet you, Utten. I've heard so much about you, and so much about your adventures. But now I have to go back inside and let someone know about Plumley. Please come back to visit us some time. You'll always be welcome here."

"You bet!" Utten yelled. Pleased, he allowed his belly to turn a brilliant blue, then he flopped over backwards into the bucket. Penny walked back to the orphanage.

"I am so glad to see you!" Cranston wailed when Utten pulled into view with the sputtering bucket. "I was worried when you and the doggy went through time right before my eyes!"

Utten climbed out of the bucket and looked around the twaddleyard. Several small junk piles were burning, and where Cranston's sofa collection once stood only a few charred bits of wood and stuffing remained. "What happened here?" he asked.

"It is okay!" Cranston yelled, tossing a bucket of water onto a pile of burning tires. "That spell you made for Woody worked really great!" From a spot on the ground behind Cranston, a tiny burst of flame erupted from Woody, lighting the back of Cranston's pants on fire.

"Hello, Woody!" Utten shouted as Cranston dumped a bucket full of water on his burning trousers. "Well, guys, I'm going to need a few things to fix this old bucket. But before we get to that, let's sit down and have a snack. I have an amazing story to tell you!"

Utten has a web page.
Visit him at
www.utten.com

ABOUT THE AUTHOR

Born and raised in Connecticut, Reade Scott Whinnem now lives on Cape Cod, Massachusetts, where he writes books and teaches high school. He enjoys sleeping late on Saturday morning and reading a good book. He has a scar on his forehead from getting clocked in the head with a swing when he was a little boy, and that scar reminds him to always watch where he is going. He loves all seafood, especially raw shellfish. Irish folk music makes his right foot tap. At night he sometimes has thrilling dreams where Godzilla is chasing him through the countryside. He enjoys a good snowstorm, though shoveling it gives him a backache. He likes to saw wood and hammer nails with his brothers and father. He likes to cook for his Mom, and she always says it's good even when it's not. He calls his grandmother Wangie, and she is a real sweetie. He lives a relatively quiet life with his cat, Elsa, and a giant poster of the king of rock and roll, Elvis Presley.

Hampton Roads Publishing Company is dedicated to providing quality children's books that stimulate the intellect, teach valuable lessons, and allow our children's spirits to grow. We have created our line of Young Spirit Books for the evolving human spirit of our children. Give your children Young Spirit Books—their key to a whole new world!

Hampton Roads Publishing Company
publishes books on a variety of subjects including
metaphysics, health, visionary fiction,
and other related topics.

For a copy of our latest catalog,
call toll-free, 800-766-8009,
or send your name and address to:

Hampton Roads Publishing Company, Inc.
1125 Stoney Ridge Road
Charlottesville, VA 22902
e-mail: hrpc@hrpub.com
www.hrpub.com